When
sparks
Fly

BOOKS BY KRISTEN ZIMMER

The Gravity Between Us

When
sparks
Fly

KRISTEN ZIMMER

bookouture

Published by Bookouture in 2021

An imprint of Storyfire Ltd.
Carmelite House
50 Victoria Embankment
London EC4Y 0DZ

www.bookouture.com

ISBN: 978-1-80019-539-4
eBook ISBN: 978-1-80019-538-7

For Elizabeth, my home.
And for my sister Breanna, who makes every day an adventure.

It's hazy, but this is what I remember: We were both a little drunk—her more than me, I think, but it doesn't really matter. The room was dark, except for the streetlights coming through the blinds. I could barely see her, but I felt her—she pushed me up against the wall, pressed herself against me, and we were kissing harder than we ever had before. Her hands were up my shirt... I unbuttoned her jeans, so fast and so clumsy, because I wanted her. I'd been waiting so long for it to happen, and finally it was going to.

Then the bedroom door flew open. The music from the party wasn't muffled anymore. The light from the hallway was so bright. Someone screamed her name...

CHAPTER ONE

Beverly High School, day one—school number seven for me. You'd think I might have gotten used to switching schools by now, but being forced to transfer a few days into my senior year is next-level suckage. The Cahills, the foster family the Commonwealth of Massachusetts placed me with, live way outside the Boston Public School District. Obviously, or I wouldn't be standing on the sidewalk staring up at Beverly High, would I?

Most of the girls walking into this place are dressed like they're about to stomp down a catwalk. I don't fit the prototype in my old Vans, shredded hip hugger jeans and oversized black Nirvana T-shirt. After falling out of bed later than I expected to this morning, I made the decision to pull my wavy blonde hair into a low, messy bun. That was a mistake. Looking like a homeless street urchin is no way to make a good first impression.

I let out a breath that blows my scraggly bangs away from my eyes, shift the strap of my ratty khaki messenger bag into a more comfortable position on my shoulder and zero in on the marquee sporting a gigantic black and orange paw print and the words HOME OF THE PANTHERS. That's when I hear someone behind me holler, "Hey, Britton!"

It's not like I have any friends in this town, so I've got a pretty good idea who's calling my name: Avery, my foster parents' biological daughter. Like me, she's a senior, but I'm certain that's where the similarities between us end. She seems to be made up of everything I am not. I'm dirt poor and mostly keep to myself. Her family's wealthy—Mom's a lawyer, Dad's the CEO of some gaming app company. She's a cheerleader, so she'll have a ton of eager groupies in tow *all* the time, and she's beautiful in a high-maintenance movie star kind of way.

I turn around to find Avery jostling toward me, pink plaid sheet skirt and white crop sweater both riding up with every stride. There's a suggestion of frustration on her face. "Why didn't you wait for me? My mom said I was supposed to drive you."

"I felt like walking." I shrug. "Besides, you were taking forever to get ready. I didn't want to be late for my first day."

She runs a hand through her long, chestnut-colored hair and slings it over her right shoulder. "I'm here, aren't I? You wouldn't have been late."

"Right. Thanks, anyway." I turn back to the school and start for the main entrance. She doesn't let me slip away unaccompanied—unfortunate considering I really don't feel like making small talk. Anyhow, I know she's only sticking close to me because her parents told her she had to escort me around.

"Do you have to get your schedule from the office?"

"Yeah."

"Okay. Let's go."

I pick up my class schedule, locker assignment and a map of the school from the secretary. "Block scheduling." I glower at the top paper. "I don't get it."

"Give those to me." Avery snatches all three sheets of paper from my hands and scans them over. "What's not to get? We've got Pride days and Panther days. They alternate. On Pride days you have Honors English, Life Skills, Biology, lunch, then Sociology. On Panther days you have Computer Science, Consumer Math, Free Study, lunch and… Tennis? Way to go on picking the lamest

Phys Ed elective ever. Today is a Pride day, so follow the Pride day schedule. Got it?" She hands the papers back to me.

"Thanks so much for being judgmental about Tennis. And yes, I've got it."

"Whatever." She waves dismissively. "I'm going to the Humanities Wing. Come with—we're in the same English class."

"You're in Honors English?"

She leers at me. "What, you think because I'm a cheerleader I must be stupid? Now who's being judgmental?"

I feel the heat of embarrassment bubbling in my chest and try to shake it off. "Touché."

She smirks.

We're about to head up the staircase to the second floor when she is ambushed by a group of girls whose barely-there attire must push the boundaries of the school's dress code. They ignore my presence and proceed to yammer at her, their voices meshing together in a wall of sound. She can't get a word in. "Guys," she says softly. When that doesn't work, she says it again, louder, "Guys!"

Everyone stops to focus on her.

She shoots me an apologetic look. "Everyone, this is Britton. Britton, this is Kylie, Amy, Liz and Tasha." She motions to each girl as she introduces them.

They all ogle me, head to toe. I can tell they're appraising my coolness factors. I lose points for my clothing, but I suppose the fact that I'm keeping company with Avery is enough for them to overlook the way I'm dressed, because they opt to speak to me.

"Britain, like, the country?" Kylie questions. Her features contort into a sour expression, like she's bitten into a lemon. I find it kind of amusing, but am able to suppress my laughter by sheer force of will.

"No, not like the country. T-T-O-N," Avery replies. "She's staying with my family for a while, so you bitches had better be chill to her."

Instantly, their demeanors soften. *Interesting.* She is the puppet master.

"So, Brit—I can call you that, right?" Tasha asks. I start to say, "I guess," but she doesn't let me finish. "Will you be trying out for cheerleading?"

Is she kidding me? Do I seem like I'm eager to join the Braindead Brigade? "I was thinking about trying out for soccer, actually."

She sneers. At second glance, I see they all do—everyone except Avery.

"Just to let you know, all those girls are lesbians," Amy says, making 'lesbian' sound like the most disgusting word in the English language—worse than 'sewage,' or 'maggot,' or 'pus.'

Should I blow their minds now, or wait until later? *Later would be better.* I'd like to get through my first few days here unscathed, maybe make some allies before I start making enemies. The problem is, on the rare occasion someone manages to piss me off, I'm really bad at keeping my mouth shut and really good at scathing comebacks. Oh man, do I have a comeback for this chick. Like, *If you're going to be homophobic, I'd prefer it if you'd call me a 'dyke.' 'Rug muncher' is also a good one.*

Avery comes to her friend's rescue without even realizing that she needs to. "Amy, seriously, refrain from spewing your shit all over the place. You'll ruin my heels."

Savage.

Amy's cheeks go bright pink.

The 8:10 bell rings; we've got five minutes to make it to class on time. Avery plasters on a pretentious smile and says, "We'd better get our ass to class. See you at lunch." She grabs me by the elbow and leads me up the steps. "Sorry. They can be dickheads sometimes," she says as we reach the second floor.

"I noticed."

"Did Amy offend you?"

Am I that transparent? Wonderful. That's exactly what I need, to live in a house with this girl until I graduate and have her feel uncomfortable around me the whole damn time—because of course the system won't let me 'age out' until I finish my public education or decide to drop out, despite the fact that my eighteenth birthday was last week. *Might as well get your social worker on the phone right now.* Am I ever going to stop fucking up and getting kicked out of foster homes? "Did I seem offended?"

"Not really."

"Then why would you ask me if I was?"

"The rainbow patch on your duffle bag, the one you were carrying when you moved in." She sucks in her bottom lip and bites down.

I forgot about that thing. "Oh."

"Listen, it's fine. I don't care." She sounds genuine, but I can't be certain.

"Are you sure? I can put a call in to my social worker if—"

She laughs, which has to be the most inappropriate reaction ever. I'm aware that I'm glaring at her like she's high on something, but I can't help it. Before I can slip my features into a more innocuous expression, she reads me. It throws me. *You're losing it, kid.*

She gathers herself and says, "The last foster kid my parents took in deliberately set fire to our garage. She was a total head-case—scared the shit out of me. If the worst thing about you is lesbianism, I'm relieved." Her eyes go wide, as though she's afraid she may have said the wrong thing. "Not that being gay is a bad thing. It's not. It's normal. I—"

"Avery, stop." I throw my hands up. I don't want her to have a political correctness-induced meltdown. "I can promise you that I'm not a pyromaniac, or a kleptomaniac, or any of those other words that have 'maniac' as a suffix. I want us to be cool with each other. Can we try to do that?"

"Yes." She smiles. It's the first time I've seen her authentic smile. *Pretty.*

"Great. So, uh, will you show me where the hell Room 232 is, please?"

"This way."

"Your locker is on this floor. Down the hall, make a right," Avery points out after English class is over. I follow her finger with my gaze, then settle on her face once she puts her arm down. Her eyes are striking, clear and crystalline, like photos I've seen of the Caribbean. Another thing about her that's different from me. My eyes are a weird ochre color, like baby diarrhea. "I've got Calculus next," she continues. "It's in the penthouse. Life Skills is on the first floor. Will you be okay finding the room by yourself?"

I check the school map. "I think I can manage."

"We have the same lunch block. Meet me outside the cafeteria at twelve."

Was that a command? I should probably make it clear that I have no intention of allowing her to become *my* puppet master. That stuff might fly with her mindless minions, but it won't with me. "Are you asking me or telling me?"

"I was asking. If you'd rather wander around the caf looking for people to sit with like some pathetic freshman, be my guest."

No. That does not sound appealing at all. "I'll meet you outside the caf."

"See you then." She starts to walk away. "By the way," she calls over her shoulder, "soccer tryouts start today at three."

Apparently, she is unable to recognize sarcasm when she hears it. I wasn't serious about that. I only said it because I like the idea of becoming an actual athlete a lot better than the idea of becoming a cheerleader. I plan to avoid becoming either. "Thanks." I keep my eyes on her retreating figure until she disappears from sight.

*

By the end of the day, I've realized there isn't a single student at this school who wants to befriend me. No one in any of my classes bothered to say a word to me unless prompted to by the teacher. It was the same in the lunchroom, save for Avery, her surprisingly pleasant jock friend Jason, and a few of his bros from the football team. I know most of the guys only talked to me because they considered me fresh meat. They had the air of hungry predators who'd spotted prey. Avery shut that down real quick. "She isn't going to fuck any of you. She's not interested in trash." It was funny, and preferable to her flat out announcing my sexual orientation to the entire cafeteria. That would have been mortifying. I've been out to myself since I was fourteen, but it's something I like to divulge to people in my own time, on my own terms.

To add to what was probably the worst first day of school anyone has ever experienced, I didn't have enough time to make it to my locker at any point, so I'm dragging three thick-ass text books and a plethora of paperbacks courtesy of English Honors around with me. It's absurd that we're only allotted five minutes between classes to make our way through, like, two thousand students and four floors. What if your B Block classroom is on the first floor and your C Block classroom is on the fourth floor—the penthouse—like mine are on Pride days? There's no way in hell I'll have time to make a pit stop at my locker. Three days a week I'll be stuck lugging every last thing I need for the day unless I cut into the forty-five minutes I get for lunch.

I find my locker, number 473, and give it an inspection. I'm not thrilled about the size of it—just high and wide enough to stuff a person into. My mind cooks up a vision of me crumpled inside, barely able to scratch at the metal, my face pressed against the grates as I gasp for every breath until I die. *Get it together*. I put my messenger bag down on the floor and proceed to struggle with the combination lock that's built into the door. "Goddamn stupid thing."

"Only frosh have trouble with their lockers. You look too old to be a freshman. That must make you a transfer," says a voice from off to my right. The locker next to mine bangs closed and my observer comes into view. She's tall, muscular. Her hair is fiery auburn, pulled up in a high ponytail. She turns toward me, and I notice her irises are the color of emeralds; they sparkle with amusement as they comb over me. I can feel my cheeks flushing. "No shame, we've all been through it. Let me help you."

I'm tempted to take her up on it, but hesitant to give my combination to a complete stranger. *Like there will ever be anything in there worth stealing.* "It's 27-9-35."

"Got it." She maneuvers into place between me and the door, hunches down to fiddle with the lock. I note the bold orange *22* and the name *Spencer* on the back of her black hoodie.

She opens the locker with such ease that it makes me feel twice as dumb. She moves away from it, gestures at the thing with a flat palm, like, 'Voila!'

"Thanks," I whisper.

"No problem." She offers her hand for a shake. "I'm Valerie Spencer. My friends call me Spence. I'm a senior."

"Britton Walsh, also a senior." I shake her offered hand, drop it a little too quickly, pick up my messenger bag and start shifting my books onto the top shelf.

"Britton, sweet name. Where'd you transfer from?"

"East Boston."

"You're from the city? Why'd your parents move up here?"

I always dread this moment, having to explain to everyone I meet that I don't have parents. I've never even met them. They gave me away the day I was born. It hurts enough knowing that they didn't want me; telling other people about it is excruciating. Naturally, I have an alternative to the truth, a well-researched and complex lie: Both my parents are climatologists who work for the United States Antarctic Program. They went on assignment to Palmer Station, so I'm staying with family friends until graduation. For some reason, though, I can't bring myself to lie to her.

She contemplates me for a moment, bewildered by my silence. "Was that a hard question?"

"Mmm…"

"We don't have to talk about it," she says coolly. The softness in her eyes tells me she means it.

Pivot, moron. "The number on the back of your sweatshirt. What sport do you play?"

She tugs her hoodie tight against her body. Below her left clavicle is a crest, the letters BHS and a soccer ball emblazoned across it.

"Soccer. Nice."

"Speaking of, sorry to cut our conversation short, I have to go get ready for practice."

"Okay."

"See ya, same place." She begins to saunter off, but stops a few paces in and turns heel. "Do you have a Study tomorrow?"

"Um." I scan my memory. "I do. G Block 1."

"That's my Study, too. Then G2 lunch."

"Same."

"Gotta love it, gives us an hour and a half to do whatever. I'm psyched to use my off-campus privileges, perks of surviving this shithole for three years."

This isn't a shithole. Roxbury Jr.-Sr. was a shithole. "Yeah."

"You want to come with me?"

I pause, weigh the invite, and her. I can already tell that I'll get along better with her than I ever will with Avery's friends. And if what they say about the girls' soccer team is true, Spence might end up being one of those allies I'm eager to make. "Sure."

"Meet me in the parking lot tomorrow at, like, 11:20? We can take my car."

I nod.

"Dope," she says, then bounces down the hall toward the nearest stairwell.

"What were you doing with her?" Avery appears at my side from nowhere.

Making out in full view of every passing student, duh. "What did it look like we were doing? We were talking."

She blinks at me. "She's trouble."

"Seems nice to me." I slam my locker door, turn to her and sneer. "I'm going out to lunch with her tomorrow," I retort, then dash away from her.

She trails behind. Once she's close enough, she snatches my arm, stops me dead. "No, you're not."

Is it absolutely necessary for her to touch me? "Yes, I am." I yank myself free from her grasp.

Her groan is almost inaudible, but it registers.

Deadpan. "What?"

Her face is a blank canvas. "I'm just trying to look out for you. You're new here, so trust me, you'd be better off staying away from Spence."

Spence, huh? "Why?"

She folds her arms across her chest, purses her lips together—secure as a dead-bolted door.

"I'd prefer to get to know her and decide for myself whether or not she's 'trouble,' alright?"

"Fine." She rolls her eyes. "If you're not going to soccer tryouts, you'll have to walk home. I've got cheerleading," she says, then marches away from me.

"No skin off my ass," I mutter under my breath and embark on my long walk to the Cahills' house.

CHAPTER TWO

I'm sitting at the kitchen table reading George Orwell's *1984* for English class when Mrs. Cahill arrives home from work. I look up from the book to find her overburdened by her briefcase and two brown paper grocery bags. I dog-ear my page and scurry over to help her. "Mrs. Cahill, let me get those for you."

"Oh, Britton, thank you." She offloads the bags into my arms. "And please stop calling me 'Mrs. Cahill.' Catelyn is fine. Cate would be better."

I suck in a lungful of air. It's difficult for me to get comfortable with calling adults anything other than Mr. or Mrs. So-and-So. Maybe it's a 'respecting my elders' thing. Hell, I think if I ever met my birth parents, I'd call them Mr. Walsh and Ms. whatever my mother's last name is. *Jesus, that's pathetic on so many levels.*

"Cate." I let her name slide around my mouth, tasting tiny pieces of it as though it were a food I've never tried before. I'm not sure whether or not I like it. I start to unload the bags, compel myself to concentrate on something other than my uneasiness.

"How was your first day of school?" she asks at my back as I'm putting a gallon of milk in the fridge.

"It was fine."

"Just 'fine'?"

Right? Should be an expert at first days. "Fine is better than shitty—uh, bad!" I spin around to gauge her reaction to my swearing.

Mrs. Cahill—Cate—is calm as can be. "You're old enough to say 'shit.' You'll hear Tom say worse. He's a potty mouth, especially when he's testing a pre-release game." A little grin flickers into being.

To say I'm relieved would be an understatement. I used to get slapped in the mouth for cursing. Was that two foster moms ago, or three, now?

"Is there something specific you'd like for dinner?" she asks, either not noticing or overlooking my reaction. "I was thinking spaghetti and meatballs, Avery's favorite. Do you like Italian?"

"Yes, I do." A lot. "Spaghetti and meatballs sounds great."

Dinner is weird. I haven't sat down at a table for a proper meal with any of my foster families in a long time. Mr. Cahill, er, Tom, is nice. I hadn't gotten the chance to talk with him much over my first couple of days here because he's been crazy busy with work. He seems pretty laid-back, precisely how I expected a guy who got rich designing video games would be.

Cate and Tom are chatty, talking about their day's grind: Cate had a debacle with a client who hadn't divulged his tendency to cheat on his wife, thereby obliterating the prospect of an amicable divorce. Tom had to talk a graphics department intern through a mini meltdown after the lead designer told her to get the fuck out of his office, then he had to scold the lead designer for being a prick to the poor girl.

Avery is silent throughout, sitting across the table from me. She's not spacing out, but not quite interested, either. Now and again I catch her watching me. Examining me? I wonder what's going on in her head. She's not going to tell me, and I'm not going to ask.

She's different at home. Quieter. Is she more at ease here, or less?

"Hey," Tom says to his daughter, "practice go well today?"

Avery rolls a few strands of her still-damp hair around her finger—she didn't bother to blow dry it after her post-practice shower. "It was a dumpster fire. No one kept up with the routines over summer. Everyone's out of shape. I'm quitting."

Cate drops her fork. It tings against her plate. "You're what?"

Avery's shoulders tense. She sits up straighter. *Less at ease. Strange.* "I'm quitting," she repeats deliberately. Defiant.

"That's not like you."

"Or maybe that's exactly like me."

Cate frowns at her, puffs out an exasperated breath.

This got awks fast.

"If you're unhappy doing it, you should quit," Tom interjects. "But if it's because you're frustrated—"

"I'm unhappy and frustrated. It's not fun anymore. It's a chore."

"It seems so sudden, is all," says Cate.

"Sudden? I was miserable last season. I only ever thought it was fun because of—forget it. It's not my thing anymore, okay? I'm quitting."

Tom reaches up, gives Avery's shoulder a gentle squeeze. "You do you, kiddo."

Her posture relaxes. *I see… she's a daddy's girl.*

Cate is placated. "You don't have to stay on the squad, but you have to do something. Join a club. How about yearbook?"

Avery hitches her chin at me. "What are you gonna do?"

"I, uh—"

"We need to have at least one extracurricular." She looks daggers at her mom. "House rules."

That's a new one for me. Most of my other foster parents didn't care what I did, as long I stayed out of their way and refrained from any activities that might bring the cops to their doorsteps. "Is there a photography club?"

The corners of her mouth prick up ever-so-slightly. "Mmhmm. I think it meets after school on Thursdays. I don't know where."

Tomorrow's Thursday. *Fantastic.* "I guess I'll check that out then."

"Me too."

I'm startled. She spots it. "You don't have to."

"It'll be good for her to try something new!" Cate exclaims. "And wouldn't it be nice to already have a friend in the club with you?"

"Wouldn't it?" Avery rests her cheek on her clenched fist. Neither of her parents catch her eyebrow wiggle.

I scrape the dinner scraps into the garbage and Avery begins the dishwashing. I offer to help. She shakes her head no. I shrug and head for the hallway.

The house is a large colonial-style Georgian with two floors—common spaces downstairs, three bedrooms and a home office upstairs, a bathroom on each level. The wooden ceiling beams are exposed in every room and the walls are painted a calming pastel blue and eggshell white. My room—so odd to say, I've never had a room to myself before—is next to Avery's, down the hall from Tom and Cate's. Overall, the place is nice—not just the size or the beachy décor, but the vibe too. More than a house, it feels like a home.

The wall along the wide staircase is lined with picture frames—art prints mostly, like van Gogh's *Almond Blossoms* series, though family photos are sprinkled here and there. There's a recent one of Tom, Cate, and Avery in front of the Christmas tree at Faneuil Hall. I love that tree. It's always beautiful. And consistent. Some Christmases it was the only tree I had.

I stop to scan a photo of Avery when she was young, seven or eight. She's missing a front tooth, smiling—not at the camera, at something out of frame. She was adorable. Bright eyes, choppy bangs. *Happy.*

An unexpected heaviness blooms in my chest. I don't have any photos of me as a child, outside of an old yearbook from middle school. I thought about tossing it a few moves ago, figuring it was just something that took up space in my duffle bag. In the end I decided to keep it as a reminder that it's okay for me to take up space.

"You good?" Avery's voice from behind me shakes me from my thoughts.

"Yeah, I'm good."

"Then, are you going to stand there all night or—should I, like, go around you?"

"Sorry." I continue the climb. She traces my footsteps. "You really don't have to come to photography club with me," I call to her as she passes me for her bedroom. "I'll be fine on my own."

"I want to. I wouldn't have offered, otherwise. I'll meet you there. I have to turn in my uniform to the athletics office first."

"Okay."

"Goodnight."

"Goodnight."

CHAPTER THREE

The day drags, until the bell signaling my Free Study rings. Then it's as if I've entered warp speed. I haven't let myself get excited about anything in ages. If I don't get my hopes up, I can never be let down. Even though I've just met her, there's something about Spence that makes me want to take a chance on her. Whether or not that's a foolish notion remains to be seen.

The student parking lot is bigger than I realized. There are different sections for different grades, and they're haphazard at best. I decide to lean against a lamppost and keep my eyes on the entrance so I'll see Spence when she comes out.

A sea of kids floods the lot, seniors with G-Block lunch or free study exercising the hard-earned off-campus privilege on Thursdays and Fridays. They're all pumped to be outside. Most kids think of school as a prison; I've always felt my freest at school, where I know none of the adults can smack me around and I'm guaranteed two hearty meals.

Spence bounces out the door. She stops for a second, throws her head back toward the sky. Her eyes are closed and she's basking in the sunlight. *Recharging her battery.* She must think it's too warm out—she peels her letterman jacket off, folds it over her arm, adjusts her T-shirt where it's ridden up her torso. Then she catches sight of me. Her lips spread into a smile. "Yo!" She greets me, still smiling.

"Hey."

"Where do you wanna go?"

No idea. "Uh…"

"Ah, right." She gets it. "What do you feel like eating?"

"I'm down for whatever."

"Alright, alright, alright," she singsongs and signals me to follow her.

Her silver Dodge Charger suits her: a muscle car, though not overly flashy; four doors, long and lean. The windows are down, music's up—not so loud that we can't speak over it, but we're both content to listen to it, for now.

She chooses a restaurant five minutes from school called Flip the Bird. Its logo is a pissed-off rooster, hunched over and scowling at the street from between its legs. I dig it. He knows you're here to devour him and is judging the shit out of you for it.

Spence opens the door for me, ushers me through. She's got manners. A lot of people don't. "Thanks."

She nods.

It's not crowded, but there are two people in front of us waiting for their food. It gives me a chance to read over the menu.

"What are you getting?" she wonders.

"Mmm. The *Ya' Basic!* with a *Flip the Bird.*" Fried chicken on a bun, topped with an egg. "You?"

"*The Cry Bird.*"

I read its description aloud, "Chicken fried in a ghost pepper and habanero batter, lettuce, red pepper jam. My mouth is on fire just from saying the words."

"I like things spicy."

I like things bland. The more boring, the better.

She tells the guy at the counter her order, and mine. "And a Coke. Want a drink?" she asks me.

"Bottled water, please," I say to the guy. He rings us up. "Uh, sorry, separate checks."

"I've got it." Spence glides her debit card through the card reader faster than I can protest.

Plenty of time to blush, though. "Next time it's on me."

"That's fair."

Her first question for me after we've sat down and started eating is, "What's your favorite color?"

It's a simple getting-to-know-you question, yet I struggle with it. There are so many great ones to choose from. "I think grey, although technically that's a shade. I like it because it's neither black nor white. It's both, simultaneously."

"A balance between light and dark. Like life," she says.

I'm amazed at her insight—wicked deep for someone our age. "What's yours?"

"Red. Not like fire engine red. Blood red."

That, too, suits her. *Spicy things.*

We talk and talk, mostly about inconsequential stuff. Until she asks about my parents, again. She isn't trying to pry; she's curious because I was cryptic. I don't have to squelch my instinct to lie, but I do have to gather my guts to tell the truth. Sometimes people act weird around me after they find out. I don't think she will, but she could. "I don't have parents. I'm in the foster system. That's why I moved here; I got a new placement."

She digests the information with her last bite of sandwich, then slurps some soda. No visible reaction at all. "Do you like your new foster family so far?"

She hasn't disappointed me, yet. We could be friends. *Not if you tell her that Avery's your foster sister.* That might be true. She wasn't shy about her aversion to Spence, so I'm sure Spence must be aware of it. Maybe the animosity is mutual. *Keep names out of it until you can't anymore.* "Yeah. They're cool." From this point on, I speak about them in ambiguities, making sure not to give too much away.

*

Photography Club meets in room 321 every Thursday at three; I checked the BHS activities website during CompSci. Today is their first meeting of the school year. I'm relieved I haven't missed anything. I take a second to collect myself, never having been much of a joiner, then head in. I count seventeen kids. They're all already acquainted with each other. A few of them set their gaze on me, though their attention is fleeting. Their conversations and comparisons between cameras aren't interrupted by my arrival. The clock above the whiteboard reads 3:05 p.m. The faculty advisor hasn't arrived yet. Neither has Avery. *She's not coming, stupid.*

The door swings open behind me. *Or is she?* In walks a young-ish, black-haired teacher carrying a small blue bin and a clipboard in his arms. He's from the history department, I think. He makes his way to the front of the class, puts the bin and clipboard on the large rectangular desk, then leans against it. "Howdy, everyone. For those of you who don't know me, I'm Mr. Warren. Welcome to Photography Club." He removes the lid from the bin, plucks out a camera case. It's small—a point-and-shoot. "Anyone who doesn't have a camera is welcome to borrow a PowerShot. You can sign it out and take it home with you, as long as you promise to baby it." He cradles the camera case in his hand and makes cooing noises at it, eliciting a round of chortles from the students. "Come on up if you need one."

Nobody moves. They all have hardcore Nikons and Canons and Sonys on straps around their necks or in cases on their desks. Just me then. Big surprise!

I keep my eyes trained on the floor as I go to retrieve my loaner. Mr. Warren hands me the clipboard. I write my name and homeroom on the top line of the sign-out sheet. "Britton Walsh," he reads my name back to me. "Good to meet ya. Pick a camera, any camera." The one I choose is in a black and grey pouch.

I'm sliding into a combo chair-desk at the back of the room when the door swishes open again. Everyone turns to gawk at the straggler. *Avery.*

"I'm late, my bad." She isn't sorry, she's indifferent. "What's goin' on, Mr. Warren?" She greets him as though they're friends. She must've taken one of his classes before and liked it well enough.

He's as surprised to see her as everyone else is, like she's never shown an ounce of interest in photography before. It could be she hasn't, and she's only here because of me. "Avery, nice of you to join us. Do you have a camera, or do you need to borrow one?"

She rummages through her enormous white leather purse, pulls out her iPhone. "I'm covered."

Mr. Warren sighs. "That's not a camera."

Her turn to sigh.

She saunters up, fills out the form, takes a camera and makes her way to the back of the class. She plants her ass in the seat next to mine, grins at me. "You thought I ditched you, didn't you?"

Yes and no.

Mr. Warren clears his throat. "Alright, so, let's talk about our first project: Autumn Landscapes."

The club wraps up a little after four thirty. We hit the parking lot as girls' soccer practice is ending. Spence is at her car, driver's side door open. She tugs the strap of an orange Adidas gym bag from her shoulder and tosses the overstuffed thing into the front seat. She looks up, sees me, sees Avery. I watch her grapple with whether or not she wants to wave. She decides to go for it.

I wave back. Avery can't subdue an involuntary flinch. There's definitely history between them. Spence hops into the car, turns over the engine and reverses out of the spot. I follow the Charger with my eyes as it guns out of the lot and onto the street.

"I take it your lunch date with her went well," Avery comments. Her tone is neutral. I check her face—it divulges nothing. I'm starting to recognize that as a talent of hers, and it's unnerving. I'm good at catching glimpses of people's feelings, but it seems when she wants to, she's better at hiding them than most. Perhaps she's even better at it than I am.

It wasn't a date. *She paid, so it kinda was.* "Yep," I respond as we slide into her azure BMW. I really don't feel like talking about it. I wish there were some music playing; she prefers to drive with the stereo off. "How did your friends react when you told them you were quitting the squad?"

She answers only after she's banged the left onto Sohier Road. "Kylie was cool. Liz and Tasha were sad about it. Amy was pissed. She's the captain and I've screwed up her roster. She and Coach Meyers have to find a spotter to replace me now."

"What does a spotter do?"

"Keeps everything from going to shit."

That makes me snigger. "How so?"

"A spotter always has to be paying attention, ready to react. They can't be afraid to catch a girl who's falling, and they can't be afraid of getting hurt."

Sharp and fearless. Hmm. That's fitting. "Sounds like an important job."

"I had to make sure no one broke their fucking neck, so yeah." Her words are flippant, though her expression is firm. She cared enough to want to do the job correctly—and well. Why did she really quit?

I find myself yearning to get to know her. It's unexpected. I'm usually satisfied by passively coexisting with my foster siblings. Rarely, if ever, have I sought any kind of relationship with any of them. Should I crush the bud, or nurture it? *To be, or not to be? That is the question.*

My window for contemplation closes as we pull into the Cahills' driveway. The simple fact that I'm not impartial for once is enough to sway me. "I was hoping to get started on this Autumn Landscapes thing this weekend. I still don't really know where stuff is around here, though, so if you have some time, you wanna work on it together?"

She purses her lips as if she's considering whether or not I'm worth penciling into her schedule. "I don't have any plans Saturday now that I'm done with cheerleading. Have you ever been to Salem Willows Park?"

"I've never been to Salem."

Her brow jumps up. "Seriously?"

Salem is a city parents take their kids to for a bit of spooky fun or cool history. Has she forgotten who she's talking to? Who would've ever taken me? *That's unfair. She doesn't know your sad-ass life.*

Then it dawns on her, and there's sympathy in her eyes. "We are so going."

My stomach does a bizarre jolty thing. "Works for me."

CHAPTER FOUR

I am so happy that my first week of school is over and I get to relax for a couple of days. Tom is sitting on the couch, folding laundry. Cate is working late and Avery is out with the Braindead Brigade. I'm glad for that. She's been stuck with me 24/7 since I moved in. I don't want her to get sick of me like I'm some annoying kid sister she's constantly required to babysit—funny, since Cate told me I'm more than a month older. Avery won't turn eighteen until October third.

At lunch Spence invited me to a party that one of her teammates is throwing tonight. I thanked her, but declined—not because I dislike parties, I can take or leave them depending on the atmosphere, but because of how hot my emotions have been running lately. That's always the case when I'm adjusting to a new environment. I'm exhausted from keeping them in check. It's a full-time job and going to a party right now would put me well into overtime.

For the moment, I'm stoked to be reading. I'm four chapters deep into *1984*—it's good, if wicked depressing—and curled up on the taupe recliner on the far side of the living room. I couldn't sink any further into its high pillowy back. Believe me, I've tried. It has to be the most comfortable chair I've ever plopped my butt into. I might sleep here. *Ridiculous. You have a bed. A friggin' nice one, too.* It is nice, a queen memory foam. The whole bedroom is nice—unnecessarily spacious, if I'm honest. There's a tall bureau, a desk with attached shelving where my school-issued Chromebook lives, and an entertainment center complete with stereo, TV, and Wi-Fi Blu-ray player. The color scheme isn't very me: pale yellows and oranges. I'm not complaining; it just doesn't seem to mesh with the rest of the house, which Cate obviously decorated. It may have been Tom's office before they started taking in strays. He comes off the type of guy who likes bright colors. That would explain Avery's affinity for them, too.

"You look cozy over there." Tom flashes me a grin.

"I am." As if on cue, I yawn.

"How are you settling in?"

"Good. Your house has a really peaceful vibe to it."

He chuckles. "I didn't think kids still said things like 'vibe.'"

"Some of us do. I like it. It's a good word."

"I agree. You and Avery seem to be vibing pretty well."

He is such a dad. "We are."

"I'm glad."

"Same."

I've had enough of *1984* and conversation for the night, so I decide to call it quits and head upstairs. I heave my messenger bag off the floor and cram the book into it.

"All done for tonight?"

"Yeah. I'm wrecked. Goodnight, Tom."

"Night, kiddo."

Kiddo. *Don't smile.* I shoulder my bag.

"Hold on a sec. Since you're going upstairs, will you bring these up to Avery's room for me, please?"

Avery's room. It doesn't seem right to go in there when she's not home. But I can't say no. That would be messed up. He and Cate are doing so much for me. "Sure."

"Thanks!" He winks, then comes over and stuffs a pile of clothes into my arms.

*

Her room is not how I pictured it. The walls, the curtains, the duvet, the carpet are all varying shades of grey—from nearly black to the color of the sky on a rainy day. Every piece of laundry in my arms is pink, yellow, baby blue, mint green, white. She wears such cheerful colors, yet her private space is so gloomy. My first impression of her was wrong. She's not the All-American Teenage Dream I pegged her to be. There's a darkness to her she doesn't let many people see. Now I'm even more intrigued.

I lay her clothes on her bed and take a last glance around before I start to feel like I'm intruding. *Leave already.*

CHAPTER FIVE

Tom and Cate are delighted to hear that Avery and I are going to Salem—Cate, in particular. She's hopeful a bond will develop between her daughter and me. From the moment I stepped into their home, she's egged Avery on—planted ideas, fun stuff we could do together. It's cute, really. Maybe she wanted Avery to have a sister, but things just didn't pan out that way for her and Tom. Come to think of it, they're the first foster parents I've stayed with who only have one kid of their own. Most had a brood. The last ones had a daughter close to my age, another a few years younger, and a precious five-year-old son I was crazy about. His name was Brent. I miss his sweet little face, and playing Pokémon GO with him. Maybe someday I'll have kids of my own. If I do, I'll play with them every day.

We're getting ready to leave and Tom hands Avery a wad of cash. Just like that, a stack of twenties she didn't ask for. Then he tries to give me one. Panic climbs my ribcage. *Not today, Satan.* Or any day. "I don't—" I want to tell him that I don't need it. I've hardly spent any of my monthly stipend. I get to decide what happens to the majority of it now that I'm a legal adult, and I'm trying to save as much as possible so I can afford tuition at a community college and a crappy two-bedroom apartment with five roommates next year. I know the Cahills aren't getting much financial incentive from the government to keep me in their home. I suspect that had a lot to do with my prior foster family dumping me. Good thing the Cahills are rolling in it, or I'd be a vagabond—preferential to another awful group home.

"No arguments, young lady!" Tom pretends to be stern. *Nah, dude, you don't possess that bone.* I accept the money. If he insists, it would be rude not to. I don't want to hurt his feelings or anything. I could always give it back to him later.

Cate kisses her daughter on the forehead and I'm shocked that Avery allows her to do it. I guess even if you've had parents your whole life, it's still nice to be shown that kind of affection once in a while. She catches me watching, and her cheeks go pink. Blushing is another reaction she can't control.

"Wait, wait!" Cate hurries to the living room, digs through her satchel briefcase, and bounds back over to us. She's holding a black rectangular thing. "This is for you." She passes it to me. It's a brand-new iPhone, top of the line. I had an LG a while ago. I never replaced it after it stopped working; I hardly used it, so I didn't really see a point. "I've preprogrammed all our numbers into it," she continues. "It's all charged up. The box with the accessories is on the dining room table."

I look to Avery, checking for a response. It would be another involuntary flinch, but there isn't one. Of course not. Why would she be envious? She wants for nothing.

It's too much. It's all too much. *Swallow that lump and do not cry, pansy ass.* "Thank you."

"You're welcome," Cate replies plainly. To her, this is nothing at all. "Go have some fun, you two."

I've got Mr. Warren's PowerShot in one pocket of my jeans and my new iPhone in the other. Sitting down with all this tech poking into me is uncomfortable. And heavy. I understand now why girls have purses—I never will, I hate them. I didn't bother to bring my messenger bag, either. I wasn't expecting to be carrying so many things.

Avery merges onto 128, accelerates to match the flow of traffic. We enter Salem's city limits ten minutes after leaving the house, but the surface roads are congested and now we're limping along, top land speed of 5 mph. "Since you've never been here before, I've thrown together an itinerary for us. Hope that's cool with you."

"Yeah, for sure." I mean it. Not that I would tell her if I wasn't cool with it. She didn't have to agree to do any of this in the first place. If she said we were only going to be there for an hour to take some stupid pictures and then turn the hell around, I'd be cool with that, too.

"Are you into history? Salem has a lot of it."

Beyond what's compulsory at school, I haven't given it much consideration. "Are you into history?" *Why you always gotta answer a question with another question?*

"Yes or no?"

She's a mind reader! "I guess."

She laughs. Was I being funny? "That wasn't a yes or a no. Allow me to demonstrate: 'Yes, I do like history. It's fascinating.'"

"Good to know. What's first on the agenda?"

"Finding freaking parking! This is nuts." We haven't seen a single unoccupied space yet. It's got her flustered.

Now, I'm laughing. I stop abruptly when the phrase *she's so cute* pops into my head. I spy an open metered spot—a gift from the gods, for multiple reasons—and point it out to her. "Over there."

"Yes!" She whizzes into the space, adjusts position, then shifts the gear to P. "I've never found parking right on Essex before. You're good luck."

The only luck I've got is bad. "Happy to help."

She fishes some quarters from a cup holder and we hop out onto the street. She feeds the curbside meter—four hours, the full allotment.

"We must have a packed itinerary."

"This is only the downtown portion of our field trip. The Willows has its own parking lot, and we're going to use it because it's like five miles from here and these shoes were not designed for that kind of walking." She kicks up her heel. Literally—they're heels. Sky blue, with an ankle strap. *Why would she...?* I glance down at my feet: well-worn Converse, the second of two pairs of sneakers I own. When I look up at her again, she does that 'come hither' motion with her finger.

Not her puppet. Screw that, I'm following her. "Lead the way."

There's a guy ahead of us on the sidewalk who'll be passing us in a few seconds, and he is rubbernecking Avery so hard it's as if he's being paid to do it. Her skirt is so short and her coat is so long that it makes her look like she's naked from the waist down. I hadn't noticed until right this second. The guy whistles at her as he walks by.

"Eww," she mumbles and goes a deep shade of red.

He embarrassed her. Unacceptable. I hit a standstill, spin around. "Hey, asshole! She's playing for the Sox and you're on Junior Varsity!" He glances at me over his shoulder, jaw slack. There. He's embarrassed, too. Good.

Avery stares at me, speechless, then doubles over with laughter. It's infectious, gets me giggling, too.

Once we manage to compose ourselves, she looks at me and bites her lip. "So chivalrous," she says, then loops her arm through mine and ushers me down the block. Oddly, I don't mind that she's touching me.

We cross Washington Street and enter a pedestrian mall section of Essex Street. The whole width of it is teeming with couples and children and tour groups. I have to jam in closer to Avery. I catch a whiff of her perfume: citrus, and some kind of sweet, airy flower. It's delectable. "You smell good." *Nice one, slick.*

"Thanks. It's Daisy by Marc Jacobs."

I nod like a bobblehead doll because I am an awkward moron.

We jump on the end of a long line in front of an old stone building that resembles a church. It has an enormous stained-glass window between two turrets—a few smaller ones off to the sides, too—and a grand, arched double door. There's gold lettering on a wooden sign: SALEM WITCH MUSEUM.

"This place is so sick at night," she says. "The windows have this red glow. Super creepy."

"You like creepy stuff?" I wouldn't have guessed that about her. Cheerleader fashionistas aren't generally into eccentric and eerie. It's something we have in common, though.

"Hell yeah. Haunted houses, horror movies, all that shit. I don't know, being scared is just exciting."

That isn't real fear. It's fun to be scared of ghosts and goblins, things that don't exist in the world. The only actual monsters are human beings, and some are as horrible as it gets. "I feel that on a personal level."

She is not at all surprised. "Nice."

"It must be awesome here in October."

"It's lit. We'll have to come back for Halloween. The costumes people wear are wild, so original and intricate."

"I don't remember the last time I dressed up for Halloween." I'm blurting out every friggin' thing that crosses my mind today, aren't I?

She ruminates on it. "Let's do it this year."

"You don't think we're too old for that?"

"You're never too old."

No, just too self-conscious. "I will if you will."

"You're on." She gives me a smile.

The museum is amazing. We watch a reenactment of a scene from Bridget Bishop's witch trial in this massive auditorium set up to resemble a courtroom. Afterward there's a tour through recreated sites of Salem in 1692.

We come to a tiny chamber, converted from a closet, with a barred door and shackles attached to the walls. The plaque beside the door says, *Coffin Cells, often no bigger than 65.5 x 35.5 inches, were used to imprison accused witches before and during trial.* Big yikes! We're encouraged by the tour guide to go inside, get a feel—he'll take pictures! Avery's into it. I take a pass. I've spent a fair amount of time locked in modern-day closets—I don't need a fake jail cell to know how it feels to be trapped.

After her mock internment is over, she asks me if I'm claustrophobic. I tell her that I'm not. Although, if claustrophobia means 'scared to death of a cramped-ass storeroom some jerk-off shoved you in as punishment for imagined crimes,' then yes, that would make me at least somewhat claustrophobic.

We're moving further into the heart of the city. She wants to show me Old Town Hall and its collection of authentic seventeenth-century artifacts. We come across a creeptastic statue of Nosferatu on the corner of Derby Street.

"Whoa, he's new." She rushes over to the bald, grey-skinned vampire with the enthusiasm of a five-year-old who's seen a puppy. My brain liquefies over how adorable it is. "Get your camera out."

I liberate the PowerShot from my pocket, turn it on—focus the lens on her and the monster she's crouched in front of. That's when Nosferatu moves. He flings his arm forward like he's going to grab her and dips his fangs close to her neck.

She screams so loudly that the astronauts on the International Space Station can hear it. She bolts toward me, seizes my waist and ducks behind me. I am cracking up. Everyone around us is, too.

I get a hold of myself, reach around my back and wrench her to my side. "I don't know what you expect me to do. I'm 5'5", 115 pounds. That badboy is a behemoth."

Nosferatu breaks character; a muffled chortle streams through his facemask. "Come back, come back! Take a selfie with me."

Avery knocks her shoulder into mine, asking *Do you wanna?* sans words.

She really wants to. I jump in front of the bloodsucker, and she joins me. I'm readying the camera when an older gentleman offers to take the picture for me. I hand the PowerShot over to him, then pose beside Avery.

"Say cheese!" The flash goes off.

The man checks the LCD screen, then shows it to me. Mr. Vamp's got his arms outstretched, total menace-mode. Avery has a mien of contrived horror, hands on the sides of her face like that painting *The Scream*. I've got my hands in the pockets of my army jacket and I'm shooting her a sidelong glance, lips in a grin.

Avery squashes in to take a gander at the pic. "Amazeballs!" We thank the man in unison. Then she rifles through her purse, goes to stick a twenty-dollar bill into Nosferatu's coffin-shaped tip box. *Wow.* Nosferatu catches the note's value. He lifts his mask, rests it on his forehead. He's middle-aged, has a close-shaved beard. "Thank you so much!"

"You got me good." She wags a finger at him. We continue on our way to Old Town Hall.

*

Her excitement is impossible to contain. There's wonderment in her eyes as they take in every object—an archaic weaving loom, a bodice dress, three pairs of antique spectacles, a tricorn hat, and a marching drum and drumsticks used to beat the procession for Washington's troops.

She doesn't like history. She *loves* it. It's the most unpredicted, captivating aspect of her personality so far. I'm enjoying learning about her even more than I am about the founding of our Republic.

The lot at Salem Willows is half empty, which, given the late season, makes sense. It's a beautiful seaside park, lush with trees and a small stretch of boardwalk boasting food stands, arcades and kiddie rides. The rides are out of commission, but the arcades and food stands are open for business. *Mmm. Pizza.*

She notices my interest in the boardwalk. "Hungry? Or do you want to get your game on?"

"I'm not big on video games."

"Neither am I."

What? How? "Your dad owns a gaming company!"

"And I am an utter disappointment to him," she says with a smirk. "Pizza?"

Stop that! It's uncanny. "Yes, please."

We grab our pizza, two slices each, and two bottles of water. It takes some coaxing, but she lets me pay for the both of us—not with her dad's money. We find a bench on the paved walkway lining the shore and take in the view as we eat.

Once we're finished, we walk around for a while. It's turned out to be one of those perfect mid-September afternoons that balances on the precipice of fall and summer, sunny and warm, yet with a cool breeze blowing in from the ocean. The leaves on the white willow trees are beginning to change—some are already a mellow gold, tinges of bronze at their edges.

I've got my camera out, lens zoomed in on a long, drooping branch. I snap the photo. *Gorgeous.*

"Hey," she breaks the easy silence we've fallen into. "How come you weren't—uh, never mind." She regards me, blue eyes shining, though I can see a hint of sadness in them. *That's pity.* It gives away her question. She's not the first person ever to ask me. She is, however, the first person I wouldn't mind answering.

"No, go ahead."

"It's probably a dumb question, but... why weren't you ever adopted? You're polite, smart. I'm sure you were cute when you were little, too. I don't understand how you didn't find a home."

Find a home. If only I'd been a kitten or a sweet baby bunny, I would have. I rub my neck—instinct when I'm stalling for time. "I was born with a congenital heart defect. I had surgery to fix it when I was really young, but I was still sort of sickly as a kid."

With this new information, her expression changes. The pity vanishes and concern takes its place. *She cares?* "You're okay now though, right?"

"Yeah. I'm fine. It's just that by the time I grew out of it I was like, four or five. Most people want to adopt babies, or at least healthy toddlers." I shrug. "I was never the most stand-out child in the room, anyway."

"You stand out to me."

A chill runs through me and I shudder. The wind is picking up, but it's pure coincidence. She doesn't know that, though. "It's getting cold." I zip the flaps of my jacket closed for effect.

"We can go if you want."

I do and I don't. "You haven't taken any pictures."

"You took a bunch. That was the goal, right?"

I nod.

She gathers her keys from her purse and we head for the car.

*

The sun is dipping below the horizon by the time we get back to the house. I'm not ready for the day to be over. She lets me set the pace as we amble side by side up the wide path to the front porch. "I had a really nice day." It's innocent enough that I don't scold myself for admitting it.

"Me, too." She smiles, then lowers her gaze to the ground.

Inside, we find Cate and Tom cuddling on the couch under a blanket. On the TV is a fully nude, very loud sex scene. They're engrossed and don't notice us at all. Avery announces our arrival: "Parental units! Quit with the porn. Think of the children!"

"No, no, it's a regular movie." Tom scrambles for the remote, clicks furiously at the power button. It's funny that he's the one who reacts that way, not Cate. I thought Tom was the more easy-going of the two. Cate laughs, and then Tom laughs, which causes Avery and me to laugh. It's the best possible chain reaction under the circumstances.

"I need a shower. I feel gross." Avery glowers at her parents. To me she says, "Dibs!" Then jets up the steps.

"Sorry!" I throw my hand up and head for the stairs, as well. Then I halt, turn around—scurry into the living room. I remove the folded stack of Tom's twenties from my pocket and place them on the coffee table. "Thanks." I make a quick exit. *Ta-ta for now.*

CHAPTER SIX

I spend every lunch block of the week with Avery and her friends—not by choice. Yesterday as we were all headed off campus, she wondered about it in that nonchalant semi-interested way: "No Spence, huh?" I tried not to show her that I was bothered by it, but I think she knew.

I haven't seen much of Spence at all, only briefly at our lockers after last bell. Every day, she'd say, "Hi," and I'd respond in kind. Then she'd close her locker, say, "Later," and hurry away. No chitchat. No invitations anywhere. Nothing.

I have a sneaking suspicion that she's avoiding me. I'm not sure why she'd be doing that, though. I don't think I did anything to mess things up between us, no accidental dropping of the Cahills' name. She saw me after school with Avery that one time, but that doesn't mean anything. As far as she knows, we could simply be in the same club.

Is she upset I didn't go with her to her friend's party? I doubt that's it. I can tell she isn't the clingy type. *You could ask her, like a normal person.* Or I can simmer and get paranoid over it like I usually do. No, I'm an adult now. I have to start acting like one. I need the practice. I'm going to be out in the world on my own soon enough. *You've been out in the world on your own since you were born.*

That's it, I'm going to confront her. It's more forward than I prefer to be, but Avery isn't the only person I'm interested in getting to know.

*

I'm relieved when the last bell rings. It has been the longest day of the longest week ever. We had a pop quiz in Biology and I'm pretty sure I flunked. I hate pop quizzes. I need to cram the night before a test, or I freeze up and forget everything we've been working on once the packet is in front of me. Call it a preference for over-preparedness, or habit—whichever you like.

"Britton!" Avery calls to me from down the long hall as I'm heading for my locker. I stop to wait for her. I must have an air of impatience or something, because she breaks into a little jog to reach me faster. "I can't drive you home today. I have detention."

"On a Friday? That sucks. What did you do?"

Eye roll. "This guy was being obnoxious in my Civics class, so I told him to shut the fuck up. Mrs. Sievers did not appreciate 'the foul language.'"

"You're not very good at subtlety, are you?"

She's stunned, as if no one has ever called her out on it before. "Not when I'm annoyed."

"Guess I'm walking, then." I let slip a sigh.

"I'm sorry." She's sincere.

Don't be a dick. She doesn't owe you anything. I need to curb my attitude. "It's fine. Shit happens." I just wish it would have happened another day.

"Okay. See you at home."

I slam my locker closed just as Spence shows up to hers. Great. The mood I'm in? My plan to talk to her is tanked.

Lucky for me, my outburst piques her interest. "You look pissed. What's up?"

"I had a crappy day—failed a test, and now I have to hike all the way to the other side of the city because my ride has to stay after school." I exhale my vexation before I have the chance to choke it back. "Sorry, I'm tired, and completely over this week."

She peeks at me around her locker door. "I can give you a ride."

"Don't you have soccer?"

"It's cancelled. My coach is sick. Serves him right, the tyrant."

I smile at that. Here's my opportunity. *Seize the moment.* "Do you want to hang out?"

She looks surprised that I asked. Why? "I would, but I have a lot of homework to catch up on."

Isn't that what the weekend is for? "Oh, okay."

"I'll still drive you home."

"It's that one, with the columns." I point to the white brick house at the very end of the street.

She pulls the car up to the curb, throws it into park. Her cheeks flush. She fidgets in her seat. "The Cahills are your foster family?"

She's been here before? *Busted.* "Did I not mention that?"

"No, you didn't."

I have to be honest with her or this friendship is going to end before it has even begun. "I'm sorry. Avery made it very clear that you guys don't get along, and I didn't want to scare you away or whatever."

"I have kind of been avoiding you." *Knew it!* "I saw you with her the other day, and then you turned down my invite to the party. I thought maybe you'd chosen her."

Chosen her. "Do I have to choose?"

She shrugs her shoulders. "I don't care if you hang out with her, but I'm willing to bet she'll have a problem with you hanging out with me."

So, it's not a mutual thing. I squint at her. "Why does she dislike you so much?"

Her eyes flit over the house. She swallows a glob of saliva. "You'd have to ask her that."

She didn't say 'I don't know.' They're on opposite sides of the same story, and neither one of them is telling it. "You know what, it doesn't even matter. What's important is that I want to be your friend. And I want to be her friend, too. But that doesn't necessarily mean the two of you have to be friends. There's enough of me to go around."

She smirks, considers the idea. "It could work." She puts her hand out. "Gimme your phone."

Bold of her to assume that I have one; it pretty much lives in my bag when I'm at school, unlike with so many of the other kids. I stick my hand into the zippered pocket of my messenger bag, tug out the iPhone stashed away inside. I unlock the screen with the thumbprint reader, then hand it over to her.

She clicks into the contacts menu, adds her name and number, then presses *Call*. Her Samsung rings out from the pocket of her hoodie—an up-tempo electronic tune with echoing chimes and deep rhythms. It's catchy, makes me want to dance.

She answers the call, hangs up quick, saves my info. "There." She flashes me a half-smile, gives the phone back. "You should be a politician when you grow up. You'd be good at it."

Lol. "Was that a compliment or an insult?"

She snickers. "A compliment. Who knows? You could establish world peace."

It would take way more guts than I possess to even begin to accomplish that. "In the interest of establishing world peace, do you really have a ton of homework or was that an excuse not to hang out with me?"

Her gaze drops to her lap and her mouth curls into a frown. *Guilty as charged.* "I suck."

"You do not suck. I understand, and I'll forgive you if you drive us to Starbucks *right now*."

That perks her up. "I could do with a Chili Mocha."

Ick! My face screws itself up. "Whatever floats your boat."

The line at Starbucks is long, swarming with high school and college kids in desperate need of a caffeine fix before their Friday night festivities kick off. There's a group of girls on the opposite side of the stanchions that I recognize from school. The black-haired girl typing on her phone has Tennis with me. We've never spoken, but I've heard her name in roll call—Olivia Takashima. I don't know the names of the blue-haired girl or the blonde.

"Olivia!" Spence hollers. *'Bout to learn them.*

With a second glance, I see that she's wearing a letterman jacket and her sport is soccer. Oh, she's a jock—that's why she gets away with half-assing through Tennis.

Olivia tears her attention from her phone, plasters it on us. "Spence!" She reaches across the rope and they dap up. Blondie leans over, gives Spence a little hug. Blue-hair nods in her direction.

Spence signals at each girl as she introduces them. "Olivia, Hannah, Mack, this is Britton. Britton, The Squad."

Squad! *Chill.*

Blondie—Hannah—gives me a wave, says, "Hi."

"Yo, we're in Tennis together, right?" Olivia asks, two fingers out, hand flapping. "What's good?" She goes to dap me, too. It's not something I normally do, but if that's her thing…

"Wait, this is the new girl you were talking about?" Blue-hair—Mack—glares at Spence, at me.

Spence gives her a hushed, "Shut up, shut up." What did she tell them about me?

The barista calls them up next and they each place their order, pay, then move to the receiving end of the counter. Hannah asks, "Meet us outside when you're done?"

*

Spence's friends manage to snag one of the black mesh tables on the sidewalk. They're sitting around it, freaking out. "What are you squawking about?" Spence pulls a chair out for me and one for herself.

"Noah asked Hannah out. I am shooketh!" Olivia answers.

"Noah Price? He's what you straight girls call 'a snack' right?"

"Snack?" Olivia pulls up his Insta on her iPhone and shows it to me. The guy on the screen is handsome: short black hair, ebony eyes, chiseled jaw, muscular arms. "Tell me he's not a whole-ass meal."

Yep, I'm still wicked gay. "Not the kind of sustenance I'm into, but yeah, he's a whole-ass meal."

Hannah and Mack side-eye Spence; they think I'm not paying attention. I'm always paying attention. And I understand now what she's told them about me—I'm the new girl she thinks is hot. It's fine. I have no say in it, anyhow.

"Hold up, wasn't he hooking up with Avery Cahill last year?" Mack questions.

Hannah shrugs. "Yeah, and?"

"She's a skank. Be careful you don't catch anything from him."

Olivia guffaws. "I'm weak!"

Spence goes stiff, peeps my way. "Chill with that," she says to Mack.

Mack goes *pssh*. "You're defending her all of a sudden? Split personalities much?"

Spence nails her with a scowl. "You're throwing shade all over today."

I realize that I have to interject before this escalates into something stupid. If it puts them off me, then whatever. "I'm friends with Avery."

Silence.

Hannah's the one who finally responds. "Don't mind Mack, she lives with her foot in her mouth." She grins at me.

I take a long swig of my coffee, then reply, "She's entitled to her opinion, even if it makes her sound like an extra salty bitch."

"Ooh, clap back!" Olivia howls. "Sick burn, sis." She thrusts her fist out for a bump and I oblige. Spence and Hannah chortle, more so at Olivia's reaction than my words. Mack rolls her eyes. So, Spence is the Head Bitch in Charge and Mack is the bottom rung of the ladder. Useful information.

After the initial hiccup, things proceed smoothly. I'd usually find a personality as big as Olivia's daunting, but her vibe is so positive that I don't. Hannah is more my speed, calmer, more introverted. Mack and I will not be the best of pals, but I'll tolerate her in exchange for Spence's friendship.

We talk for hours—they talk a lot; I spend most of the time listening—and it's after seven o'clock when Spence drops me off at the house.

Tom meets me in the entryway and gives me a once-over. "Hello."

You done fucked up. "Um, hi."

"Ah, shit, listen, I'm not good at lectures. Please just give me or Cate a heads up if you're going to disappear for hours, okay? We like to know you're safe. Also, checking your phone once in a while would be a good idea."

I scramble for my phone in my messenger bag. I have a missed call and three texts. The call and one text are from Cate, the other two texts are from Tom. "Crap. I'm sorry. It's been on vibrate in my bag the whole time."

"I figured it was something like that. I'll let you in on a little secret"—he lowers his voice—"my wife's a bit of a worrywart."

Yeah, she's the worrywart. "Got it. Won't happen again."

"Good. Alright, well, Avery's out with her friends and Cate is out for drinks with some co-works, so we're on our own for dinner tonight. The only thing I can cook worth a damn is breakfast. Pancakes and eggs?" *Breakfast! Fave.*

He's so genial. How do people get that way? I try to be courteous, but I'm standoffish even on my best days. "Wicked."

He shoots me a double thumbs up, and we shuffle into the kitchen.

CHAPTER SEVEN

It's another perfect fall Saturday—a tad nippy, though not unpleasant. Fortunate for me, because by afternoon I'm smacked by an urge to take some pictures. I've always been interested in photography, just haven't had the opportunity to take it up until now. East Boston High had a Camerawork Club, but I couldn't go. After school I had to pick up Brent from kindergarten, take him home, make him a snack, keep an eye on him. His bio-sisters were the ones who got to do extracurriculars. I was the convenient, live-in child minder. I had no problem with that; he deserved more attention than they were willing to give him, and I was happy to provide it.

I throw on a pair of jeans, my Vans and my new, official Beverly High School Photography Club hoodie—an advertisement of my normality; I don't want to seem like a creeper for taking pictures of randoms. I yank the PowerShot from my desk, then go knock on Avery's door. She isn't much for putting in the work, but she still shows up to club on Thursdays. She really did only join for me.

There's no answer. Actually, I haven't seen her around the house since breakfast. She's probably out doing typical teenager things with her typical teenager friends. I can't begrudge her that; she's had a more ordinary existence than me. I wonder what the world looks like through the eyes of someone like her, someone less jaded—probably a little sunnier, more alluring, less calamitous. It's hard to get bogged down in the shittier parts of life if you've rarely had to experience them.

I recall Tom's advice—warning?—from last night, and turn up the volume on my phone. I find him and Cate sitting across the dining room table from one another, both absorbed in their laptops. "I'm gonna go out, if that's alright with you guys." Cate looks up at me—Tom doesn't; he's wearing a huge pair of headphones. I hold up my camera to her, like she needs a reason.

"That's fine. Give us a shout if you need a lift home."

I wander aimlessly through Prides Crossing, the Cahills' neighborhood. It's upscale—I'm talking mansions and Maybachs—and close to the ocean. I feel out of place. It's definitely the fanciest area I've ever lived in. *It's the only fancy area you've ever lived in.* East Boston was fine, Roxbury was outright dangerous. Before that, Lynn—junkie paradise. It ain't called The City of Sin for nothing.

I take a right onto Haskell Street and happen upon a common I didn't know existed. *Dix Park*, the sign attached to the chain-link fence reads. It's scenic—lots of oak trees donning their autumn hues, and a charming playground with a big plastic castle, slides and a swing set attached to it.

There are kids playing, their mothers sitting on a bench close by, chatting and loosely watching. I power up my camera. One of the moms gives me a quick inspection, reads my shirt. I show her a smile and give a wave. *See, not some pedophile!* Her smile and wave are broader than mine. She's okay. All the adults around here are strangely amiable. I suppose it's because they're all affluent, as though having money makes them more secure in themselves. *Of course it does, you fucking pauper.* Rich people are safer in so many ways they don't even know about.

I snap some pics of the playground, a few with children swinging in a hazy background. I capture this amazing sequence of a little blonde boy leaping from his swing in mid-air, catching some serious height, then landing on his feet, knees bent like he's about to fly away Superman-style. It's adorable and innocent and fun, the epitome of what childhood should be. For the briefest of moments, I'm a little envious of him.

I meander further into the park, closer to the wooded part. There's a pond over this way. A flock of ducks—two adults and seven ducklings—are splashing around in the water, and there are lily pads with frogs on them. So cute! Snap. Snap. Snap, snap. This place was a good find.

In the distance on the right bank of the pond there's a young brunette sitting alone on a bench. The collar of her tan trench coat is popped; huge dark sunglasses obscure half her face. I'm looking at her three-quarter profile with a feeling of familiarity in my stomach, but I don't realize why until she removes her sunglasses. It's Avery.

The soft sunlight bathes her in an ethereal glow, kissing her high cheekbones. She looks like she belongs in a Renaissance painting, all contemplative and melancholic. This is who she is on the inside—grey, like her room. She only lets it out when nobody's looking. *Mesmerizing.*

It's intrusive and I shouldn't do it, but I do. I want to know all of her colors. Snap. Zoom. Snap Snap. Zoom. Snap.

Her phone rings, shattering her stillness. The grey falls away from her, replaced by pink. I hear her say into the receiver, "Hi, Tash."

The longer she listens to Tasha, the more irritated she becomes, until she sputters, "Hun, I broke up with him six months ago. I really don't care who he dates... No, honestly, I don't." More from Tasha. She sighs, "Let it go. He's trying to move on and be happy."

I've had enough—starting to feel stalkerish—so I power down the camera, shove it in my pocket and approach her. She catches her first glimpse of me. "I've gotta go. Yeah, I'll call you later. Bye." She ends the call.

"Hey," I say once I'm close enough.

"Hey." She scooches over, makes room for me on the bench.

"I had no idea there was a park so close to your house."

"I used to come here all the time with—" Her voice disappears. The inner corners of her eyebrows draw up; she pouts her lower lip. And then the look is gone. "I like it here. It's relaxing."

Was it Noah she used to sit next to on this bench? "It is, but you didn't look so relaxed on the phone just now."

"Tasha had to ruin it, call me up to spill the tea."

"I know. Your ex-boyfriend is dating Spence's friend now, huh?"

"News travels fast."

"I was with Spence and her friends at Starbucks yesterday… Are you pissed about it?" I saw her face when she told Tasha she didn't care, and I'm almost certain she meant it, but I don't want to give myself away.

"No. I'm the one who ended things. Noah's a good guy. I'm glad he's gotten over me." She huffs, "And Hannah's alright. She's pretty, anyway."

Go on, ask. "If he's a good guy, why'd you break up with him?"

She sucks in a noisy breath, rubs her palms against her thighs. "He's more interested in expanding his muscles than his mind, so conversation got boring real fast. That just left the physical stuff and he was terrible in bed, always finished right as I was starting to get into it." I blush, and it makes her laugh hard. "You're so red right now! Omg, are you a virgin?" She asks it effortlessly, as if the answer doesn't make a difference. I guess it doesn't.

"Maybe I'm blushing because I don't want to talk about your extremely boring cishet sex life in public."

"Yeah, you're a virgin."

I don't know why I'm insulted. "No, I'm not. Not with girls, anyway." I've actually had a lot of sex. It still amazes me, seeing as how I'm not the best at forming attachments. That's probably the reason I've had so much of it: I couldn't manage to keep one girl for too long. They'd get tired of my hesitancy to talk about anything that mattered, my past, my future, my feelings. The last girl I dated—Paige—called me 'aloof' when she broke up with me. There are two things about her I'm positive of: that she's going to score well on her verbal SAT, and that she was right. It's not like I aim to be aloof. It's conditioning. At this point, I don't know how to be any other way.

"How many girls have you had sex with?"

Nunya damn business. "How many guys have you had sex with?"

"Two," she replies, unabashed. "And your number is..." She rolls her hand, leading me.

"I lost count." It's not true. I'm trying to shock her. She's not shocked. She knows it's a lie, and wouldn't care if it weren't. "Five."

"So you're a player!"

I feign bravado. "It's not my fault girls like me." *Until they don't, and then it is.*

"Cocky." She studies me, moistens her bottom lip. "Were you in love with any of them?"

To be in love—the warmth that starts in your core and blossoms all over, the longing to be around the person all the time and missing them when you can't be, wanting them to be happy and safe, the willingness to do almost anything to make them happy and keep them safe. I understand the hypothesis, but I have never proven the theory. No one has ever been in love with me, either. "Not really." I shrug. "Were you in love with either of yours?"

"Not really."

Two loveless girls sitting on a park bench. How unromantic.

"What are you doing here, anyway? Walking around alone like a loser?" The question is playful, no malice behind it.

Uh huh, that's exactly it. "Continuing my unending quest to find something worth photographing."

"You're getting super into this club thing."

"You're not getting into it at all."

"I've been taking pictures."

"Right."

Her mouth goes a little slack and her forehead wrinkles. She dips her hand into her purse, pulls out her loaner camera and waves it at me. "I carry it around now and everything."

"Oh."

"Ha!" She drops it back in her bag.

And then we're silent, looking at one another for what feels like half an aeon before she peels her eyes away. Never mind the world, I wonder what she sees when she looks at me? "I'm starving." *Another lie. Tsk tsk.* "You want to go somewhere and grab some food?"

She nods. "There's a deli down the block that makes an incredible meatball parm sub."

"Whaaat? Take me!"

She grins, hops up. I shadow her the whole way there.

CHAPTER EIGHT

Spence, Olivia, Mack, Hannah, Noah and I are going out for lunch together—it's becoming an end-of-week ritual for us. It's cool to have people to hang out with, even if Mack can be grating, sometimes. I had friends at East Boston, but not close ones. I suppose the term 'acquaintances' is more apropos, casuals who didn't mind either way whether I showed up for or skipped out on plans. I prefer those types of people—the blasé ones; they're the easiest kind to deal with, few commitments, fewer complaints. These girls are in no way blasé. They care about one another on a deep level. It's starting to pierce my consciousness, might bud into something scary. *And refreshing.*

Olivia wants burgers from a place called Scotty Dog and Hannah is craving a smoothie. No one else has an opinion, so I suggest they play a round of Rock, Paper, Scissors—a very democratic solution to the most trivial of life's disagreements, I've found.

"Yo, you mad smart!" Olivia says to me.

We gather around a picnic table in the rear courtyard and watch them pound the sides of their fists into their palms. "Rock, Paper, Scissors, Shoot!"

Olivia throws paper. Hannah throws scissors; she gives a little 'Woot!'

"Ah, no, sis, best two out of three." Olivia balls her fist to throw again.

Hannah wags her finger. "Nuh uh, *sis*. You lost. We're going to Rocket Juice."

"We don't have all day," Mack says. *Way to ruin a good time.*

They consult Head Bitch in Charge, Spence, for her decision. "Hannah won. It's smoothies. Let's go."

Mack gestures to Hannah with a curt nod. Hannah turns to Noah and says, "Can we take your car? I think I'm getting a flat."

"Bet," he affirms.

Hannah, Olivia and Mack all sprint to the parking lot. Noah glares at Spence, the closest thing he has to a bro in this group. *Poor guy's so out-numbered.* "What's with them?"

"I don't know. Girls, man."

He takes off after them, leaving Spence and me to each other's company.

"Your friends…" I say to her. "I like them, but they're kinda strange sometimes."

"You have no idea."

We rock up to Noah's ride, a lime green Honda Fit, the small-est possible automobile that can still be legally classified as a car. "Sorry there's not enough room for everyone," Noah says to us. "This thing sucks on space."

"No worries, we'll meet you there," Spence replies.

Olivia gives Spence a smile, then scoots into the car, and Noah drives away.

Ahh. They planned it this way so Spence and I would be alone in her car. I'm sure Hannah's tires are fine. Was Spence in on it? *One way to find out.* "I think they set us up."

Her lips go sideways, make a *pfft* sound. "Yeah, they did."

It was not her idea. "Uh huh. My question is, why?"

"Short answer? I haven't dated anyone since last year and they highkey want me to find a girlfriend—I don't even think they care who, anymore. They've been trying to hook me up with every chick they know who's into chicks." She smirks bashfully.

Any chick who's into chicks, like, 'Sure, whatever, the new girl will do.' That's offensive. But Spence doesn't realize it, and it isn't her fault, anyway. "It's sweet that they care about you so much, but um, maybe you shouldn't let them play matchmaker anymore. They're not at all discreet."

She chortles. "They have no clue what that word means." We approach her car; she snaps her carabiner from her belt-loop, tosses her keys to me. "Wanna drive?"

I leer at the jangly things as though they're proof of alien life. "I can't drive. I don't know how."

Her forehead crinkles. "For real?"

You're the proof of alien life. "No one drives in Boston, everyone takes the T."

"Okay, but, you never wanted to learn?"

"I did. I do, I just haven't gotten around to it yet."

"Nope nope. You live on the North Shore now. Here, we drive. So, you, me and Sweet Caroline are going to work on that this weekend."

"Sweet Caroline?"

"My baby." She pats the roof of her Charger, sings the Neil Diamond song that plays at Fenway every game.

"So good, so good, so good!" we chant together.

Then I laugh and toss her keys back to her. "Red Sox fans are hardcore."

"Yes. Yes we are."

*

Saturday around noon, my phone pings. It's a text.

Spence: Scoop U in 10.

Shit, she was serious? She's got follow-through, admirable. I rush to get dressed and scarf some food. Tom had to go to his office to handle some emergency with a new game and Cate's at the grocery store; I leave them a note on the whiteboard in the kitchen. I'm headed for the door when Avery catches me. "Going out?"

"Yeah. Why, something up?"

"No. Tasha and I are supposed to go shopping in a bit, figured I'd extend an invite."

"Oh, I… Spence is coming to pick me up. But If you want to hang out—"

"Like, the three of us?"

"Uh, yes?"

She makes a face like she's gotten a strong whiff of dog shit. "Not with her. Not in this lifetime. Or the next."

Harsh. "Okay. Then have fun with Tasha."

"I will."

Another text. *Spence: Outside.*

"Bye."

Spence rolls down the driver's side black-out window, sticks her head out a little. "Suh? You ready for this?"

Am I ready to get behind the wheel of a two-ton monster I can kill people with? No. Do I want to tell her as much and come off as a terrified little bitch? Hell no. "I'm ready."

I'm about to reach for the passenger-side door handle when Cate's white Mercedes pulls in the driveway. I spot a guise of trepidation on Spence when she sees it. *Odd.*

"Hold up," I tell her, and wait for Cate to get out of her car.

"Hiya." She slams her door and calls to me.

"Hi. Do you need help with the bags?"

She spies Avery's car beside hers in the drive. "That's okay. I'll get Avery to help. You go on and—" She dips her head to get a good view into the Charger. She sees Spence and her face goes on an absolute rollercoaster ride of micro expressions: recognition, curiosity, despondency, delight. *What's all that about?* "Valerie Spencer," she says. "Goodness! How are you? I haven't seen you in ages."

Spence is restless, but she squelches it. "Hi, Mrs. C. I'm good, how are you?" *Mrs. C.*

"Good, good. What are you two up to this afternoon?"

"She's going to teach me how to drive," I answer.

"That's nice, Spence." *Spence again.*

Spence shrugs. "Reese taught me; I'm just paying it forward."

I don't know who Reese is, but Cate's eyes change at the mention of her. At the edges of her mouth, the hint of a grimace. "Well, have a nice time and be careful."

"We will. Take it easy, Mrs. C." They give one another a wave and Cate disappears into the house.

We're a ways away from the house, close to the school, where, Spence informs me, my lesson will commence in the empty faculty parking lot. She wants me to get a feel for driving without panicking about hitting any other cars. It takes me this long to get up the nerve to ask, but my curiosity gets the best of me. The familiarity between Cate and Spence, Cate's reaction to that name... "Who's Reese?"

If I had punched her in the face, Spence couldn't be more startled. "You don't know?"

Did I stutter? I shake my head.

She's quiet for a minute. I can see her weighing her options, deciding exactly what, or how much, to tell me. "A girl I used to know," she says, her voice low and dejected. That's all she's willing to say about it. *Leave it alone.*

I look around, note the handles protruding from the interior roof. "It's a good thing Sweet Caroline has 'Oh Shit' bars. Once I'm in control, you're gonna need to hold onto something."

She squeezes her lips into a thin line and her eyelids flutter. "I don't doubt that."

Hey, idiot, she took that someplace you didn't intend it to go. "Oh, stop!"

She chuckles. "Sorry." She taps her temple. "Dirty mind… Man, I need to get laid."

Now, I laugh. "You really do."

CHAPTER NINE

Avery and I arrive at room 321 to find an all-caps note taped to the door: PHOTOGRAPHY CLUB RELOCATED TO COMPUTER SCIENCE LAB TODAY.

We eye each other, nod, and head upstairs to the penthouse.

We're the last arrivals—everyone is already sitting in front of a PC. Mr. Warren welcomes us, "Hi, ladies. Take a seat anywhere." People turn to see who he's speaking to, and we make our way to the center of the room under scrutiny. We sit down next to each other at one of the unoccupied, long white console tables. Avery puts her gigantic purse on the seat to her right. *She could murder someone with that damn thing.*

"As I was saying," Mr. Warren resumes, "you've been working on your Autumn Landscapes projects for a few weeks, and today we're going to start the editing process—just the basics, enhancing color, light and shadow, adjusting focus on either the foreground or background. Please take your memory cards out of your cameras and insert them into the card slot in your computer tower."

"Shit," Avery says as she retrieves her camera from her purse.

"What? You said you've been taking pictures, right?" I remove the card from my PowerShot.

"I have been." She pops her memory card out. "But I didn't say I was any good at it."

Huh. This is the first time I've heard her articulate any kind of self-consciousness. She always projects such an incredible air of confidence, like no one's opinions of her even register, much less matter to her. This minor crack in her armor is… appealing.

"Why are you staring at me?"

Caughttt. "I'm not."

She grumbles, slips her card into her computer. I do the same.

"We'll be using the Polaris program. Find the purple PRS icon on your home screens, double-click on that and—" I tune out Mr. Warren. Nothing he has to say is as interesting to me as Avery and this new part of her she's allowed me to see. I can figure out the software on my own; if I hope to figure her out, I'm going to need her help.

Eventually, I do try to work on my own stuff, but my attention keeps flitting to her screen. She opens a file and a bunch of thumbnails spill out. She hovers the mouse cursor over one, drags it into the editing studio. In the foreground, a little blurry, are the backs of Tasha, Kylie, Amy and Liz's heads; they're planted on a bench. I recognize the rear courtyard of the school. The background—the focus of the shot—is a line of dead trees across the parking lot. They're pitiful, dry and deformed, innards exposed. Some are falling over, needing their neighbors to prop them up. But the lighting is gorgeous, cold and haunting, like something out of a fairytale. *Hansel and Gretel.*

"That's an awesome picture." I can't stop myself; it pours out.

"You think?" She tilts her head at it.

"Yeah, it's really evocative. Looking at it, I feel… despair. Hopelessness. There's no coming back for those trees, they're goners."

She looks at me, into me, with fierceness in her eyes. She knows I've captured a glimpse of what she keeps hidden away. "Whatever. I was just fucking around."

If that's how she wants to play it. "You should fuck around more often, then, because that"—I point at her computer—"is spectacular."

Eye roll. She turns back to her screen. She doesn't see me catch her smiling.

"Alright guys, it's time to wrap up," Mr. Warren announces. "But first, I want to take a second to talk about a very cool opportunity we have coming up. Photography Club has been invited to show some of our work at the Art Department's Fall Gallery Night." There's excited murmuring all around. Mr. Warren talks over it: "It'll be in October. The date is tentative at the moment, so I'll get back to you once it's finalized." As we all start gathering our things and getting ready to leave, he adds, "Your Chromebooks are equipped with Polaris; please try to get some work done at home."

As we're headed for her BMW, Avery wonders, "Are you going to submit any pictures for the gallery?"

"I think so. Will you?"

"No. You're the artsy one. I'm along for the ride because I didn't want you to be one of those pathetic emo kids who has no friends." I thought that, too, at first, but I'm not so sure anymore. She grins, then says, "Kidding."

And she is. In actuality, I think she likes hanging out with me. *Def like hanging out with her.*

CHAPTER TEN

Cate and Tom go out for a 'date night.' It's sweet, seeing as they've been married for twenty years—although, the house is eerily quiet when they're not home. I'm at the kitchen table, editing some of the pictures I've uploaded to my Chromebook and trying not to get creeped out by the silence. I started off up in my bedroom, but I wasn't happy with either the overhead light or the desk lamp; they're both too soft, too yellow to be true white. The kitchen has bright, fluorescent LED bulbs recessed in the ceiling—an enormous improvement for editing purposes.

This could be considered a lame way of spending a Friday night, but I don't care; I've got like, two hundred pictures to edit and I'm digging every second of it.

"Britton?" I hear Avery call from the foyer.

"Kitchen!" I reply, not shifting my focus from the laptop.

"You want to watch a movie or something? I'm bored." She's in the kitchen, now. I spin around in my chair, peep the time on the clock above the entryway. It's 8:30 p.m. *Why is she even home right now?* Spence told me there's a party at Jason's, the only mutual friend she and Avery have. There's no way Avery's presence wasn't requested, insisted upon, even.

"Aren't you going to Jason's thing tonight?"

"It's not really my scene." Her custom chillness.

"Oh." *Legit shocking.*

"What are you up to?"

"Messing around with Polaris."

She ducks her head around the cabinets for a better view. The picture on my screen is blown up, corner to corner; the warmth filters are tuned up high, giving it a lush, silky glow. The background is in soft focus and the foreground in sharp. All of this would be fine if it weren't a photo of her—sitting on the bench in Dix Park, her hand on her neck, head resting against it, staring idly at nothing, but in a contented way.

"Wow," she says. *Here it comes, a well-deserved telling off.* She waltzes up to me, leans over my right shoulder. Her long hair tickles my ear. I feel her warmness, radiating against my skin. "You made me look beautiful."

I almost guffaw. "No, I didn't. You are beautiful." *Fucking idiot, that's an inside thought!* I watch for her reaction. She opens her mouth to say something, then snaps it shut. We lock eyes. *Those eyes.* She bites her bottom lip. *That lip thing, Jesus.* "Uh, what movie did you want to watch?"

She stands up straight. Too straight. "Something with zombies."

That's all she needs to say. "I'm in."

We've turned off all the lights. Avery made a giant bowl of popcorn that neither of us is interested in. We're sitting next to each other on the cushy blue sofa—closer than is necessary, considering the size of it. *Too late to move now.* We've been scrolling through Shudder for a good ten minutes and she still hasn't settled on anything. "How 'bout this one?" She hovers on the preview screen of a film called *The Horde.* It's in French, subtitled. I took French in school for two years and was pretty decent at it; I doubt I'll need the subtitles.

"Looks good to me."

She presses play.

*

We're two-thirds of the way through the movie, and she's fallen asleep. How? There's been screaming and explosions and gunfire gushing from the TV speakers this entire time. My mind flashes back to the conversation we had about her being a spotter. *Brave.* Then I think about her reaction to Nosferatu and smile. *Maybe not so much.*

Her head is resting on my shoulder. She nuzzles into me, makes this low 'mmm' sound. She has a little subconscious jerk, and her hair falls into her face. I inch across to brush it behind her ear—try to do it as gently as possible, but end up waking her anyway. She sits up, yawns and stretches. Then she's wracked with an expression of pure alarm. "Was I sleeping on you?"

"Yeah."

Her cheeks go rosy. "My bad."

"I don't mind." *Shut up, stupid.*

"'Kay, I'll get right back to it, then."

"You can if you want." I pluck the remote from the table, lower the volume, set the thing down next to me on the arm of the couch, and recline, all easy-like. "There."

She sniggers and her head falls back against the cushion. "I missed too much, what happened?"

"You didn't miss anything. Most of the group is dead, that big dude with the machete was bitten but is sticking around to kill as many zombies as possible before he turns, and in about twenty minutes the final girl will be the only one to make it out of the building alive."

"Argh! Predictable."

Snort. "Were you expecting a twist?"

She shakes her head. "Wrong genre for a twist; that's suspense thriller, sometimes romance."

"A romance with a twist? Right! I could be into that, if they existed."

"Ooh, Imma hook you up!" She leans across me, snatches the remote. *So warm.* "*Big Time Love*, best rom-com ever." She scooches herself up, folds one leg under the other. Then she yawns again.

"We should finish this movie and call it a night. I think we're both too tired to start another one."

"You're right. Raincheck on the rom-com?"

Definitely. "Sure."

The credits of *The Horde* scroll up the screen. She pushes off the couch, goes for the bowl of popcorn. "I'm going to toss this."

"I'll take care of it. You're beat; go to bed, already."

"Thanks." She grins. "Night."

"Night."

When she's gone, I google the trailer for *Big Time Love*. The movie's a few years old, starring Kendall Bettencourt—wicked hot—and some other actress I don't recognize... and the twist is totally homo. Best rom-com ever, huh? *Straight girls are allowed to like LGBT movies, it's not illegal!*

I pick up the popcorn, bring it into the kitchen and dump it into the garbage.

CHAPTER ELEVEN

"Brit!" Tasha calls to me from the far end of the hallway as I'm twisting my combination lock. She's got Kylie and Liz in tow. They've been warming up to me, despite me not giving them much reason to. Still, they don't usually bother with me when Avery's not around—only ever on the days I eat lunch with their group—so I'm caught off-guard. *They are too damn cheery for this ungodly hour.* I'm barely functioning with one open bloodshot eye. Adding to the oddity of the scenario, they're acting sketchy, huddling in close to each other and scheming in whispers as they sidle toward me.

"Uh, hey, good morning."

"Morning," they all say. Liz gives me a smile. Tasha and Kylie look at me with uncertainty in their eyes, evaluating whether or not to say whatever it is they want to say to me.

If we ain't gon' talk, skurt. "What's up?" I open the locker, sift through my stuff, start pulling out textbooks and binders.

"You know how Avery's birthday is next Saturday?" Kylie asks. She brings her high ponytail over her shoulder, plays with the ends of her bleached platinum hair.

"Yeah." I shove a book into my messenger bag.

"We were thinking about throwing her a party—not like, a surprise party or anything, that shit's dumb. Jason's got a mad nice house and his mom is never home, so…"

"Okay." That's actually really thoughtful, but what the hell does it have to do with me? *Godspeed, ladies.* "I'm sorry, is there a question in here somewhere? Because I'm not sure how much help I can be; you guys have known her way longer." Probably not any better, though.

"It's just," Liz starts, "she doesn't really do parties. But we've been thinking she might be okay with it, since it's a special occasion."

"And if you talked to her about it, she'd be more receptive to it," adds Tasha.

What, me? "Where'd you get that idea?"

"If you told her you wanted to go to a rager, she'd take you to one."

Is she for real? "How do you know that?"

"She told us when Jason invited us to his last week. We expected her usual 'hard pass,' but she said if you wanted to go, she'd be into it. And then Jason never got around to asking you, so she obvs let it drop."

Wow, okay. So, she does like chilling. "I mean, I'm not sure she'll be down, but I'll ask her. I'll let you know her answer either way."

All three of them squeal, their faces alight with excitement. Tasha throws her arms around my neck. It's a quick hug, but I still go stiff.

The first bell rings and I catch Avery in the corner of my vision. She's approaching fast. Mmm, English class. "Guys, she's coming," I whisper.

"Hi, Avery!" Liz waves to her as she reaches us. "Come on, Tash, Mrs. Sievers will kill us if we're late again." The three of them blow past Avery without so much as a goodbye. Why don't any of these kids comprehend the concept of finesse? *Because they've never needed it, dumbass.* Right. Their parents probably encourage honesty and openness, the kind of guardians who'd never hurt a child for saying something they didn't like or speaking out of turn.

Avery gawks at her friends' backsides, then glowers at me. "What the hell was that?"

"Your friends asked me to convince you to let them throw you a birthday party. I don't know why."

"No," she says without hesitation.

"Alright. I've been instructed not to ask, 'why not,' after you inevitably say no, but it's going to eat at me, so, why not?" *Fully fabricating stuff now...*

"I told you I'm not into parties."

"But you're turning eighteen. It's a milestone."

She gives a fervent headshake. "I said no, I meant it."

New tactic. "I really would have liked it if I had friends who cared enough about me to throw me a party for my eighteenth, but I didn't." I soften my eyes, pout my lips, let them quiver just a touch—the most adorable Sad Homeless Puppy face I can muster. It's a valuable skill, manipulation through guilt. Not a muscle I'm particularly proud to flex, though.

"Oof." She grimaces as though my words were a wasp sting. "That's not fair and you know it."

Right in the feels! I go from puppy face to serpentine grin in two seconds flat. "It might not be fair, but it's true."

She groans. "If I say yes, will you come?"

Abso-friggin-loutely. "If you want me to."

She's bewildered, or insulted—she's faltered just enough to let something show. "Don't be stupid. I wouldn't have asked if I didn't want you to."

"Then say yes and I'll be there."

She nibbles on her lip. *They do look scrumptious.* "Whatever. It had better be the most fire event of the year."

Snicker. "I'll stress that to them."

"Good," she sneers. "Class?"

"Yeah."

I hang around near the cafeteria doors, waiting for the Braindead Brigade. *Don't be a douche, they're okay.* The lobby is filling up with kids. Even so, I'm confident I can catch them. They're unmissable; the energy they exude is palpable as soon as they enter a room.

I spy Kylie and Tasha in the crowd. I kick off the wall, head them off halfway to the caf. We gather in the alcove of an empty classroom. Tasha's hazel eyes are full of anticipation. Kylie is a bit calmer. "It's a go."

"Yas!" Tasha replies.

Kylie says, "I knew you'd come through."

As promised, I add, "I cannot stress enough how imperative it is that you throw her the most incredible party ever thrown."

"I heard that," Tasha says.

Kylie nods. "Bet."

"Cool."

They bounce to the cafeteria. I stay put, standing against the wall, wondering whether it was a smart move to get involved. It's my ass on the line, even though it's their brilliant idea.

Avery, Amy and Liz are approaching, beaming at whatever funny thing Avery said. They're about to walk right past me without even noticing that I'm there. At the last second, Avery's gaze flitters over me. She shoos the others on, then squeezes into the nook across from me. She slips her purse from her shoulder, dangles it in her hand. She rests the back of her head against the wall, closes her eyes, exhales slowly. I have no idea what's happening. "Are... you okay?"

"Do you ever wish—" She opens her eyes, and I'm sure they're bluer than I have ever seen them. "You want to get out of here?"

"Er, it's Wednesday." No off-campus privileges until tomorrow.

"I didn't mean for lunch."

"I'm supposed to meet Spence inside."

"Right." She starts to move away. I grab her wrist, pull her back, willing her to stay here with me in this moment for a little while longer. She stares at my hand, at my hand holding onto her. And then her eyes are glued to mine. They're pleading with me: 'Come with me or let me go.'

"Let's get out of here."

She's so eager to escape that she bolts. I tail her up the steps, out one of the side doors, straight to the parking lot to her car. No one tries to stop us.

"Where are we going?" I wonder out loud once she's jammed the keys into the ignition. I suspect she hasn't thought that far ahead.

"I don't care, as long as it's someplace you've never been before."

"There are far too many of those for me to choose from."

"Name one. We can go anywhere."

Make her smile, pick someplace ridiculous. Straight-faced, I go, "The Grand Canyon."

She cackles. And suddenly, she's okay again. I see the tension leave her body as though it has tangibility, a molecular structure of its own. "You're really funny. I feel like I've laughed more in the time I've known you than I have in years."

Ah, yes, humor—one of my special skills, and one of a handful of coping mechanisms I've developed. At this moment, it's by far my favorite. "That's a good thing, isn't it?"

"So good." Her expression… Again, I can't name it. I like it, all the same. "We can go back inside, if you want."

"Back inside, hell! You promised me the Grand Canyon."

That gets her laughing again. "How about we go to Japan instead? The caf is serving sushi today."

"Yes, sushi! Ugh, I should weigh as much as a whale with how much I love to eat."

She gives me a thorough examination. "You're good." A redness creeps up her neck, and she adds in a hurry, "Sorta scrawny."

Jerk. "In that case, I suppose I'd better get some sushi into me."

She flashes a smile. "You simply must."

As we're paying for our food, she says, "Sorry I cut into your time with your friends." I try to say, "You're my friend, too," but before I can get the words out she's already saying, "I'll catch you later." Then she takes her tray and goes to find the Cool Kids table.

I yank my phone from my pocket, type a text to Spence: *Change of plans. Gonna eat with Avery. Sry.* The 'read' notification pops up next to my text bubble. I wait a few seconds, but don't get a reply.

I shuffle over to Avery's group. When she sees me, the corners of her mouth slip into an understated grin. She elbows Amy and says, "Slide over." Amy looks up at me. There's disbelief on her face as she vacates the stool beside Avery—I've stolen her position in the starting lineup and she's been relegated to the sidelines. Avery either doesn't notice or doesn't care. I decide not to care either and take a seat.

CHAPTER TWELVE

There's a knock on my bedroom door. I open it to find Avery standing way back in the hallway. She's so far away from the threshold that she's almost in the bathroom. *What is this, a fresh version of ding-dong-ditch?* "Hi."

"Hi." Her eyes dart around my room. She's standing stock-still and perfectly straight—a sunflower stretching toward the sun. Or a deer about to be run over by a tractor-trailer. She's looking through me, not at me, and it's making me squirm inside.

"Do you wanna come in?"

Her shoulders go taut and her lips downturn.

"Really, you can come in. I won't bite you or anything." Thinking about it, she has never knocked on my door. Seriously, not once. It's been Cate or Tom every time. Did something crazy happen to her in this room before? Could it be that her pyromaniac ex-foster sister attacked her over something as innocuous as a knock on a door? I would never do that to her, or to anyone, but it's possible the last girl did. Foster kids can be extremely fucked up. Most of us have been through some shit. I know how fortunate I am never to have been raped or beaten half to death by a bio or foster parent.

She chances a step forward. *That's right, I won't hurt you.* "Dad sent me up here to get you. Family meeting in the living room."

Family meeting. What the hell did I do now? "Okay."

*

Cate and Tom are on the love seat. The TV is on, but muted. The TV being on is a good sign. Whatever's happening isn't so grave as to require my utmost undivided attention. I'm not going to be screamed at or slapped. Although I'm almost positive neither Cate nor Tom are the type to set me straight with violence, it's always a situation I'm prepared for. *They could stuff you in the kitchen cupboard.* Fucking hell.

Avery takes a seat on the couch and I join her. The closer I stick to her, the safer I'll be. It's hardly ever the bio-kids who get the brunt of things, and once in a while I've known them to step in if the situation gets too out of control.

My focus is fluttering back and forth between Cate and Tom. Neither of them seem annoyed or angry. They look unperturbed, like this is a totally normal thing.

Avery leans forward, rests her elbows on her thighs. She lets her hands loll over her knees. "What's good, parental units?"

I feel my muscles relax.

"So." Tom drags out the 'o.' "I have to go to Japan for a week, see what it'll take to get the Asian market interested in our first shooter game."

Avery is surprised. "You haven't gone on a business trip in a long time."

"I know. I don't like to leave you guys alone. I've been able to send Uncle Jimmy most places, but our new PR partners will only deal directly with me. I'm leaving Monday."

Avery doesn't know how to feel about it; Tom is upset. "I've tried to put it off until after your birthday, but I can't swing it. I'm really sorry, kiddo."

She sits up, scrunches her lips to the side, steals a minute to collect her thoughts on the issue. "It's cool, Dad. You've never missed any of our birthdays before, even when you were traveling all over the place. I can let this one slide as long as you promise to get me turnt up for my twenty-first." Her smirk is straight devilish. *This girl is unreal!*

Tom and Cate both chuckle, and so do I.

"Do you think I'd have it any other way?" Tom replies. "But since I can't be here for this birthday, I'd like to have a daddy-daughter day this weekend, like we used to when you were younger. I thought maybe the three of us could go to Franklin Park Zoo on Sunday."

Avery splutters, "The zoo?"

"Wait, you want me to come?"

Everyone's gawking at me. Was that a stupid question? "Of course!" He says it like it's the most obvious answer in the world, as if the alternative never crossed his mind. "That is, if you want to. You don't have to."

"She absolutely does have to!" Avery exclaims. We look at one another. "If my ass is getting dragged to the zoo, so is yours." She gestures between us.

I have no objections. I went to Stone Zoo once on a class trip in fifth grade and really liked it. Maybe Avery is too cool for that now, but I'm not. "I'd like to go."

"Great!" Tom's eyes sparkle.

Avery peeps at me, shows me the suggestion of a smile; I've let something novel slip, and she finds it amusing. There's nothing I can do about it now.

CHAPTER THIRTEEN

Spence is uncharacteristically quiet at lunch. That isn't to say she's ever rambunctious or even loud; she's sociable, doesn't have to search for words, but is also very good at listening... which is why I'm worried. I don't want her to shut down on me. We've had a few driving lessons now, and I've enjoyed them a lot. She's patient and kind, never gets flustered even when I stomp too hard on the brake or catch some air over a speed bump. If I'm honest, I don't care if we're sitting around doing nothing; I like her company. I don't need anything more from her than that.

So observant, yet so staggeringly obtuse. Oooh, that's it! She feels the same way, and she's being weird because I blew her off for Avery the other day. Our friendship must bother her more than she's willing to admit. Sometimes I hate that I can be so crappy at grasping normal social mores. It's hard not to cave to my impulses when one grabs me by the crotch—it's such a rare occurrence that I have no defense against it.

How do I fix this? "Spence, do you want to go to a movie or something Saturday?"

The conversation going on around us screeches to a halt. Olivia, Hannah and Mack all glare at me, at Spence. *It did sound like you were asking her out.* Whatever. I can't afford to obsess about verbiage right now. There'll be time for that later once I've salvaged this, wrapped some insulation around it, given it the warmth it deserves.

She deadpans, "I don't really like movies."

Denied. Everyone else goes back to chatting, embarrassed for me. *Be suave.* "That's why I said, 'or something.' We can do whatever." I don't add, *I just want to hang out with you,* despite wanting to.

She smiles. *Got her.* "Ever been rock climbing?"

Say what now? "Um… like, up a mountain?"

She titters. "No, indoor. At a gym."

"I have not. Sounds fun, though." No, it doesn't. But if that's what she wants to do, I'll nut up and do it.

"Want to try?"

"For sure."

"Dope. I'll pick you up Saturday at like, one?"

"Perfect." I catch Olivia leering at me as I say it. Oh God, okay. She for sure thinks I've asked Spence out. *Bookmark it. Address it in the future.*

*

I don't know what the appropriate attire is for scaling rock walls. I could ask Avery—she's an athlete, she'd probably have a better idea. But if I do that, she'd ask me why I'm asking her, and I don't feel like playing twenty questions. *The hassle.* She isn't home, anyway. She went to the football game. She asked me to come with, but obviously, I couldn't. I didn't tell her I had other plans, just said, "Maybe next time." *Yo, dummy, Cate goes to the gym.* Problem solved. I find her and Tom in the living room watching TV. No sexy stuff this time around, thank the Lord. "Cate, can I ask you something?"

"Shoot."

I do this awkward shuffle thing for a second. I'm not one to seek advice, especially not about stupid shit like clothes; it feels weird. "Do you know what a person should wear to go indoor rock climbing?"

"Hmm." She sits up. "That depends. Is the person going for a workout, or is it a date sort of thing?"

This is too complicated. "It is a non-romantic one-on-one hangout thing." *Could you be a bigger loser?*

She chortles. "Let's take a look at your wardrobe."

"Uh, cool."

Cate and I pick out a heather grey, loose-fitting racerback tank with an outline of Massachusetts on it, one of my nicer zip-up hoodies, and the only pair of leggings I own—black. We hit a snag on the shoes. "Vans won't do for climbing. You don't have sneakers with better grip?"

"No."

"That's a problem." She taps three fingers against her lips, makes a humming noise. "What size shoe do you wear?"

"Seven."

She snaps her fingers, "Wait here." And then she's gone for maybe two minutes. When she returns, she has a pair of black and pink Nikes in her hand. "You can borrow these."

She actually wants me to put my funky-ass feet into her nice-ass sneakers? Is this something that moms and daughters do—swap shoes whenever? I take them from her.

"I think you're good to go." She winks at me.

"Thanks for your help, and for the sneakers."

"Anytime."

Spence rings the doorbell. Why not send a text? I fly down the stairs, reach the door half a second before Cate can get to it—not that it helps at all, the windowpane is only slightly frosted. "I won't be out late."

"Have a blast," Cate singsongs.

Spence is in a very tight maroon Metallica T-shirt and very tight grey cargo pants. Her hair is pulled up into a neat ponytail. And... she's wearing a touch of makeup: a light layer of green eyeshadow, eyeliner, clear lip gloss. Shit. She thinks it's a date, too.

"You look nice," I say without thinking. *Hey, asshole, is this or isn't this a date?*

She gives me a half-smile, does a quick assessment of my attire. "So do you."

Gulp. "Listen, I have to tell you that if I die today, I'll be very upset about it."

That earns me a full smile. "Not gonna happen." She gestures toward Sweet Caroline, and we're off.

We arrive at an enormous warehouse that's been painted an obnoxious purple. There's a yellow sign above a set of glass doors: Rök. I tug one of the doors open before Spence can reach for the handle, and she's taken aback. She likes being the one to do the chivalrous stuff, holding open doors, pulling out chairs. *To reiterate, is this or is this not a date?*

Inside, there's a large reception desk manned by two women. I'm ready to pay them the price of our admission when Spence takes a membership pass from her pocket and presents it to them. They wave us through to the gym.

The climbing area is sprawling. It has twenty rock walls of various heights and difficulties, along with five small ones for the kiddies.

Spence leads me to this colossus of a wall, hundreds of colorful foot- and handholds protruding from it. There's a warning on red plasterboard at its base: *Recommended for expert-level climbers.*

No. Nope. Fuck that noise. "You told me I wasn't going to die today!"

"And you won't. I guarantee it."

A muscular guy in a purple Rök-branded polo comes to greet us. "Spence! Back again, huh?"

"You know it. Wayne, this is Britton."

"Hi, Britton." We shake hands. "I'm going to be your instructor for today." He regards Spence. "What are we doing this time, bouldering? Lead?"

"Top rope, my dude. Britton's a noob."

"Let me get the equipment." He heads over to a storage bin, removes two harnesses and two helmets, then comes back to us and hands us one of each. "Here you go."

The helmet is straightforward; I pop it on, fasten the clip. The harness has too many straps for me to know where to begin. Spence hops into hers and secures it with no problem. I'm still standing in the same position, harness hanging from my hand. "I don't usually have such a hard time *strapping things on*."

She snickers at me and goes, "Need some help?"

"You have to ask?"

"Come here." She takes my harness from me, gets down on her haunches. "Step in." I steady myself, hand on her shoulder. I put my right leg in—*shake it all about*—then my left. She slides the contraption up my thighs, adjusts the straps, then clicks the snap-clips in place around my waist. She tugs on the belt and I jolt toward her. "How's that?" She's so close to my face that I can feel her breath, balmy on me—minty, hints of vanilla. *How smooth.*

"Good," I respond evenly.

I've gotta give it to her, the girl's got game. All I have to do is refuse to play. *Or not.*

I'm stuttering through my climb, slow as a snail. Up a goddamn baby wall. *Almost there. Keep going.* True to her personality, Spence has infinite patience with me. She's belaying me, shouting words of encouragement with every new handhold I grab.

I really want to like her. *Like* like her. Though I don't know if I can. She's attractive, there's no question about that—an Amazonian stunner. But something's missing... the spark, or whatever other dumb cliché they use in love stories.

And... I'm falling. *Oh fuck!* I bang against the wall, scrape my shoulder.

"Whoa! I gotcha." Spence takes all of my weight, stabilizes me.

"Damn it! Sorry."

"It's okay. Want me to bring you down?"

"Please!"

When I'm close enough to the bottom, she catches me—helps me plant my feet on the ground again. She holds me a second longer than I need her to, and I let her. *Come on, spark!* I gaze up at her, see the concern in her viridian eyes.

"Are you hurt?"

Nothing. Damn. "I'm fine. Thanks." I step out of her arms.

No, this is not a date. *Aloof.* No shit.

Tom and Cate are out when I get back to the house. Avery's lounging on the couch, reading *1984*, wearing glasses. They're square, pink and black, semi-rimless. How is she even better-looking in specs? It's not fair. "You wear glasses?"

Her head snaps up from the book. "My contacts were bothering me. How was your date with Spence?" She's irritated.

"It wasn't a—"

"Please. My mom was gushing about how adorable you were, making a big deal over what to wear."

"That's not... I'm not used to athletic activities, that's all."

"If you say so."

Pivot. "How was the game?"

"We lost, big surprise. Our football team belongs in a dumpster, not on a field."

Ha! "Then why'd you go?"

"For the squad, not the team."

She's a good friend. I wouldn't go to a football game to watch the cheerleaders. *The hell you wouldn't.* Okay, fine, but I'd go for the skirts, not the sport. "You still owe me a raincheck on that movie. Can I cash it in?"

She closes the book, tosses it onto the coffee table, then sits up straight and pats the couch beside her. I plop down, watch her set up the TV. She's not even doing anything out of the ordinary, and I feel like I've got a bunch of Cirque du Soleil acrobats in my stomach. *What was that about sparks?*

No! She's straight, and it wouldn't matter if she weren't because she's so off limits that she's the human equivalent of Chernobyl.

Thirty-four minutes and forty-three seconds—that's the build-up to the first kiss between the two leading ladies, though I knew it was coming right at the start of the scene. It's tame, yet I'm fidgeting like a total prude. I take a look at Avery. Okay, so she 'sparks' me. Thank God it's one-sided; I don't want it to be mutual. That would complicate the shit out of everything, and I really don't need that kind of aggro. I just want to ride out this year, nice and easy, so I can get on with adulting.

Sixty-five minutes and seventeen seconds: next-level lesbian love scene, crazy for a rom-com. Everything about it is sensual, the soft lighting and lingering close-ups, the hair-tugging and tongue action. I know I'm redder than a baboon's ass. I don't dare glance at Avery, not this time. If she were to catch me, she'd be able to read me, for sure.

I don't breathe until it's over.

Yeah… this year isn't going to go smoothly, *at all.* Somebody kill me.

"What'd you think?" she wonders as the credits roll.

"I didn't expect the ending. I thought Allie was going to go through with marrying Heather's brother."

"No. They were meant to be friends. She was always going to end up with Heather."

Hmm. "It was good. I like happy endings." There aren't enough of them in real life.

"So do I. But things don't work out that way." Alright, seriously, she is psychic.

"They did for Kendall Bettencourt. She and her wife have been together for years, since they were, like, our age. I read online that they're having a baby soon, too."

She grins. "Fine. I guess sometimes they do."

CHAPTER FOURTEEN

Tom is more excited about heading to the zoo than either of us actual kids. It's about a half-hour drive to Boston given the traffic, and he is giddy the entire way. Avery is in the front seat, being so cute about it—indulging him as he relays every part of the afternoon's schedule: Serengeti Crossing first, then Kalahari Kingdom, Giraffe Savannah afterward, so on and so forth.

It's sweet, these two are wicked close, have such a strong bond. I haven't witnessed a connection like this between a dad and daughter since my second foster home. The dad's name was Alan, and he tried to include me in family things, but his youngest daughter, Jade, was not having any of it. She hated me, constantly tried to get me in trouble. The last straw for her parents was when she kicked their dog Milo—really hurt the poor sweetie, too—and blamed it on me. I tried to tell Alan and his wife the truth, but they didn't believe me. Well, Cindy almost did; Alan never sided with me over Jade. I gather it's because he didn't want to acknowledge that his favorite child was a fucking psychopath. But then, what parent would want to admit that about any of their kids? *She's gotta be in juvie by now.* Man, I hope so.

Tom parks the car. The lot is packed, tons of people trying to cram in a visit before the weather turns bitter. There are families with little kids all around us as we head to the ticket booth. Not too many teenagers, I notice.

The line is long-ish, though moves fast. When it's our turn, Tom purchases three tickets. I am prepared—Spence stopped at an ATM for me on the drive back yesterday. I take my wallet out of my pocket, flip it open, snatch a twenty and go to hand it to him.

Avery shakes her head as Tom turns his toward me. His eyebrows squeeze together as he catches sight of the money. "What the hell is that?"

What kind of response...? Just like his daughter, funny and unbefitting.

I'm frozen. *Speak, stupid.* "It's for my ticket."

"That's not how it works, kiddo. I give you money, not the other way around." His smile is so kind. So are his eyes. Avery's got his eyes, brilliant and lovely.

Say thank you. "Thank you!"

He hands a ticket to Avery and one to me. I slide it and the twenty into my wallet, then the wallet into my back pocket. He claps his hands, rubs them together. "Let's do this!" He scurries through the gate with extra springy steps. Avery and I ogle each other. She huffs. Then, we scuttle to catch up.

We see so many exotic animals from all over the world—Australia, Africa, the tropical rainforests of South America. Avery is blah about everything, save the big cats. I saw her face when the tigers were playing with these huge cardboard boxes all around their enclosure, pure delight. She must be a cat person, which would make sense—she's sort of cat-like herself, sweet when she wants to be, surly when she's aggravated, and preternaturally untouchable in comparison to most other creatures.

As for me? I am in awe of every single beast we come across. Lions, zebras, giraffes, kangaroos, the lot. They're all exquisite in their own ways. But when we enter the Aviators exhibit, I know that it's going to be my favorite part of the day. There's an entire section dedicated to birds of prey: hawks, harriers, falcons, owls. *American bald eagle!* I scamper over to our national bird and snatch my camera from my jeans. *Pictures! Lots of them.* Snap. Snap. Snap. "You're such a handsome boy," I murmur to him between shots. "Can you spread your wings for me, bud?" He does it!

Avery pops into place beside me. "I see you like birds."

"Mmhmm." I love birds. Raptors, specifically. They're so majestic and so untamed. Imagine, to have that kind of freedom; the ability to soar high above the earth on the winds and go anywhere I please. "If I could've chosen to be born as anything, it would have been a peregrine falcon." Why'd I tell her that? *Embarrassing yourself as usual.*

I can sense her grinning. "They have one here."

My head snaps to the side and I see that she is grinning. "No…"

"Oh yeah." She reaches out, wraps her fingers around my wrist, drags me clear across the exhibit. It happens with such swiftness that my stomach doesn't have the chance to do jumping jacks.

There are a few different species of falcon living together in a giant netted enclosure—brown, grey, black, saker, peregrine. "Which one is the peregrine?" She's facing me, still holding my wrist. I free myself from her grasp, point to the bird. It's perched on a long branch, its blue-grey back to us, wings ready to carry it away. She steps closer to me, follows my finger with her eyes.

"They're the fastest animal in the world," I say, a little too close to her ear. "They can dive for prey at over 200 miles per hour."

"I get why she's your favorite. She's beautiful." Her voice is hushed and thick with awe.

Oh boy.

"Yeah." I take a picture.

"There you are," Tom calls to us. We turn, find him with a leaflet in his hand. He thrusts it out to us. "There's an aerial demo and info session in fifteen minutes!" He's too excited. *He's not the one who just squeed out loud, fool.*

Avery examines me and cracks up. "We'd better hurry to the arena if we want to get good seats."

On our way to the amphitheater, we find a concession stand; the line is growing exponentially. "Do either of you want a soda or something?" Tom asks.

"I'll take a Diet Coke. Ooh, and a soft pretzel please, Daddy?" Avery's tone is saccharine, like a five-year-old who's begging for a new toy. Tom melts over it, a chocolate bar forgotten in the sun.

"Anything for you, Britton?"

"I'm good, thanks."

"Okay. You two head over. I'll meet you there."

Once he's out of earshot I say to Avery, "You've got him wrapped around your finger."

"Always have." She winks.

The small arena is already swarming by the time we walk in. All the seats at the bottom of the bleachers are full. Avery puts her hand to her forehead, blocking the sun from her eyes, and scans around. "Up there." She points. "We'll have a killer view and the birds fly in from back there, right over our heads."

Do not squee again. "Sweet."

We clamber up to the very top row of the bleachers. Our backs are against the broad post of a tall wooden fence. I look around, check out the view for myself.

There, across the showground, I see a face I've prayed and prayed I'd never have to see again. I squint hard, hoping that my mind is misinterpreting the woman's aged features, morphing a complete stranger into my worst nightmare. But it's really her, still decked out in the same style of hideous floral muumuu she was so fond of. Susan Goddamn Brichard.

I was with her for half a year when I was twelve. Those were the longest six months of my life. The thing I remember most about Susan's house is the pantry. It was so tiny. And it locked. I recall: the sound of the door being slammed and bolted behind me— *thunk-cha-chink*, hours and hours in the dark, bloody knuckles from pounding incessantly to be let out, the blue mop bucket I had to use as a toilet—the putrid fucking smell of it.

My heart is pounding so hard, so fast. *Thumpthumpthumpthump*. How long can it keep that up before it gives out, even if it is healthy now?

Either my lungs have stopped working or every last molecule of oxygen in the atmosphere has been sucked away, because I suddenly can't breathe.

Shit. ShitShitShit! What do I do? What the hell do—

"Are you okay?" *Avery.*

Gasping. No words, only gasping. God. Oh, God. What is this?

"Britton, look at me." Her hand on my cheek. Now, her eyes. *So blue.* "Focus on my chest. Breathe with me. Deep and slow. In… and out." Inhale. Exhale. I watch her chest as her lungs expand and contract. It rises and falls. Rises and falls. Measured and steady. *With her. In and out. In and out.* Huff. Puff. "That's it. Just like that. You're doing great." Her palm in the middle of my back, rubbing. "You're going to get through it. Deep breath in… and out. In… and out."

Is this going to last forever? Please, please, just let me die soon. I can't—*gasp*—huff, puff. Hiccup. Inhale. Exhale. *Avery, please stay with me.*

"I'm right here. I'm not going anywhere."

Did I say it out loud? The heat of her skin through my shirt… I shut my eyes. *Breathe. Breathe.* Hiccup. I open them; she's still with me.

My face is wet. Why is my face wet? *Tears.* Wipe. Wipe. *Breathe.* Hiccup. Huff. Puff. *In and out.*

Inhale. Exhale. Rinse and repeat.

My heartbeat is starting to slow down, and it's becoming less difficult to take in air.

She is still touching me, her voice calming as whitecaps crashing against the shore. "What do you need, Brit? Do you want to leave?"

Brit. That's me. "Yes."

She takes my hand. Leads me down the bleachers, step by step. Then, outside, beyond the wooden fence.

She steers me to a recessed nook. There's a boulder with a flat top. She sits me down on it, stands in front of me. So close I could... I rest my forehead against her abdomen. I'm sapped, no energy at all; it's this or fall on my face. She strokes my hair, again and again, gentle fingers combing through long strands. *Feels nice.* "It's okay. You're okay, now," she murmurs.

"What's going on?" I hear Tom ask.

Avery keeps doing what she's doing, doesn't move away—not a single inch. "I think she had a panic attack."

That's what it was?

"Britton?" He sounds too close. I turn my head, find him with one knee in the dirt. The food and drinks are in a box on the ground beside him. And then I see the worry on his face. "Let's get you home."

CHAPTER FIFTEEN

I'm in my bed. *What the fuck?* It comes back to me in pieces. The zoo. The aviation show. The amphitheater. Susan Goddamn Brichard. Avery. Her eyes. Her hands. She didn't leave me.

I remember the car ride back to the house, Avery sitting next to me in the back seat. My temple against her shoulder, her arm around me, her hand rubbing the crown of my head. And then Cate bringing me up to my room, tucking the covers in tight around me.

The sunlight streaming through my windows tells me that it's early afternoon. It was near sunset when we got home from the zoo. *So friggin' parched. Need water.*

I climb out from under the bedspread. My feet are bare against the downy coral carpet. I'm wearing sweatpants and a muscle tee. When did that happen? *Cate helped you change.* How humiliating.

I drag myself out of my room and down the stairs. The TV is on in the living room, volume turned down low. Avery is on the couch in a pair of pink plaid pajamas and her glasses. *Those things are great. Please wear them all the time.* She sees me, pushes herself upright. "How are you feeling?"

I gather some saliva and swallow it. "I imagine this is how it feels to get struck by lightning." I rub at my forehead. "What time is it?"

She glances at the cable box, back at me. "12:27. On Monday."

"What? Crap, I slept through school! Hold on, why are you home?"

"My parents had to go to work, but we didn't want you to wake up to an empty house, so I took a sick day."

"You didn't have—"

"When are you going to realize that I don't do anything I don't want to do?" She motions for me to come sit beside her. I pad across the living room, collapse backwards onto the couch. "What happened? And please don't say 'nothing,' because one second you were fine, and the next you totally weren't. It's like something set you off."

Ah, balls. I was hoping I'd never have to tell this tale to anyone again. I wanted it to die with the cops and my social worker. But I don't have the mental prowess right now to make up a believable lie. And anyway, I don't want to lie to her. She was so compassionate throughout the whole mess, she has more than earned the truth.

I take a breath, steel my nerves. "Do you remember when you asked me at the Witch Museum if I was claustrophobic, and I told you I wasn't?"

"Uh huh."

"I lied. I am, kind of. And at the bird show, I saw the foster mom who's the reason why. Anytime I did anything she didn't like, she'd stick me in this horrible little pantry, leave me in there for hours—an entire weekend, once." I sigh. "Sometimes I think it would've been better if she'd have just hit me." Physical scars are nothing compared to mental ones.

"God, Britton." She scoops my hands into hers. "That's fucked up. I'm so sorry." There are tears welling in her eyes.

Please, don't cry for me. "It's fine, I—"

"It's not fine! Of course you'd react that way to seeing her again. She traumatized you. It's called PTSD." She drops my hands, balls hers into fists. "I want to hunt her down and beat the shit out of her!"

"That's sweet in a twisted way. And the way you talked me through it was really sweet, too. I appreciate it."

"It's nothing."

It's everything. "How did you know what to do?"

"I learned it in Life Skills last year. Hella glad I did, too. The way you were breathing, I was afraid you were going to pass out."

I'm struck with guilt from out of nowhere. "Sorry I ruined your day out with your dad."

"You didn't ruin anything. We were having fun, then something happened that was beyond your control. And hey, you got me a three-day weekend, so…"

Ha. I fold my arms across my chest. "If that's the case, the least you can do is make me lunch as a thank you. You're so rude."

"You skinny little wiseass." She giggles, then signals toward the kitchen. "You're on."

We raid the fridge and find gold, all the ingredients for Italian subs. We make two overstuffed sandwiches, sit at the table across from one another, and eat and talk about stuff I've never talked about with anyone.

"What do you want to do when you grow up?" she probes.

I was always too focused on surviving into adulthood to consider what I wanted to do once I got there. "I think I want to be a photographer—wildlife, maybe, for National Geographic or something." That's it. That's what I want. "What about you?"

"Historical archivist."

I have never heard anyone, ever, answer that question with 'archivist.' "You want to spend your life in a musty basement somewhere doing research and collecting old stuff?"

"Yes, that sounds fabulous." She is 100 percent for real. I admire the hell out of her for it.

"That's awesome. Do you know where you want to go to college yet?"

"Northeastern. It's my first, second and third choice. They have an unbelievable history department, world-renowned faculty." She rolls her eyes. "And a 19 percent acceptance rate."

"You'll get in."

"You don't know that."

"Yes, I do."

The Lip Bite. What goes on in her head when she does that? I can't figure it out. "Where do you want to go?"

"I don't know. I'll probably end up at North Shore."

She straight up crows. Why does she react that way all the time? *Why do you like it so much?* "You will not go to North Shore," she asserts. "You're too smart to waste your time at a community college."

"Too smart to, too poor not to."

She kicks her chair back a little. "No. No! I'm not tryna hear that. Where do you want to go, in your heart of hearts?"

"MassArt." Huh? I guess so.

She smacks the table-top. "Yes! That's your school. You're going to study photography at MassArt, and then you're going to become a famous wildlife photographer and the entire planet is going to fawn over your work."

"Stop."

"I will not stop. You're doing it. Pinky promise me." She throws her fist up, pinky out.

"If you promise me that you'll go to Northeastern like the undercover smarty-pants that you are."

"Deal."

We pinky swear. *Skin like cashmere.* I don't want to let go, and she doesn't let go. We sit there, fingers hooked together for I don't know how long. Right as my heart is about to burst through my ribcage, she moves. She picks up our plates and takes them to the sink.

I go over to her. "I can do that."

"I've got it." She's austere all of a sudden, her muscles rigid. But then she checks herself, bites it back. "Seriously, it's already done. Why don't you go find us something to watch on Netflix?"

"Are you in the mood for anything in particular?"

"Something funny."

We're next to each other on the couch, deep into the first season of a show called *Curb Your Enthusiasm* and we've both been dying of laughter. "I can't take this Larry guy. He's so uncouth, it's out of control."

"It's not Larry. It's everyone else," she says.

"What? No way."

"Yes! Like that Shoe Whore thing. He didn't start that, he wanted to pay the man his commission."

"Okay, but the thing with his 'abusive' uncle and the director's meltdown. That was all his fault."

She brays. "I don't care, it was hilarious."

"It was, but still."

"What's going on in here?" Tom pokes his head into the living room.

"Hey, Dad. We're watching TV."

"I heard you guys laughing. It's good to see you're feeling better, Britton."

"I am. Thanks."

"My wife is going to make a big deal over cooking for you tonight, so, better get an idea of what you want," he says before disappearing upstairs.

Avery nods her agreement. "Mom's like that with food. If you're stressed, she cooks for you. If you're happy, she cooks for you. Grandma's Italian, that's where she gets it from."

"Um, that's perfect. You know how I feel about food."

"Yeah, I do, Scrawny." She pokes her finger into my stomach and I squeal like the Pillsbury Doughboy. Her eyes go wide. "You're ticklish!" She attacks my sides. I writhe against her, bat at her hands, grab ahold of them. She stares at me, smirking. "You've thwarted me for the time being, but I know your weakness now. You are forever screwed."

I hate being tickled. I don't like being touched, in general.

And I like both as long she's the one doing them. I am forever screwed.

CHAPTER SIXTEEN

Photography Club is in the Computer Lab again. Mr. Warren informs us that Fall Gallery Night is next Wednesday and he wants us to use today's meeting to choose and prepare the eight photos we're each allowed to display. He's loaded two of the badass mega-printers at the back of the room with glossy 8" x 10" photo paper.

Avery and I have cued up some of our pics and are standing around waiting for them to appear from the ether, transformed into real-life pixels. I had to convince her to do it; it took some prodding, but she relented after I told her she didn't have to hand them in even though we were asked to. The Dead Trees photo is the first of hers to print. She snatches it from the tray.

I tap its top corner. "You should hand that one in."

"No."

The next picture to print is one I took of her, the one she caught me editing. My turn to snatch.

"Is that for the gallery?"

No way; this is mine. *Okay, freak.* I shake my head. "I wanted a hardcopy to see how it looked on paper." She's relieved, but doesn't say so. *Bad enough you snuck the dumb pic.* "I should've asked you first, before I snapped it."

"It would've been forced, then. This is… authentic."

So, she's fine with me seeing her, the veiled her, as long as I keep it between us.

My pictures are starting to backlog the tray. She gathers them up and scans them over—a seascape and a landscape from Salem Willows, the American bald eagle, the peregrine falcon, and the series of the boy on the swing. "These are so good."

Face reddening to commence in three, two, one. "Thanks."

Another of her photos pops out onto the tray, a close-up shot of her friends cheerleading at a football game. Kylie is at the top of the lift, Liz and Tasha make up the base. They're all fixated on the crowd, beaming. *She misses it.* I want to come out and ask her why she quit, but if she wanted me to know, she would've told me by now. Instead, I say, "That right there is a yearbook photo."

She inspects it. "You might be right."

"There's a game tomorrow night, isn't there?"

"Yeah. Away at Danvers."

I don't care much for football. And I don't get cheerleading at all. Still, I want to go. For her. "Are you gonna take me, or what?"

Her eyebrows try to climb off her face, as if that was the most startling question anyone has ever asked her. Then, she smiles. "Totally."

*

Friday night we go to the game. Danvers's field is nicer than ours, in addition to their team being on a whole other level. By the end of the second quarter we're down 28–6—shameful for everyone save the kicker—and the sun is gone from the sky. The stadium lights are wicked bright, but do nothing to stop me from freezing my funbags off. *Cate said to wear something warmer than jeans and a hoodie, stubborn mule.*

Avery, the paragon of foresight, brought a thick fleece blanket as backup to her long wool trench coat. She notices me shivering and strips the blanket off her shoulders. She scoots closer to me, wraps it around us both. Then my hands are in hers and she's rubbing heat into them. "What the hell is wrong with you? It's like you've never been to New England in October before."

"It was humid earlier!"

"Again, it's New England. In October."

"Alright, I get it, I'm a terrible Masshole."

She chortles. "You are." Now her eyes are on me as well as her hands, and my gut does that somersault thing. Damn it. It's so weird, and so nice. Or, it would be nice, if it were caused by someone else.

Dance music pumps through the sound system and the crowd gets loud. I glance down at the field and see that both schools' cheerleaders are on the fifty-yard line. Avery lets go of my hands and shifts her attention to the pitch. "Whoooo!" She adds a piercing whistle. I watch a rush of enthusiasm take hold of her as Beverly gets the cheer-off started.

I'd have loved to see her out there. Our squad has some sick moves, for sure, but I'd bet a fat stack on her being the best of them all. *Hey, look, skirts! Really short ones.* If only I gave a single shit about any of those other girls.

The cheer-off is over faster than it began, and the girls are already headed back to the sidelines. Avery stands up. I look at her, confused. "I'm going to say hi, and then we can leave."

"You don't want to stay for the rest of the game?"

"The best part about quitting the squad is that I can bounce whenever I want. I saw what I came here to see. Plus, we're losing and you're cold." She motions for me to follow her down to field-level, and I do.

Her friends are glad that she came—even Amy, who's always kinda bitchy. Avery gives them a few glowing words on the performance and a round of high fives. She shoots the shit with them for a while, looks over at me just in time to catch my teeth chattering. "Okay, ladies, I gotta get Brit someplace warm before she turns into a sad, skinny meat popsicle." We say our goodbyes, and then we're out.

CHAPTER SEVENTEEN

Cate is up earlier than usual for a weekend morning; I hear her bang into something downstairs in the living room and squeal, "Crap!" She and Tom are both the type that like to sleep in—sometimes to nine, if they can—and who could blame them? I would if I could, but my stupid body never makes it past seven o'clock no matter how late I may go to bed or how tired I am when it happens. Except in the case of a panic attack. And that was the most terrifying experience ever, 10/10 would NOT recommend.

Coffee? Yes, that's what that aroma is, coffee; how astute. *Get some immediately.*

I shamble out to the hallway and meet Avery as she's exiting the bathroom—white tank top wrinkled, one leg of her bright pink-and-aqua tartan PJs scrunched up around her calf, hair looking like she had a heaping helping of electricity for breakfast—and she is still breathtaking. *Forever screwed.* Understatement.

"Morning," she says through a yawn.

"Good morning, birthday girl."

"Fuck." She smooths her hair.

"Did you forget?"

"About my birthday? No. About the party?"

"Yes."

"I just want to sleep."

That's troubling. "Are you sick?"

"No, I feel fine." She pouts. "Can we say I'm sick? I'd love to skip it."

"After I threatened your friends with death to ensure that you get the best party ever? I don't think so."

"You're lucky I like you," she groans.

I'm not lucky I like her. "We're going to have fun tonight, okay? I'll hire a clown to make balloon animals if that's what it takes."

"So cute," she says under her breath. Her face goes rosy; I wasn't supposed to hear that.

What's cute, me or balloon animals? *Lol, 'me.' Been huffing paint?* "I need coffee."

"Mmm. Caffeine."

I let her go first, follow her down.

"Birthday huuugs!" Cate clobbers her as she saunters into the kitchen. Avery's a good sport about it and hugs her back. "My little girl is all grown up! I can't believe it. Seems like only yesterday we brought you home from the hospital."

That's all Avery is willing to endure. "Okay, Mom." She pats Cate's head and pushes out of her arms.

These precious moments between her and her parents make my heart swell. I don't know if she realizes how #Blessed she is. I really hope she does.

"How would you feel about doing a birthday brunch? Since you've got your party tonight and you won't let me make a big dinner because it 'takes too long.'"

Avery gawps at me. "You see what I have to put up with?"

I know she's joking, but I want to be snarky about it, anyway, like, *Oh, your mom loves you and wants to celebrate your birth? The horror!* Instead, I smile and say, "Now, now."

"Yes, we can do brunch."

That was the right answer. Cate is thrilled.

Avery pours herself a cup of coffee, and one for me. She takes hers black, as always. She ladles two spoonfuls of sugar into mine and adds a pinch of milk. When she hands the mug to me, she asks, "What?"

What 'what'? *Your stupid jaw is hanging open.* "You know how I like my coffee?" *Yew knyo mehmehmeh.*

"I paid attention." Her phone rings in her pants pocket. She snatches it, looks at the screen; her face has joy written all over it. She peeps at her mom and says, "It's Daddy," then answers the call. Cate and I can hear Tom singing "Happy Birthday" into her ear as clearly as if he were on speakerphone. She's beaming throughout the whole song.

Avery chooses a swanky gastropub downtown called Taro for brunch. Their menu is chock full of ornate dishes: cinnamon apple bostock—I have no idea what that is—and fried egg with hazelnuts, chanterelles, blackberries and green garlic. Avocado, egg and bacon waffle sandwich. Honey and ricotta scone? *Who eats this boujee crap?*

The waiter has taken Avery and Cate's order—an egg and cheese soufflé and strawberry-cream cheese crêpes, respectively—and I still haven't decided what I want. *Should've asked for the damn kids' menu.* "Um, can I get regular, plain waffles?"

The waiter regards me with mild contempt. "Plain waffles," he repeats. "Okay, miss."

Cate taps his arm after he's written down my order, motions for him to come closer. He bends, and she mumbles something unintelligible into his ear. When he stands, he says, "Certainly," and then leaves us.

"And now…" Cate reaches into her purse, removes a small, blue snap-lid box with a dainty white bow on top, and slides it across the table to Avery.

Avery pops the box open. Inside is a rose gold ring in the shape of a crown, clear diamonds embedded in each of its points, and a delicate chain-necklace is strewn through it. "Mom, this is—" Her breath hitches in her throat. She has tears pooling in her eyes.

"Happy birthday, sweetie," Cate says. There's sadness in her eyes, such a contrast to her smile. She reaches out to Avery, touches the back of her hand. "Wear it close to your heart."

Avery dabs at her eyes, then removes the necklace from the box and turns to me. "Can you help me put it on?"

I nod, take the chain into my hands, undo the clasp. She bunches her hair in her palm and swooshes it off her shoulders. I slide the necklace around her neck, redo the clasp. She lets her hair drop, then straightens the crown, rolls it between her fingers for a second. She regards her mother. "Thank you so much. I'll wear it every day."

"You're welcome."

The meal concludes with the presentation of a piece of tiramisu, a tall lit candle stuck in the middle of it. A small group of staff gathers around our table and sings an off-key rendition of their own birthday song. When they've finished, Avery looks to me. "Blow it out with me."

"You need help for one candle? You've gotta quit smoking."

"No," she titters. "You weren't with us for your birthday, so we'll celebrate it now."

Cate goes, "Aww."

Please, don't let me blush. Please. *No deal, hunny; here's your pink!* I clear the lump from my throat. "On three?"

"One, two, three." We extinguish the flame from existence together.

The staff gives us a round of applause, then disperses. Avery plucks the candle out of the cake, slides the plate between us and hands me a dessert spoon. "Happy super belated birthday." She holds up her spoon for a cheers.

"Happy actual birthday." *Clink!*

Cate watches us, grinning, as we delve into the sugary treat.

CHAPTER EIGHTEEN

Avery flies down the steps, taking them two at a time. It's nine thirty; we're half-an-hour late to her birthday party. *Is she wearing jeans?* Yes, skinny, shredded ones, and a pair of white and pale-blue Nike high tops. *Well, I never...* Her shirt is more what I'm used to seeing her in—baby blue, long-sleeved and off-the-shoulder, short enough for her midriff to peek out from below its hem.

Her hair is pin straight and up in a high ponytail, bangs jagged. She usually wears it down and wavy. There's almost no makeup on her face. She doesn't need it, anyway, she's prettier without it.

I've gone the opposite direction, made way more of an effort than I ever do. My hair is loose around my shoulders, with a 'sexy mermaid' style crimp, rather than trapped in my preferred low messy bun. I'm in a pair of tight black pants, a white button-down, and a fitted military jacket—also black. I've got dress shoes on my feet, bought special for the occasion. I'm even wearing eyeliner and friggin' lip gloss! I feel like an imposter, a Pod Person. But I must admit I look good.

"I'm ready if you are." She takes her first solid glance at me of the evening. Her left eyebrow arches and her mouth goes a tad agape. If she were someone else, I'd have a pretty good idea of what she's thinking, but because it's her, it isn't that. She's surprised that I've gone through the trouble, is all.

"I've been ready."

"Good. Let's go."

Cate says, "Be careful. If you need a ride home, call me. No matter how late." Her mouth contracts into a worried scrunch. Why? I don't think Avery's the type to get behind the wheel drunk.

"I will!" Avery grabs her car keys from the hook, and we're out the door.

Kylie, Liz, Amy and Tasha followed my recommendation to make this the best party ever; they've gone all out. There are some decorations—a giant rainbow *Happy Birthday* banner strung across the living room archway and a few bunches of balloons here and there—tasteful, not like at a child's party.

The kitchen counter is stocked with every variety of alcohol known to mankind, and there's a fat beer keg sitting in a big green bucket of ice on the floor. *Wonder how they got it all.* There's a stack of pizza boxes on the table, too, and some chips and dips in bowls.

The music is loud, thick with heavy bass and smooth synths. The house lights are low and they've set up string lights that flash in time to the beat of each song.

There must be a hundred people here and it's only ten thirty. If this keeps up there's no doubt the cops will show up within the hour. Maybe Avery would prefer that, to have this shindig broken up early. *Get 911 on speed dial then, toolbag.* Nope.

"Avery, happy birthday! This party is lit." Her friend, I think his name is Kevin, slinks his arm around her and hugs her tight to his letterman jacket. "It's good to see you out again. You haven't been to a party since—"

"Have you gotten a drink yet?" she yells over him and pats his shoulder. "There's a massive keg in the kitchen. Get your ass in there and tap it!" She gives him a shove in the right direction, then grabs my forearm and hauls me in the other.

People are congregating in the living room—some are dancing, others are sitting around talking and laughing and drinking. Avery doesn't seem interested in doing any of it. Truthfully, she seems stressed-out. I want to help her relax, but I can't do that if I don't know what the problem is.

"I need to get some air. It's too hot in here. Wanna come outside with me?"

She gives a curt nod. I take her hand, somehow don't freak about it, and tow her through the sea of kids to the back door.

There's no one outside. We've got the patio to ourselves for a little while, at any rate. There are plenty of places to sit, yet she chooses to park next to me on the small loveseat. The sky above us is clear; the moon and stars are so brilliant, they're the only light we need.

"Nice night."

She looks to the heavens. "It is."

"Your friends did a good job. This party really is lit."

"Yeah."

"Here." I pull out the small, flat package I've had buried in my front pocket for hours and hand it to her. "Happy birthday."

"You got me a present?" Her appreciation is sincere. Her eyes are overflowing with it.

"It's not much." I don't have a lot to give. I'd have done more if I could've.

She knocks her shoulder into mine like she's heard my thoughts, then tears at the corners of the sparkly-green wrapping paper. When it falls away, she gasps. "How did you know I needed these?" It's a pair of pink, wireless-charging knock-off brand AirPods—I could never afford the real ones on my stipend—but these are supposed to be of comparable quality.

"I heard you mention to your mom before your run the other day that your old ones weren't charging right."

"You notice everything, don't you? I mean, you're like, hyper-aware of your surroundings."

She picked up on that, huh? No use lying to her about it—not after she had to coddle me at the zoo, definitely not after she heard one of the shittier parts of my life story. "This is going to sound messed up to you, but it's a survival skill. I've had to watch my step a lot."

She takes my hand, slips her fingers between mine. "You don't have to do that with us." She doesn't say, *we'll never hurt you*, though that's what she means.

"I know." I honestly do.

The ranch sliders glide open and a handful of tipsy kids spill out onto the patio. She drops my hand, jumps up fast and shoves the earbuds into her jeans pocket. "I should head back inside. It doesn't look good if the guest of honor bails on her own party."

"You're right."

She cuts through the small group—all of whom slur out birthday wishes—and ducks into the house. She doesn't check to see if I'm behind her. What is her deal? She's so hot and cold, sometimes. *You're one to talk.*

"Do you want a drink?" I ask once I've caught up with her.

"No, thanks. I'm okay."

I amble to the kitchen alone. I'm not much for alcohol, though I opt to pour myself a beer. As I finish, I hear her shout so loudly that it trounces the music, "What are you doing here?" She's perturbed more than pissed, but definitely both.

She's not in my line of sight; I can't see who's on the receiving end, although I have a solid idea. I leave the beer on the counter and rush into the living room. She is face to face with Spence.

Spence's posture is tense, stiff as a board. Her fists are clenched at her sides.

Avery's not much better, with her arms folded across her chest. "I asked you a question."

People are gawping at the spectacle as if they're expecting a physical fight. *That's not what this is.* What is it, exactly? I know they don't like each other, but this is beyond awkward.

Spence's jaw slackens. "Jason invited me."

Avery's eyes are glassy. Is she going to cry? "Can you leave?"

Spence doubles down. "This might be your party, but it's his house. I'm not leaving unless he asks me to."

Avery scans around for Jason. He's nowhere to be found.

Damn it. I have to squeeze through two muscular-ass football players to get to Spence. "Hey, you." I flash her a smile, focus on her and only her. *Everything's cool.* "Come get a drink with me." It takes a tiny nudge to get her moving.

"Dope. I need a beer." She nails Avery with a look I can't quite place. "Happy birthday."

I steer her around Avery and we disappear into the ocean of bodies.

Spence hops up to sit on the counter. I have a 'she came with me, she's leaving with me' policy when it comes to large gatherings, but I might have to break it this time. "Do you want to go?"

"Nah. She's being a bitch. Screw her," she says. She doesn't mean it. Her expression tells me that she's hurt, not heated.

I reach around her to grab a cup, fill it with beer, and hand it to her, then pick up the one I left on the counter. "Drink."

We dance, song after song. I'm afraid to let her stop. As long as we're swaying together, she's not looking for Avery. Neither am I. I haven't seen her in a while. I hope she's okay.

A new tune pumps through the speakers, older but so damn good—Zeds Dead "Lights Out." It has a slower, sexier sound than the previous track. The bass reverberates through my torso. The singer's voice gives me goosebumps.

Spence puts her hands on my hips, pulls me closer to her. *Please, don't.* She does, bows her head to make up for the height difference between us and plants her lips on mine. She helps herself to a little taste of me with her tongue. *One more try.* I grant her entry to my mouth.

Her lips are soft, and she's a good kisser.

Still, it's wrong.

I hate having to turn girls down. It's never easy, but it's better than stringing them along. *Please don't let this ruin our friendship.* I palm her shoulder, push her gently away. "Spence."

"I had to shoot my shot." She smirks. "I think we're both tops."

We erupt into raucous laughter. By the start of the next song, we're right back to dancing.

"It's almost midnight. Turn the music off!" Amy yells to whoever's playing DJ for the evening. "Where's Avery?"

"Right here!" Avery stands up from the couch. Or, she tries to stand. Her legs are wobbly and about to quit on her.

"Get over here, birthday girl!"

That's not gonna happen. She's blown past buzzed, gone straight for crunk.

I'm about to leave Spence and go to Avery when Kevin jumps to his feet. He slithers an arm around her waist and takes more than a little bit of her weight. "Here we come!"

Tasha flicks off the lights. Liz and Kylie present the cake, ablaze with enough candles to burn the place to the ground. "Happy birthday to you…" Everyone, including Spence and me, joins the chorus.

It takes everything Avery has to blow out the candles. She turns a sickly green the instant the last flame dies.

Funny how your body functions when you're drunk; one minute you can barely stand on your own, the next you're able to run to the bathroom unaided. The bathroom is where she's hauling ass to now. Kevin's too embarrassed for her to follow and make sure she's alright.

I go over to him. "I've got this one."

"Cool," he says, relieved.

Avery's hair is still in its ponytail—I've secured her bangs behind her ears—so I don't have to hold it off her face. Instead, I rub her back. The sound of her retching is bad. The smell of Jägerbombs and bile is worse.

She finishes vomiting her guts into the toilet. I hand her some TP so she can wipe her mouth. She sits, back propped against the ceramic sink basin, and gapes up at me. "You're soft in there." She smiles and points at my heart. "Reminds me of my sister."

HER WHAT? "I didn't know you had a sister."

A vexed snort leaches out of her. "Why would you? Not like anyone ever talks about Reese." She slurs her sister's name. *Reese!* "Don't even have any pics of her in the house. Guess it's easier to try to forget she ever existed than wrap your head around what happened."

"What happened?"

"She died two years ago."

Holy weeping Christ. That's why no one has ever mentioned her; it's too painful for them. "I'm sorry."

"Yeah, me, too."

"How…" I shouldn't ask—it'll sting for her—but I need to know. "How did she die?"

Her head lolls back. She squinches her eyes and swallows hard. "Not tonight. Not on my fuckin' birthday."

"Okay." My voice is so hushed, it's near a whisper. "Come on, I'm taking you home."

Her arms are wrapped around my torso and I have my arm slung round her shoulder. She's leaning against me so hard, neither of us can walk a straight line. I have to get her home, but I don't want Cate to see her like this. *Wishing you had a license now.* Shit. I could call a cab, but I don't have any cash on me. Uber might be an option...

And then Spence is with us.

"I hate to ask—"

She stops me. "No worries. I got you."

I pour Avery into the backseat of Sweet Caroline, slide in next to her and slam the door. Spence turns over the engine, and shoots us a look in the rearview mirror. She's seen this spectacular shitshow of Avery's before, perhaps more than once. *The hell?* Oh my God, Reese.

Avery's eyes are closed and her head is resting on my shoulder. I smooth her hair. It's a long ride and a short one all at once.

"Can you get her inside?" Spence questions from the driver's side window.

Avery's a tad more put together now after her micro-nap. "Yes. Thanks for the ride."

"No problem."

She idles at the curb until we're in the house, then I hear her drive away.

It's one in the morning. The house is silent. Cate's asleep. We take the stairs slowly, quietly. She's got her arms around me, again.

I flip the switch in her bedroom and the overhead light flickers on. "Too bright," she growls. I lower her onto her bed, turn off the overhead, switch on the desk lamp.

I grab the garbage pail from beneath her desk. "I'm leaving this here for you in case you need it." I show her the pail and exactly where I'm putting it.

"Mmm." She unbuttons her jeans. Please let her be able to get undressed on her own. "Can you get me a shirt? In the… thingy…" She flaps her hand at her bureau.

I choose an oversized tee from the top shelf. By the time I turn around again, she's in her bra and panties. I look at the carpet, study its geometric patterns as I hand her the shirt. My work for the evening is done. Without another word, I leave, turning off the lamp and closing the door behind me.

CHAPTER NINETEEN

I'm startled awake by the sound of Avery's voice passing my door in the hall. It's not angry, necessarily, more annoyed. "You can't just barge into my room! I've asked you a hundred times to knock. God, I'd kill for a door that locks."

Then comes Cate's voice, collected. "Your car wasn't in the driveway. I was making sure you were home."

Avery chokes back her exasperation. "I know. Sorry."

It's silent for a moment. I figure it's as good a time as any to intrude. I open my door and poke my head into the hallway. "G'morning," I say, wiping the remainders of sleep from my eyes.

"Good morning," Cate replies.

Avery says, "Hey."

I step out, close my door behind me.

Cate smiles at me. "I'm making breakfast. Hope you're hungry. I mixed too much batter, there'll be about a thousand pancakes."

My stomach rumbles at the mention of food. "I think I could eat a thousand pancakes on my own."

She perks up. *Good answer.* "So, you accept the mission! Excellent, excellent. See you down there." She bounds downstairs.

Avery's mascara has run amok. I want to reach out to her, wipe away the black streaks from under her eyes. "You look like shit." The words creep past my lips without permission. *Such a charmer.*

I anticipate indignation, but she chuckles, then winces. Her hand rockets up to her right temple and she massages it. "I feel like shit."

"Wash your face and brush your teeth. It'll help."

She shuffles to the bathroom. "Thanks for everything last night, by the way."

"You should thank Spence. She's the one who gave us a ride."

Her mouth curves into a frown.

I can't stop staring at either of them over breakfast—or even hours after, as the three of us laze on the couch in the living room watching TV.

Reese.

I've seen the incredible amount of love this family has for one another, and I have never felt so fortunate not to have a family of my own. I cannot imagine what it's like to have a piece of my heart torn away the way they have. I don't want to imagine it. Yet both Avery and Cate—and Tom, so cheery and positive all of the time—are so normal, carrying on with their lives as though they aren't suffering. Maybe they aren't suffering every minute of the day, not anymore, anyway; maybe two years has given them some time to heal. But still… A single second of that kind of heartache is enough for an eternity.

All of a sudden, I feel unbelievably stupid. Blind. I never even noticed it.

No, that isn't true. I've caught glimpses of their sorrow, droplets that seeped through tiny fissures. But those crevices were always plastered over so quickly I wasn't able to make sense of it. Now that I know, I wish I didn't. I hate being aware of their burden. I hate that they have to bear it at all.

I hate that I know I'm living in Avery's dead sister's room and that's why she was so freaked out about knocking on my door. I hate how awful it must be for her, the loneliness she must feel, and how she'll never ever say it out loud.

I hate that I know Reese and Spence were friends, and that's why Cate was so surprised and happy to see her that day. Because regardless of whatever happened between Avery and Spence, Cate still cares about her dead daughter's friend—she's the kind to nurture even guttersnipes like me.

What I hate most of all is how helpless I feel; there's nothing I can do to make it better for any of them. I'm a spectator observing the aftermath of their calamity, useless as a glass hammer.

"It's getting late, honey." Cate pats Avery's thigh. "Why don't I drop you off at your car?"

"Okay." She turns her attention to me. "Wanna come?"

"Yeah."

I notice her messing with her ring-necklace when we're stopped at a red light on the way back from Jason's. It's not the 'getting used to new jewelry' kind of absentminded fiddling; it's purposeful, introspective. I understand why—it isn't just another pretty bauble to add to her collection. I gesture to the miniscule crown. "That belonged to your sister, huh?"

She's caught off guard by my insight. She crumples her lips, determining what she wants to disclose. The light turns green. She puts her foot on the gas, then nods and says, "My parents gave it to her for her last birthday. It was the only piece of jewelry she ever wore." A subtle smirk. "She wasn't into glitzy girlie stuff, unlike me. Sometimes I wondered where she came from, the two of us were such opposites."

"I've seen that between siblings before. I think it's common."

We turn onto Haskell, and she brings the car to a stop in front of Dix Park. She used to come here with Reese. They probably grew up playing here—countless hours on the swings, or pretending Princess and Knight in the castle. It must be excruciating for her to be here now.

She looks at me. "Last night you asked me how she died. Do you still want to know?"

"Yes, I do." And she wants to talk about it.

She turns the engine off, pulls the keys from the starter. "Take a walk with me."

We head for the playground. She's quiet the whole way, hands jammed in her coat pockets. I'm glad the sun is setting. It's starting to get chilly; all the children have gone home. She jumps on a swing, kicks up mulch. "It's a long story."

I make myself comfortable on the swing next to hers. "I've got time."

"I've never told anybody before, not even my parents."

"I'm listening."

She takes the deepest breath, exhales hard. "Spence and I… we killed her."

What the ever-loving fuck is she talking about? This girl has her secrets, and I'm sure Spence does, too, but this would be too heavy for any two people to keep quiet. "Wait. That doesn't make sense. Start at the beginning."

She pinches her bottom lip between her thumb and forefinger, gives it a slight twist, lets it go. "Reese was a little more than a year older than me, a grade ahead in school. And she was so cool. I was the typical baby sister, wanted to do everything she did. She got into cheerleading, so I did, too…" *Ahh. Okay.* "I don't know if you know this about Spence yet, but she's really good at math. Like, so good they put her in eighth grade Algebra when she was in seventh grade. That's where she and Reese met. Reese sucked at math, and Spence, being the nice person that she is, wanted to help her. They got along really well, and after a while they were inseparable. Reese was an awesome big sister, she always included me in everything they did. We were a trio, The Three

Amigos, you know? For a long time, it was great, up until the end of sophomore year."

She fidgets a bit, takes another breath. "That's when things started to change between Spence and me, got... physical. It started with a kiss on the cheek and then the next thing I knew we were sneaking away from Reese all the time to go make out. I told myself it was hormones or something, that I wasn't actually into her. But I was into her. It was so confusing—I had only ever liked guys before. We agreed to keep it lowkey, and we managed to do that for a while. Until one night over summer vacation, there was a party.

"It's hazy, but this is what I remember: We were both a little drunk, her more than me, I think, but it doesn't really matter. The room was dark, except for the streetlights coming through the blinds. I could barely see her, but I felt her—she pushed me up against the wall, pressed herself against me, and we were kissing harder than we ever had before. Her hands were up my shirt... I unbuttoned her jeans, so fast and so clumsy, because I wanted her. I'd been waiting so long for it to happen, and finally it was going to.

"Then the bedroom door flew open. The music from the party wasn't muffled anymore. The light from the hallway was so bright. Someone screamed her name. It was Reese. She didn't even give us a chance to say anything, just stomped out. I chased her all the way down the street, begging her to talk to me. Eventually she turned around and yelled, 'You've been lying to my face, the two people in the world I trust the most!' The last words she ever said to me were, 'Find your own way home' before she got in the car and drove away."

She wipes tears from her cheeks. "The craziest thing is she wasn't even drinking that night. We did a coin toss and she lost, so she was the DD. She must've taken a curve too fast. Her Jeep kind of tumbled off the road and wrapped around a tree. Do you get it now? Spence and I killed my sister."

Reese. Spence. Avery. Finally, she's in full focus—sharper than she has ever been. Grey wasn't always one of her colors; she used to be pink, unadulterated. And then she lost too much.

"You did not!" I'm surprised at the sternness, the loudness of my voice.

She edges her swing away from me. *Too firm.* This is a delicate conversation; I can't be so adamant. "I've had foster parents who had two daughters—even a set of twins, once. Trust me, I have seen some arguments. Sisters fight all the time. You had a mis-understanding with yours, and she stormed off—that's normal. She wasn't thinking clearly. She had an accident and she died. It's horrible, and I'm sorry that she's gone, but it wasn't your fault." It wasn't Spence's, either.

She sighs. "The worst part is Reese probably would've been cool with it. Like, who cares if I'm bi or whatever, right? I could marry a woman tomorrow if I wanted to. I think it was the lying she couldn't stand. I'll never know for sure."

"It's not the easiest thing, realizing you're different and owning it. It can be scary. When you care about people, their opinions of you are important. You might think they're evolved and open-minded, but there's always a chance you're wrong."

"That's true. But I knew Reese, she loved me. I should've trusted her."

"You can't beat yourself up about it forever. You can't beat Spence up about it forever, either." *Poor Spence...*

She rubs her forehead. "Things got way too fucked up between us to ever salvage. It's best for both of us to stay away from each other."

"I understand."

"Now that you know what happened, I'd appreciate it if it could stay between us."

I have to tell Spence that I know, otherwise, I'll always feel like I'm lying to her about this terrible, mountainous thing. More importantly, I want her to know that this is a secret she doesn't have to keep anymore. Now, there are three people in on it. *Three's a crowd.* And one is the loneliest number. "I'm not going to say anything to anyone." Anyone who didn't live it.

Cate is still curled up on the couch when we get home. Avery sits down beside her and I drop onto the recliner. "You were gone awhile," Cate says.

"I told her."

Cate sees the look on her daughter's face; she doesn't have to ask what I was told.

"I... I am so sorry, Cate." It's inadequate, but it's all I have.

"Thank you," she says with a wounded smile.

CHAPTER TWENTY

It is the strangest day. There's been a knot in my stomach since I woke up. I want to talk to Spence about the knowledge Avery dropped on me, but at school…? No. Too many prying eyes and ears, and I don't know how she'll react, so privacy is best. I shot her a text between E and F Blocks asking if we could hang out after she's done with soccer, but she hasn't seen it yet.

Avery and I have an exam on *1984* in English tomorrow that's worth a third of our grade for the marking period. Mrs. Henry gave us an updated question guide this morning. We're having lunch together to get a jump on cramming. I don't know what made her think that studying in the cafeteria would be feasible. It isn't. It's too noisy. Her friends don't seem to understand the concept of studying, either—they keep interrupting us after every other question.

"Yo, Brit, are you and Valerie Spencer a couple or just smashing?" Tasha asks.

Avery's head snaps up from her notecard. She shoots Tasha the nastiest look I've seen her give anyone, to date. The scowl makes Tasha wither, a flower at the mercy of a killing frost.

I'm thrown by the question, too. "What?"

Tasha surveys Avery, asking 'Permission to speak?' without words. Avery's lips are pursed, brow raised. She's waiting for her cue to strike. Tasha goes, "Like, the entire school saw you guys making out at Avery's party, and you're always together."

And? "Would you have a problem with it either way?"

She shakes her head. "It's your business, not mine."

"Then why the fuck did you ask her?" Avery spits. "Because you have to stick your nose in everyone's business, right?" To me, she says, "You don't have to answer that."

I let myself touch her shoulder the way I've seen Tom do sometimes, hoping it will pacify her and giving little thought to what it'll do to me. "It's okay, I don't mind." I glare at Tasha. "Spence and I are just friends."

"Uh huh," Tasha retorts, then looks down at her food tray, stabs her fork into the pile of potatoes.

Why bother? The zipped pocket of my messenger bag vibrates. I open it, grab my iPhone.

Spence: Yeah. Come 2 practice?

That's something jocks ask their girlfriends to do, come watch them practice. *Boring.* But this is my chance to talk to her. I skim my eyes around the caf and see her at our regular table, phone in hand.

Will do.

I turn to Avery and notice her leering at my phone before she can flick her eyes away from the screen.

Got ya. "I'm gonna stay after school. I'll catch a ride to the house later."

"'Kay." She holds a flash card close to her face. "Winston commits thoughtcrime by writing what in his diary?"

"'Down with Big Brother'."

I watch girls' soccer practice from the middle-section of the bleachers. Spence and her coaches run it like they're equals, divvying up groups for passing drills and, later, a mini-scrimmage. She's impressive, really knows the game and her teammates' individual skills. I wouldn't be surprised if she goes professional someday. *Gotta catch one of her matches.* I like soccer. It's one of the few sports I understand.

The coaches call it a day, and Spence heads for her bag on the sideline bench. She signals for me to join her on the field as she's toweling the sweat from her neck.

"Suh?" She throws the cloth at me.

I shriek like a total priss and lob it back at her. "Gross."

She chuckles, stuffs it in her gym bag. "Ready?"

"Mmhmm."

"Did you have an idea where you wanted to go or…?" she asks.

"Someplace quiet so we can talk."

She wasn't ready for that response. It concerns her. "Uh, okay. I know a place."

She pulls her car into Balch Park, right up to the deserted baseball field. She gets out of the car and I follow her to the diamond, where she glides onto the bench in the Home dugout. "This work?"

I peep around. There's no one in sight. "Yep." I slide in next to her.

"Man, you're so serious right now. What's goin' on?"

I don't know how to start. There's no delicate way to phrase it. It's a Band-Aid covering a bullet hole. *Rip that bitch right off.* "Avery told me about Reese—about how she died, and everything that led up to it."

She folds her hands together, brings the sides of her knuckles to her lips, lets a puffpuffpuff out against them to warm them. Then she drops them into her lap and concentrates on me. "Everything?"

"Everything." Not a detail spared.

She lets out a disbelieving snigger. "I wasn't sure she'd ever have the balls for that."

"Well, surprise."

"I'm relieved. Not being able to talk about it has sucked for me."

"We can talk about it, if you want."

She smacks her lips together. "What's there to say? My best friend died and my first girlfriend ever pushed me away because she blamed it on our relationship. I loved them both, then just like that"—she snaps her fingers—"I didn't have either of them, anymore." She lets out a breath. "My run-in with Avery at the party? That was the first time we've spoken in almost two years. Everyone figured we drifted apart without Reese around, like she was the only connection we had, and I couldn't say any different because outing her would've made me an asshole. It was a clusterfuck."

She tries to stop herself from tearing up, but fails—falls into a deep, silent, body-shaking kind of sobbing.

It breaks me.

I don't hesitate; I wrap my arms around her neck and tug her into the tightest embrace. Her hands climb my back, grasp swaths of my hoodie. "You can let it go now," I whisper into her ear. "Let it all go."

I hold her for the longest time as she quietly cries.

Her eyes are still bloodshot when she drops me off at the Cahills', but she seems lighter in every sense. "Remember that thing I said about you being a politician when you grow up?" she asks as I'm about to hop onto the curb.

"What about it?"

"I take it back. You should be a therapist. You even got Avery to open up to you."

"I didn't do anything. I just listened."

"It's more than that. Something about you made her want to talk. Same with me. I guess what I'm trying to say is, thanks."

That makes me smile. "Anytime."

I missed dinner and forgot to let anyone know I'd be out. Cate's cool about it, though. She meets me in the hallway outside the living room, takes one look at me and asks, "Are you feeling alright?"

"Yeah, sorry. I lost track of time."

"It's okay. There're leftovers in the fridge."

"Thanks. I'm gonna go study. Big test tomorrow."

As I head up, I run into Avery on the second-floor landing. I know there's something off about me and I can't hide it, because she squints at me and wonders, "What's with you?"

I hardly have enough room for all of my own baggage, so dealing with other people's takes a lot out of me. Sometimes when they get really emotional, it makes me feel like I'm drowning—a symptom of empathy, I suppose. The last two days I've been hit with wave after wave and… "I'm so tired."

She does something so unexpected that I can't do anything but capitulate: She hugs me. My arms snake around her waist, and suddenly we're holding each other. Funny how a single reflexive motion can turn a hug into a hold.

Her citrusy scent inundates my consciousness. Every part of my body feels warm, all of my muscles slack. I could get used to feeling like this. Safe. *Safe in her arms.* I tear myself away from her. "I know we were supposed to work on those test questions for tomorrow, but I need to go to bed."

"It's not a problem. Get some sleep."

"G'night."

CHAPTER TWENTY-ONE

Reese's premature departure from the world is something that we all know about now, nothing more than that. Neither Avery nor Spence seem to want to talk it over any further. I haven't heard her name at all in the last two days. It's fine, better than never having heard it to begin with.

Tom got back from Japan around midnight last night—I heard the security alarm beep when he came in. He knows that I know what happened to his eldest daughter; I overheard Cate tell him as much before I walked into the kitchen for breakfast. He doesn't mention it to me.

He hands me a package wrapped in washi paper. "Souvenir." He grins. "Next time, we're all going. Family trip."

Family trip... I know better than to question him, so I opt to gulp down my discomposure and open the package. There's a folded cloth inside. I unfurl it. It's a tapestry of *The Great Wave off Kanagawa* and it is stunning. "It's beautiful. I love it."

He winks. "Thought ya might."

"Dad!" Avery bounds into the kitchen, leaps onto her father's back. Tom goes, "Oof!" Then scoops her into a bear hug. "Hey, kiddo!" He kisses her forehead and produces another package from the back pocket of his jeans. "For you." He smirks as he hands it to her.

She opens it, pulls out a cream-colored card stamped with Japanese characters, and below those: "Kan-za-shi," she reads. She plucks the present from the box. It's a traditional Japanese hair-stick with a strand of white-pink faux cherry blossoms attached to the end, gold filigree on each leaf. "This is gorgeous!"

"Two for two." He pumps a triumphant fist.

Avery takes a gander at my tapestry. "Oh, cool!"

Cate's at the stove making omelets, which is insane. I don't know how she manages to cook breakfast every morning, forget when she has to spend her day in court. I know when she's going to be in front of a judge, her outfits are smarter than when she's headed to her office: skirt-suits, dark blues and greys, rather than colorful business-casual dresses. "And where's my present?"

"You'll get yours later." Tom gives her a naughty eyebrow wiggle.

Gag!

Avery goes, "Eurgh!"

Cate chuckles and plates the eggs. "Let's eat!"

I'm not hungry anymore, but I make myself scarf my omelet, anyway.

Midway to school, Avery says, "So, Gallery Night. Are you excited?"

No. I'm petrified. Mr. Warren told me that my photos were "really lovely," but that's his job, to encourage us. No one else has to say nice things. They could call my work straight trash and I'd have no choice but to swallow it. "More like nervous."

She shoots me a glare that lets me know it's the dumbest thing she's ever heard. "Don't be. I told you your stuff is good, and tonight everyone else will see that, too."

"Mmm. Maybe."

"Not maybe. Definitely."

Damn it. Sometimes I can't stand it when she's kind. It makes me like her more. "Okay, definitely."

"Better." I catch her beaming.

*

I aced the English test. The only thing left to dread is Gallery Night, which starts in thirty minutes. Photography Club arrives early to the auditorium to finish last-minute prep. The place is set up to look like a real art gallery. There's a section for paintings, one for sculpture, one for performance art pieces, and one for photography. Avery and I are sitting at a table in the photography section, mounting photos on grey mat boards that Mr. Warren gave to us—he said it would be more professional if they were displayed that way and I decided to take his word for it.

I've numbered each of my eight pictures to show that they should be viewed in order from left to right. The first two—the eagle and falcon—are cool-toned and natural, the next four—the series of the boy on the swing—grow gradually warmer, and the last two of Salem Willows are overwhelmingly vivid, their red-orange tones and saturation tuned up high. It's a theme, to be sure: Beauty comes in many forms. I wish I could've shown a pic of Avery. She's got all the forms covered.

Mr. Warren calls to me as I finish mounting the last picture. Avery and I both look up. He's approaching the table with a tall woman who looks like she time-jumped out of the seventies— flowing brown skirt, beige tunic top, curly brown hair down to her waist. Everything but a crown of flowers. "Britton, Avery, this is my friend Sara Roscoe. She's a professor of photography at Boston University."

"Hello." She shakes our hands.

"Hi," Avery says.

"Professor." I nod.

"Sara," she corrects me. "Do you have a moment to discuss your work?"

I peek at Avery. Her eyebrows are raised and she's sporting a simper.

"Sure." I pull out the folding chair next to mine and Sara sits. She picks up each photo and is quiet as she examines them.

"The gradation of color is very striking. Can you tell me a little bit about your reasoning behind grouping these shots together, and why in this particular order?"

"Uh, yeah." I motion to the left side of the table. "These are raw, no editing at all, exactly how I captured them. And as we move to the right, the photos become more and more heavily tweaked, light and shadow, color intensity, blurring or crispness. I was trying to highlight the difference between real and manufactured, and how both can be alluring in their own ways."

"And Mr. Warren told me that all of your photos were taken with a basic point-and-shoot camera. Is that right?"

He talked about my stuff with her? *Duh, simpleton, why else do you think she'd be wasting her time with you?* "All I had to work with was a Canon PowerShot, so, yes."

She covers her mouth with her fingers, scours over each picture again. "These are fantastic. I'd love to see what you could do with more advanced equipment. You have an eye for the truth of things, the stuff that exists beneath the surface, and that's a rare gift. I hope you continue to nurture it."

"I'm going to try. My plan is to major in Photography next year."

"Glad to hear it." She reaches into her clutch, pulls out a business card and hands it to me. "If you need advice on putting together your portfolio—say, for an application to BU in the fall—I'd be happy to help."

I'm gobsmacked. "That would be great. Thank you."

"You're welcome." She stands. "Keep taking pictures. Avery, it was nice to meet you." She goes to rejoin Mr. Warren, who's setting up the refreshments table.

Avery's rubbernecking me. "A photography professor just critiqued your work, called it fantastic and wants to help you get into college. How are you not flipping out right now?"

"I am. On the inside."

"You can do it on the outside, you know. You should."

I'm too practiced at keeping heartfelt joy to myself—I never know how fleeting it might be, and I like to hold onto it for as long as I can. If no one else knows about it, no one else can wreck it for me. She's seen my worst, though, so that has to entitle her to my best, too. "Okay okay, that was so cool!" I throw my head back and squeal into my hands.

"There you go," she says through her laughter.

I've been posted up near my photos and haven't heard a negative comment on any of them from anyone so far—baffling, since kids can be cruel. I've had a bunch of strangers talk to me about them, ask where I took them, what software I used to edit them. I've gotten a ton of "Wow" and "Pretty" and "Nice." Even the art teachers have expressed their appreciation. It's beginning to get overwhelming, all these compliments. I never was any good at taking them.

The auditorium is getting wicked full. Loads of parents are piling in to view their kids' artwork, as if this were a professional exhibit, their son or daughter's big break. It's bittersweet for me. I'm happy that so many of my peers have parents who care enough to show up for them, and I'm sad that I don't.

"Yo, Brit, these are sick AF."

Olivia? And Mack, and Hannah, and of course, Spence. Good thing Avery's off checking out the sculptures. "I can't believe you guys came."

Spence screws up her features. "You were stoked enough about this to invite us. We knew it was important." She throws her arm around my shoulder, makes me stand in front of my display. It's the hundredth time tonight, but this time feels special.

"The ones of the little boy are so cute," Hannah comments.

Mack adds, "The color's nice, too. Crazy blue."

Olivia moves her face closer to the picture of the peregrine. "Eh, yo, what kind of bird is this? A hawk?"

"It's a falcon."

"Bruh, what's the difference?"

I let out a puff and launch into a mini anatomy lesson of raptorial birds.

The five of us chat for a bit, until Spence spies Avery approaching. She elbows Mack. "Let's go look at the sculptures, guys."

"Aight," Olivia responds. "Deuces." She daps me.

"Nice work," Hannah says, and gives me a high five.

Mack nods at me. "Good shit." It's the most polite thing she's ever said to me.

Spence puts her arm up for a hug. "Thanks for inviting us. It was very cool."

The dam's been broken. Hugging is going to be the way it is for us now, and I'm good with that. "Thanks for coming."

When they've gone, Avery sidles up beside me. "Guess who's here?"

"Who?"

She points to the rear of the auditorium. There, coming through the propped-open doors, are Cate and Tom. "You invited your parents? You didn't even submit any photos."

"They're here for you, dummy."

Oh. Wow. That's… something else. There's a heat rising from my chest, splashing out, out, all over me. I know this feeling. *No crying!*

Tom spots us first, points us out to Cate. Both of their faces light up once they realize I've seen them. They edge over to us through the crowd. "Hi, girls!" Tom says. Cate waves, then goes straight for my pictures. Tom joins her.

I don't want to stand too close to them. I still haven't gotten rid of the lump in my throat, and if I overhear their hushed words to each other—especially if they're praising—it won't bode well for my No Crying mandate.

After a while, Cate seeks me out. Her eyes are bright and soft. "These are wonderful, just gorgeous." She clasps my hand, gives it a little squeeze, lets it go without any urgency.

Tom echoes the sentiment, "You did a great job, kiddo! I'm proud of you." He pats my shoulder.

Proud... of me? *Don't you dare tear up!* "I'm glad you like them. Um, excuse me for a minute."

I head out of the auditorium as fast as my feet will carry me without breaking into a jog. The bathroom across the lobby is empty—a mercy. I turn on one of the taps, splash some cold water onto my face. Drip. Drip. I stare at my reflection in the mirror until I'm certain the threatening torrent has dissipated.

Tom and Cate stay the entire evening. The four of us stroll around, taking in the artwork. Tom gets really into a performance piece called Shadowplay, self-explanatory: colorful paper screens, a spotlight and the shadows of gyrating bodies. Neither Avery nor I understand the appeal, but different types of people like different types of art.

At nine o'clock, the head of the art department closes the night with a speech thanking all the visitors and asks for a round of applause for all the student artists. Cate, Tom, and Avery make a show of clapping for me, and I can feel my cheeks flushing. Afterward, I take my photos down from the canvas, then Avery and I walk her parents to Cate's car.

"Thank you for coming tonight, guys," I say. But it falls flat. They showed up for me in a way no one else ever has; the least I can do is give them each a hug. And I want to, so I go for it—Cate first, who's so gentle about it, and then Tom, who gives me what must be the best version of a dad hug in existence, little 'rawr' included, just like with Avery this morning.

As they drive away, I decide that I wouldn't mind if mom and dad hugs were to become a more regular occurrence in my life. *Within reason.*

Avery keeps shifting her attention between the road and me on the drive to the house—harried glimpses stolen when she thinks I'm not looking. *She gonna say something or not?*

"My parents really like you. Dad said you're 'a good egg' and I was like, 'Okay, Boomer,' because who even says that anymore?"

I chuckle. It's exactly what I needed. "I like them, too."

"Yeah, they're alright."

No, they're extraordinary.

"I love the picture of the boy jumping off the swing, the shadowy one where he's blocking the sun. Can I have it?" she asks as we're entering the house. I'm carrying all of my photos in my hands, piled on top of each other.

"I'll trade you."

"For what?"

"You have to let me take your picture, legit, full knowledge and permission."

"What, like, right now?"

"Whenever you want. We'll do a photoshoot in the park."

She does her lip-bite thing, mulls over the proposition. "If you promise to make me look as beautiful as you did the first time."

"I told you that wasn't me. It's all you." *Whew, ballsy.* Where'd that even come from? And there's the trill in my goddamn stomach again.

She pushes her hair behind her ear and drops her gaze to the floor. "Okay, it's a deal."

I flip through the photos, pull out the picture she requested and hand it to her. "Advanced payment for services to be rendered."

She goes *tsss*. "You'll never make any money with a bartering system."

I shrug. Who needs it, anyway?

CHAPTER TWENTY-TWO

All anyone can talk about at school Thursday or Friday is something called a Pep Party that's going down tonight. The concept of this particular social gathering is completely foreign to me: All the senior athletes across every sport from every season get together to throw this huge celebration of their jockdom, as if that's the only interesting quality any of them possess. *Big yawn.* It's semi-sponsored by school, meaning that coaches and other affiliated adults are welcome, but I've heard that some kids sneak in alcohol right under their noses, which is the most high school thing ever—tactless and excessive. There are enough unsupervised house parties for under-aged alcohol consumption, they could stand to give it a rest around their coaches.

Olivia is psyched about going. Spence is not. She seems uneasy over it. The bell signaling the end of lunch block rings and, as we're herding out of the caf, I ask about it. "You want to skip the Pep Party? We could do something instead."

"I'm a captain. Captains can't swerve it."

Oh, I see. This school has its own traditions, like the Fall Ball in November instead of a Homecoming dance at the start of the autumn sports season. I guess it's to make everyone feel included, not just the people who've earned letter-jackets. "I can see you're thrilled about it."

She lowers her voice. "I don't know if Avery's going to be there. She quit cheerleading, but…"

For fuck's sake, these two can't parley long enough to honor something they both think is monumental? I was hoping now that they've each gotten it off their chest things would be a bit better, at least semi-tolerable. "I could try to get her not to go…" How, ask her out to dinner and movie? *Like she'd say yes.* Bisexuality doesn't mean 'attracted to every individual on Earth.' Foster sisters have to be doubly excluded.

"No. She has as much right to be there as I do. I'll give her the sidestep."

"I'd offer to come with, but I'm not even jock-adjacent."

She stares at me like I'm a genius. "You can come."

I shake my head. "I'd feel like I'm crashing."

"If she asked, you'd go?"

Shit. "I doubt she'll ask." Even if she did, I couldn't accept now. It'd be too unfair to Spence. I refuse to choose sides or play favorites, despite the ridiculous crush I have on Avery.

*

Avery's ready to leave for the party around seven. She's wearing a black and orange Beverly High Cheer T-shirt. *Sparkly megaphone, duly noted.* "Are uniforms the required dress code for this get-together?" I wonder from my spot on the recliner—my official favorite seat in the house.

"Traditionally, yes, for the fall sports. Since I don't have mine anymore, this will have to do."

"Give 'em hell."

She splutters. I think that's the end of it, but she reverses course, walks into the living room. "You wouldn't want to come, would you? I'm just putting in a cameo." She makes a half-hearted attempt to hide her hopefulness.

Parties seriously aren't her thing. Not since Reese died leaving one. "I really wouldn't." Damn her and her dejected eyes.

I hear the *ding dong* of the doorbell from my room and look at my desk clock—seven forty-five.

"Britton!" Tom hollers. "You have a visitor."

Footsteps pound up the stairs. There's a knock on my door. I open it to find Spence, long auburn locks loose and flowing over her soccer jersey that's half tucked into her jeans. "Hi? Come in."

She takes a hesitant step through the threshold and peeks around. "It's weird being in here again. The furniture's different."

I want to tell her that Avery can't stand it, either. "So… What's happening?"

She slips her hands into her back pockets. "You weren't at the party."

"Avery didn't invite me."

She folds her arms across her chest. "I call bullshit."

"Okay, fine. I didn't feel like going."

"Why not?"

"I don't want to get stuck taking care of her again if she gets plastered." It's only half untrue. Her birthday was a disaster, and I honestly didn't like seeing her that way, but I'd be alright with taking care of her if she needed me to. The whole truth is I don't want to be a shield for either of them; I want them to hash it out. They can't go on egg-shelling it indefinitely.

"Don't take care of her, then."

"I'm not built like that."

"No, you aren't." She relaxes, smirks. "We'll take it as it comes. Let's go, get dressed."

She wants me to be there badly enough to have left the damn party to come get me. How can I say no to her? *Try, 'If I can't go in*

my pajamas, then I can't go.' Sigh. "Give me a sec." She doesn't move.
"You know you have to get out for me to get changed, right?"

"Bashful?"

"You're incorrigible."

"So I've been told."

I give her a joking elbow and she shuffles out to the hall.

She tells me that the Pep Party is being held at Kevin's house—
his dad is the assistant coach of the boys' basketball team—and
he lives on the other side of town; the less-rich part, on the
Beverly-Salem border. We turn down a road that edges up against
Kernwood Country Club and it becomes clear to me that there
is, in fact, no 'less-rich' part of this town.

The road transforms from paved to unpaved and the tree line
on either side of it gets thicker. "You're not taking me into the
woods to murder me, are you?"

"Nah, I like you, wanna keep you around."

We pull up to an expansive stone ranch house. The gravel
driveway is overflowing, cars spilling onto the manicured grass.
Spence doesn't care anymore than anyone else; she parks on a
patch of the green stuff.

A few spots ahead of Sweet Caroline is Avery's BMW. We
saunter past it and Spence's entire body goes rigid. She's already
seen her once tonight, so why? *It's hard for her, too—every single
time.* "You are way too tense. Want to hear a dirty joke?"

"Please?"

"What do Chinese food and pussy have in common?"

She's already snickering. "What?"

"An hour after you've eaten, you're hungry for more."

She guffaws. "That was dirty to you? You should hear my
brothers."

"I haven't had the luxury of brothers, so that's the best I can do."

"It was good." She palms the doorknob and we enter the party.

It's basically Avery's birthday 2.0, except everyone's in costume, er, jerseys, and there are grown-ups; not the legit kind, the overly-friendly-with-teenagers, desperately clinging to their lost youth kind.

Spence says a few hellos to athletes from other sports, Volleyball mostly. They're all in full uniform, must've come from a game. Their shorts are practically underwear. How do they, like, jump or whatever without those things bunching into their assholes? The poor girls.

We find her teammates. There are six of them gathered around the billiards table, shooting pool and chatting. I've only ever talked to her and Olivia, so I'm out of my depth. Still, I can fake comfort pretty well in group settings. She introduces me to everyone. I mingle, smile and laugh along with them.

It isn't true that they're all lesbians, I come to find as I'm cajoled into a discussion about which past or present Red Sox player's ass looks the best in baseball pants. Most agree on Xander Bogaerts and Dustin Pedroia, with an old school Johnny Damon thrown in.

"What do you think?" a girl named Erin asks me.

"I've gotta tap out on this one."

Olivia says, "An ass is an ass, don't matter who it's attached to."

"Uh, Big Papi?"

That answer earns me a round of giggles.

"Oh, fam, you are full homo, hundo p!"

"I said I wanted to tap out."

"Great song," Spence interjects. I strain to hear it over the din of voices. "What I Need" by Hayley Kiyoko.

"Oh yeah." I tug her onto the makeshift dancefloor.

She knows all the lyrics, sings along as we dance—she has a nice voice, right on key. It's the most laid-back she's been all night. I like it, it's the best version of her—the way she should always be, no stress or sadness weighing her down.

And then I see Avery. Liz and Amy are working the bar, doling out sodas or beers to the adults and, no doubt, spiked juice cocktails to the kids, and she's hanging around with them.

The song changes and I stop dancing so abruptly that it knocks Spence off her groove. "Sup?"

"I want a drink. You?"

"Yes." Her mouth curls into a frown as she spots the drinks station.

No more goddamn eggshells! "Cowboy up, Valerie!" I take her hand and drag her to the bar.

Avery sees us coming, tosses a glare at Spence. I hear her say, "I'm gonna dip," to her friends, and she's off.

"Cowboy up," Spence stammers a touch above audibility. She grabs Avery's wrist as she's passing us and yanks her to a halt. Avery tries to snatch her arm away; Spence won't let her go. They lock eyes and I see the pain on Spence's face—bare, inescapable. "I miss Reese, too, you know. She was my best friend. And I miss you."

Avery's gaze darts over to me. Yes, we discussed it. Then it's back on Spence, and her jaw droops open.

Spence knows what she's thinking, adds in a hurry, "You know what I mean, how tight we were before all that. I wish we could go back to the way it was."

"Not gonna happen!" Avery barks. Then, quieter, "Every time I look at you…"

I know that she's not just angry; she's choking on guilt and grief, but all I can seem to concentrate on is her anger. And it makes me angry. Because the two of them had something rare and beautiful before everything went to hell: sincere friendship.

For once I don't censor myself. I don't even care that there are people around us. "You're an idiot, Avery!"

Her eyes are ready to pop out of her skull. "Excuse me?"

"You're an idiot," I repeat, lower this time, and take a step closer to her. "You can't accept that accidents happen, and you're either too blind or too stupid to see how much Spence cares about you. I would burn the whole world to the ground for a friend like her. Honestly, do you think your sister would want to see you two like this? 'Cuz I don't."

"What do—"

I throw my hand in the air. "I don't want to hear it." Then I'm pulling on Spence's arm. "Get me out of here." She looks startled but leads me away in spite of herself.

"Go fuck yourself, Britton!" Avery yells at my back.

I don't turn around.

Indignation, righteous or not, isn't something I'm used to emoting. It's too frank and too dangerous. I'm drained, leaning against Sweet Caroline's trunk. Spence is wearing a guise of utter astonishment, scarcely visible in the dimness of the landscape lighting. "I can't believe you said that to her. Nobody talks to Avery Cahill that way."

"She's not the fucking Queen of England."

"She knows that now. I think everyone does."

"I did get loud for a second, didn't I?"

"Uh huh."

"Well, you're both my friends and I don't like that you can't even be in the same room with one another because of something that wasn't anyone's fault. There's no blame to place here."

"I know that."

"And I really don't like that there's nothing I can do to make her feel better."

"No, that's on her."

I huff. I want to help her get there, but she has to want to get there herself.

"Thanks for sticking up for me."

"That's what friends do, isn't it?" *Isn't it?*

She grins. "Yeah."

CHAPTER TWENTY-THREE

I manage to avoid Avery on Saturday by holing up in my room, only leaving for the occasional foraging trip to the kitchen. I even skip dinner—sitting at the table with her is a nonstarter. I tell Tom and Cate that I'm feeling unwell when they come to check on me, which technically isn't a lie, although it's my emotional wellness that's suffering. Cate's maternal instinct shines its brightest. She even goes so far as taking my temperature. She's relieved when the thermometer flashes 98.6. I hope it doesn't make her suspicious. "It's probably allergies. Mold," I say. This is true, but we've had a mild autumn so far, very little rainfall.

Tom runs to the store for Claritin. When he returns, he has a glass of water at the ready. He undoes the child-safety cap and breaks the aluminum seal, then pours a pill into his palm, presents it and the water to me. "Down the hatch." He really does think I'm a child in need of a father. *You are, pitiful orphan.*

It's so heartwarming, I can't take it. I do as I'm told and swallow everything.

Once they're gone, I pop in a Blu-ray, one of a handful that I own, the classic sci-fi horror *They Live*, and fall asleep.

*

By late Sunday afternoon, it has become intolerable. And we still have another day off. Our first—with a bit of luck, our last—argument had to happen on a three-day weekend. I wouldn't have expected it to go down any other way; fate was always going to make sure I'd have a remarkable amount of time on my hands to brood over it.

Avery's been out for a while. When I ask Cate about it, she tells me she's at the mall with Amy and Kylie. Her absence is advantageous. I can let my guard down while I plant my ass in the recliner and figure out the best way to remedy the shit-uation. Groveling for forgiveness won't work; that would annoy her. A simple apology won't be enough. Why the hell did I act without considering the consequences first?

I could cry? *That's some weak shit.* The only acceptable time for tears is during a panic attack when my logical brain goes into hibernation and my primordial lizard brain takes over.

I could write her a note? *You want her to forgive you or laugh in your face?*

I could buy her flowers? *Lol, wut?* No, that's weird. Total wifey move.

The front door opens and closes. I shut my eyes. Please be Tom. I open them again and see that Avery is standing in the hallway with about fifteen bags in her hands. Retail therapy.

I scamper to my feet. "Hey."

"Hi."

"You need some help with those?"

She holds out her left hand. I bundle the handles and take the bags from her. "Come upstairs with me?" she asks.

We head to her room. She closes the door. I place the bags on the floor, then turn around and squirm under her gaze. She puts the rest of the bags down on her desk. "We should talk." She motions to the bed. "Sit down."

Not her puppet. Or her dog. I sit. Her mattress is the same as mine, comfortable, shape-conforming. She takes a seat beside me.

"Look, I wanted to apologize. I shouldn't have told you to go fuck yourself. That was out of line."

"I deserved it. I wasn't the most gracious version of myself, either. I'm sorry, too."

"I know I can be a bitch sometimes, all the time when Spence is involved." She groans, "I hate it, that I can't just, like, chill out when she's around. I even switched my gym elective last year because I couldn't handle being in class with her for forty-five minutes."

"It's the same for her." That's not my truth to share, but she needs to hear it.

"I know. I broke her heart."

That's another thing she can't forgive herself for. "Broken hearts mend. What she can't stand is that her presence hurts you."

She rolls some of her wavy tresses around her finger. "I can't wait to graduate."

Graduation. The only thing I have ever looked forward to: my first step toward freedom—getting to decide what's best for me, living on my own, never having to fear being screamed at or slapped or locked in a goddamn pantry ever again. Now, I'm wishing it would never come. What happens to us when we're not forced to be together under the same roof, at the same school? I couldn't bear it if our relationship were temporary. Regardless of anything else, I care about her. I want her in my life.

"Anyway, I got you something." She leans forward, plucks a paper shopping bag from the desk. She digs inside, pulls out a medium-sized box wrapped in white paper, a rainbow ribbon tied around it, and hands it to me.

I stare at it, at her. "What's this for?" *Compensation for guilt.*

"You need a reason?" She shrugs. "I saw it and thought of you. Open it." She scoots a little closer to me. I feel her body heat.

I yank at the ribbon and it comes undone, then glide my finger beneath the taped flaps, careful not to rip the paper. Unwrapped, the box reads *Nikon D7500, 18-55 VR Kit*. It's a DSLR camera—a very expensive one. My breath catches in my windpipe. "This is too much. I can't accept it." And I can't look at her. Her eyes are all over me, though; I can feel them as if they were her hands.

"Yes, you can. You need a good camera, not that shitty one Mr. Warren lets you use. Besides, I owe you a photoshoot, and it sure as hell isn't going to be with a PowerShot."

I don't know if it's because of the sudden influx of honesty, or the absolute deluge of emotion, but I lose my damn mind, forget who the hell I am. I kiss her... on the lips.

When I move away, she lets out a tiny breath, the ghost of a breath.

Fuck me dead. "I am so sorry! I—"

She laughs so hard that it shakes the bed. "And you called me an idiot."

"What?"

She can see that she's going to have to explain it to me like I'm five. "Spence showing up to my party wasn't the worst part of the night for me. The worst part was when I saw you kissing her. I wanted to be the girl you were kissing."

"Oh." After that thing in the caf with Tasha, I thought she might be jealous, but of me, not of Spence.

"Come 'ere..." She wraps her hand around my neck, tugs me in for another kiss. Her tongue slips into my mouth. No, I let her slip her tongue into my mouth. And then I slip mine into hers. She tastes sweet, like strawberries. I crave more of her.

My arms encircle her waist; she more than allows it, she's eager for it. She lies down, wrenches me on top of her. Her fingers slide into my hair. My hands are on her hips. Our legs, entangled.

Jesus, I could kiss her forever.

Yep, full on making out with your foster sister. Shit! I push myself away from her, sit up, breathless. "Wait, Avery, I—I don't think this is right."

She sits up, too. "Feels right to me." She reaches for me again. I catch her wrist.

"No." There's a difference between something feeling right and being right.

Her mouth twists into a pout. Disappointment? Frustration? An amalgam of both. "I already have a sister. I don't need or want another one. What I want from you is this."

This thing between us has never been sisterly. We both understand that much, maybe even have from the very beginning. "Your parents…" I was just starting to get comfortable in their house, and with them. *That's tanked.*

"I get that you're scared this could screw things up with them, with your living situation. Honestly, right now I'm not even ready to tell them that I like girls, let alone that I like you. So, if you like me, too, can we try? You and me, no one else has to know until we're both ready."

We could keep the same secret for different reasons. *What is her reason?* 'Who cares if I'm bi or whatever, right?' She knows who she is, but if she says she isn't ready, then she isn't ready—the 'why' is what matters. She still blames that part of herself for Reese and doesn't feel like she has the right to be happy. Her motive for keeping it a secret isn't about me; her eyes are imploring me to say yes. She does want this.

What do I want? I want to not have to agonize over the possibility of her parents finding out, hating me, and kicking me out onto the street. *And her. You want her.* God, do I. "I don't know."

She sighs, launches off the bed—pads over to her door and opens it. "Let me know when you've figured it out."

I swallow my heart, stand up. There's nothing left to say, so I leave. She closes the door on me.

CHAPTER TWENTY-FOUR

The Silent Treatment, day one—it's not the first time I've ever been on the receiving end. I've never minded it before, but because I'm getting it from her, it kills.

She's the one who holes up in her room today. She doesn't come down for breakfast, or lunch, or anything else. I spend hours loitering around downstairs, waiting for my chance to say… anything. Every time I think we might end up in the same room, I'm wrong. It's as if she's checking around corners with a mirror, making sure I'm nowhere in sight before walking through the door.

After a while of simmering, I text Spence. She's at a state training camp in Boston, so she can't hang out. Olivia's there, too. Hannah's working on a research paper. I still haven't gotten around to getting Mack's number.

I take a walk to Dix Park and watch some kids play. It doesn't help.

I try the little pond. Sitting on the bench, my mind is flooded with thoughts of Avery. *Destroyed everything with a kiss.* How could I have done something so asinine? So thoughtless. It isn't like me at all. I've always been so careful when cultivating my connections with people. Since moving here, I've changed. Spence, Avery, Tom and Cate—they've overwhelmed my barricades. My ammunition is depleted, and I have no cover from them. This is going to be the battle that causes me to lose the war.

Perhaps it was only a matter of time, but I think it's just them, who they are as individuals, the best of humanity—sad and sensitive and imperfect, yet still warm and thoughtful and accepting. I wasn't prepared for any of it. It's terrifying and wonderful, and even if I've ruined it, I wouldn't trade it.

Avery. Damn it.

Cate doesn't allow her to miss dinner. We sit across the table from each other in our usual places. She avoids looking at me as much as possible.

I am a street scamp begging for scraps. I want her gaze. I want her smile. I don't care if it's to call me a 'motherfucking-rat-bastard-cowardly-piece-of-shit,' I want her silky voice saying whatever words she's willing to say.

I thought I'd take an actual bullet before I met a girl who hit me like one. I think I'd have preferred the bullet. *So dramatic.* Accurate, though.

*

The Silent Treatment, day two—she leaves for school without me. She told her parents she had to go in early for extra help with a Calculus assignment, which may or may not have been the truth. My money's on not.

Tom isn't put out about giving me a ride. It's the first time I've been inside his black BMW SUV, and the newness of it gives me something else to concentrate on for a while: the tan leather interior, the chrome dashboard accents, the huge touch screen recessed in the console. Lots of knobs to turn and buttons to mash. I press a button and accidentally open the sunroof. Tom doesn't mind. He grins and says, "Enjoy the weather while it lasts. It'll be snowing soon."

Snow. School cancellations. Twenty-four hours trapped inside with Avery hiding from me like I'm death, personified. Winter is gonna be awful.

I lean back in the seat, shut my eyes. It's been a day and a half, and I don't know how much more of it I can take.

English class. She's been sitting at the desk beside mine since my first day. This morning she sits on the opposite side of the room, way up in the front. The boy who usually takes that spot is confused. He asks her to move. I hear her say, "Sorry. I'm waiting for a new box of contacts. Do you mind if we switch for a while?"

The kid's so elated that Avery's even talking to him, all he can do is nod. *Feel ya, bro.* He ambles to the back of the room, glides into the seat next to mine and goes, "Hello."

Yeah, sure, whatever. "Hi."

I don't know if she's going to leave me to my own devices this afternoon, but it's better to be proactive. At lunch I ask Hannah if she can give me a ride to the Cahills' after school. She's surprised. "Avery has a doctor's appointment." I'm so good at lying; it's such a shitty character trait. Avery's not bad at it, either. Are all people good liars, or is it only the people who are broken?

"Yeah, no problem," she responds.

"Thanks." She's great at this friend thing. They all are. I think I could've asked Mack for a ride and she would've said yes, too. I need to work on becoming a better friend to them. And to Avery. If I keep telling myself that all I'm interested in is her friendship, can I convince myself it's true? *Can you teach a fish to fly?*

I arrive at the house to find the Nikon on the floor in front of my bedroom door. There's a bright orange, heart-shaped sticky note attached to it. *You forgot this.—A*

Oh, you fucked up so bad. I'm still fucking up. How do I stop? Giving her what she wants—what I want—is the worst idea in the history of ideas. But will this ever end if I don't? *It might not.* Do I deserve for it to end? My idiocy knows no bounds.

*

I've been persona non grata for ninety-six hours. Somehow, Tom and Cate haven't noticed it. Or if they have, they've decided to let us settle our problems on our own. If I weren't already aware of it, this would be their tell that they raised two daughters for sixteen years. I'm thankful for their parenting style; it would be awkward if they insisted on getting involved. What could I tell them: *I have a painful crush on your daughter?* What could Avery tell them: *I want to bang the orphan girl you brought into our home?* Holy crap, this is bad.

On the subject of bad, the car ride to school this morning... Avery waited for me, and it would've been better if she hadn't. She put the radio on. It was louder in her car than it has ever been, but for all the wrong reasons—no banter, no laughter, none of the stuff I've come to enjoy.

I don't know where to begin to fix this. When you upset and humiliate someone, you can't take it back with, "Whoops, my bad!" It's exceptionally hard to make things right when you hurt someone like her, someone who's so careful with their emotions that they guard them like they're vile, perilous things. *Oh, so, someone like you?* Yes. Except she has never done anything to hurt me. To the contrary. All she has shown me is kindness.

I wish it had never happened, not just this awkwardness I've caused with my indecision, the kiss, too. How is it possible that it was the best and worst kiss of my life?

The entire situation blows big donkey dick, going all the way back to the start. If I had met her under different circumstances, I would be 100 percent all about her. What complete moron wouldn't be? It's so unfair that she has to be the daughter of the most decent, friendly—no, genuinely caring—foster parents I've ever had.

They've been good to me in ways I didn't even realize parents could be. They go out of their way to include me in everything. They're there for me. They want me to be comfortable in their home. More than that, they want me to feel like their home is my home.

Thanks so much, fate! You could've at least kissed me before you bent me over and fucked me.

This is the first time I've ever felt hatred for my birth parents. When I was younger, I was sad about not knowing them, but how could I bring myself to hate people I've never met, and further, the two people who were responsible for bringing me into the world? Right this moment, though? Screw those selfish, useless assholes! If they had just made an effort, even a crappy, half-assed one, who knows where I'd be right now? Although, if they had, maybe I wouldn't have met Avery, and then I never would have felt anything real for anyone. Because what I'm feeling right now… it's real. I don't have the vocabulary to describe it, but I'm aware of its existence and that's plenty.

"Ay, Brit, you good?" Olivia interrupts my silent contemplation, a stone tossed into a pond. *Raging rapids, more like.*

"I'm good." I grab my water from the lunch table, take a sip. *Should be thanking her, sappy fool.*

"Aight. Yo, so, Spence, I was reading Salem's stats. They're 9-1-0 this season. They got a First Team All-Stater on their roster, too, their goalie."

Spence huffs. "Of course, they're good this year. I'm the captain, they have to go and make things hard for me."

"I don't see the issue, you're All-New England, Olivia's All-State," Mack comments. "And aren't you guys 10-0?"

"Barely. Last week Marblehead put one in early, then held us scoreless until the sixty-third minute." She nods at Olivia. "You saved our asses that day, man, got the ball rolling, literally."

Olivia shoots her a grin. "I do what I can, sis."

"Wait, is the Salem game your last one?" I should probably already know the answer to that. *Welp, you've def established yourself as a garbage friend.*

"No, but it's our rivalry match, and it's away, and as far as I can tell, they're the only real threat left to our perfect season." She rubs her eyes with her thumb and forefinger. "I hate Salem."

I don't get high school rivalries. They're so minor in the grand scheme of things, yet jocks treat them like they're this huge deal. I suppose most kids don't have bigger things to worry about. Must be nice.

"You should come to the game," Hannah says to me. "We could use another voice cheering for Spence."

"People yelling your name, that doesn't throw you off?" I ask Spence.

"I do better under pressure."

"Okay, I'll be there." I force a smile.

The conversation veers off in a direction I can't follow. *Avery. Avery. Avery.*

*

Night, day five. We almost collide in the hallway as I'm exiting the bathroom. At first she looks alarmed, the result of a near miss, then her mien morphs into sadness. It's the closest we've been, physically, since...

I cannot continue to live like this. I'd rather be shoved into a pantry. "This obviously isn't going to work for either of us anymore. I'm gonna call my social worker."

"Don't." She glowers at me. "My parents won't understand why you want to leave. They'll think it was something they did and feel like assholes over nothing for eternity."

That's where she gets it from, the upshot of having a big heart. "I can't—"

"Not here."

Right. Tom and Cate have gone to bed; having this discussion outside their door is not advisable. I don't want to have it in her bedroom, her space, either. I know my room is out of the question for her, though. "Let's go to your room."

She flinches at the suggestion, but relents. I follow her. The door creaks as I close it behind me.

She sits on her bed. I opt for the rolling chair and notice the photo of the boy on the swing pinned to the wall above the desk.

We stare at each other in silence until it gets too uncomfortable for both of us.

Talk, you invertebrate. "I know this is my fault, and maybe we'll never be the same again, but I miss spending time with you. And it's only been what, five days?"

"I miss it too. I don't..." She gulps. "I don't think I can be alone with you. It's too hard when all I want to do is—"

"I get it." I really, really get it. Her eyes are on me, all soft and longing. I wish she wouldn't look at me like that. I can't take it. Then, from nowhere, I'm hit with the smartest, stupidest proposal ever. "I have an idea, and I need you to hear me out before you respond."

"Okay?"

"I want to go to Spence's soccer game tomorrow night. It's the biggest match of the season, and it's away at Salem. They're our arch enemies or whatever, right?"

"Uh huh. If you want to go, go. You've never asked my permission to hang out with her before."

"Firstly, you're not doing an awesome job of hearing me out. Secondly, I'm not asking your permission, I'm asking you to come with me."

"Seriously, this is the solution you come at me with?"

"Sometimes you have to force yourself to chill in difficult situations. It'll suck way less than feeling like garbage every time she walks into a room."

"Yeah, but—"

"Do you know what it took for me to talk to you after days of nada? A hell of a lot."

"That's different. Soccer is her thing, like, her arena. You should go with your friends."

Olivia's on the team. Hannah and Mack plan on going, and I could go with them. "I don't want to. I want to go with you. It's in public, there'll be lots of people there, so you won't… get any ideas." I waggle my eyebrows at her. *Please laugh.*

She does. *There she is!* It's the best gift the universe could've given me.

The tenseness between us begins to waft away. I amp up what little charm I have to eleven, smile real wide. "Come on, you were a cheerleader, you're supposed to have school spirit. Show me how it's done?"

"I'll consider it if…" She lets her words hang in the air.

"If?"

"If you kiss me. Right now. Like you mean it, not a lame peck on the cheek."

Clever. A round of tit-for-tat. Except I'm playing checkers while she's playing chess. It's not a game to her. It's a prompt: *Remember that I'm still here, waiting for you to choose me over fear. I'm willing to do the same.* I don't need a reminder of how amazing it felt to kiss her; that's not something I could forget. "I'm pretty sure this is blackmail."

"You came up with the barter system, not me." She shrugs her shoulders. "It's a big ask, so that's the trade, take it or leave it."

It is a big ask, and I very much want to kiss her, but I shouldn't—not two seconds after I've made progress. *Not ever.* If I don't do it, things will just go back to being horrible. To hell with it.

I scoot the chair closer and reach out to her. She closes her eyes as I take her face into my hands. I press my mouth to hers and my heart goes crazy. Her lips are warm and smooth. She still tastes like strawberries. I feel the tip of her tongue brush against my lips. *Too much, restraint is waning.* I break the contact.

She opens her eyes, exhales. "I'll come with you."

CHAPTER TWENTY-FIVE

Salem High School is older than ours, Bertram Field more time-worn. Their stadium is bigger, however, and it is packed—Beverly fans on one side of the field, Salem supporters on the other, a divided sea of school colors, orange and black, and scarlet, white and black, respectively. Panthers vs. Witches.

It takes some perusing, but I find Mack, Hannah and Noah in the stands. Avery and I go to join them. "Hey, guys," I greet them as we take our seats. "You all know Avery."

"Hi," she says, without any shyness.

Mack's taken aback by her presence, but covers it quick. "Yo."

"Hey." Hannah gives her a smile and a wave. She's so mature. How many girls our age would be so chill around their boyfriend's ex?

Noah takes Hannah's hand, a show of reassurance. "Sup, Avs."

I check for a reaction from her. Nothing but a nod in his direction. Unruffled. She must have loved Spence, although I don't think she would admit it if I asked. I wonder if they'd still be together had things not happened the way they did. Maybe she'd be out to her family and friends. Maybe she'd be happy. I think eventually love gets too big to contain and you have to share it with the world or you'll erupt like a volcano.

Pangs of jealousy hit me. Unjustifiable. They'll never be together again, and we'll never be together at all. I puff them away through clenched teeth.

The whistle blows and the match is underway.

*

Avery gets wicked into it, yelling and cheering, even shouting the occasional word of encouragement to Spence. Her school spirit trumps everything. She was an incredible cheerleader, I'm sure of it.

Damn it, why does she have to be so stunning? And magnetic. And lovely. And... *Watch the friggin' game!*

The match is rough, bordering on dirty. The ref is worthless, calling almost nothing a foul. Spence has been getting knocked around more than her fair share. Salem has come prepared. They know she's an All-New England Forward and want to keep her off the ball by any means necessary. Somehow, she's maintaining her collectedness, waiting for the perfect moment to get even. Her every move is calculated, deliberate—every pass immaculate, even the ones that fly clear across the field. I can see, in real time, how good she is at math. This sport is very much about geometry, and she's nailing it.

Eighty-six minutes into a ninety-minute contest and neither side has scored a goal. Beverly came close twice, but Salem's goalie is too good. Just as I'm starting to think this thing might end in a draw, Spence sees her opportunity; she slide-tackles the legs right out from under Salem's attacking striker. It's legal, no whistle. She comes up with the ball in her possession. And then she takes off down the field. She has support from Erin on her right flank. But she has no intention of giving up control. This is her house now.

The dogged determination in her is palpable to everyone watching. The whole crowd is on its feet. Salem's fans are shouting, "Get on 22! Stop her, stop her!" Our fans are shouting, "Go, Go! Come on, Spence!"

Salem's midfielders can't catch up to her; she's a rocket. She splits the defense, jukes the sweeper. It's between her and the goalie, matched for talent. *Nope, not even close.* She flicks the ball from her right foot to her left and launches a missile right over the keeper's head and into the net. The sideline official sounds her whistle. It's a goal.

"Yes! Yes!" I squeal, fist in the air.

"Woo! Yeah, Spence!" Avery shrieks. She's clapping like mad.

Every Beverly High School player near Spence leaps on top of her, whooping and hollering. They're patting her head, her back. Olivia sprints all the way from the backfield to give her a hug. She's about to be the hero of this game.

Celebration over, the players start jogging back to their positions. Salem's goalie kicks the ball into play; her team is too deflated to mount any kind of comeback.

A minute or so later, the referee checks his watch. He puts his whistle up to his lips and blows out three bursts. It's over. *One game closer to her perfect senior season.* And I'm so close to tears, it's preposterous. This is what it's like to feel proud of someone? It's wonderful!

Avery is in my arms. I'm in hers. We're smiling, jumping. If this were another place and she were another girl, I'd be kissing her right now. *Stop.*

*

The team is making their way off the field. We descend the bleachers, head toward them. We meet Olivia first, extend congratulations, a "Good game" from Avery and a "You were awesome" from me.

Spence is lagging a bit behind. I turn to Avery. It's enough that she's here; I'm not going to make her speak to her. "I'm gonna talk to Spence. Meet you at the car?"

She gives me a headshake. "She obvs won the game for us. I can choke back my shit for a quick congrats."

Is she taking my advice? *Weird.*

Spence sees Avery. Avery sees Spence. Neither of them look to be on the verge of crying. I hug Spence, no reluctance. "Great game! You were incredible."

"Thanks."

"Nice goal," Avery says.

Spence smiles, nods her appreciation.

The moment is interrupted by a commotion behind us. Someone yells, "Hey, 22!" We all spin around. The Salem striker Spence tackled is stomping toward us. "What was that dirty-ass tackle?"

"Flawless is what."

She's in Spence's face now. "Fucking dyke."

"What'd you call me?"

I've never been in a fight, but I know what the start of one looks like—the split second before someone pops off. This girl is teetering on the edge. She shoves Spence. "You heard me!"

Spence isn't going to let it go. *Aw, hell.* I'm about to jump between Spence and the girl. Avery beats me to it. She's got her arms up, hands waving. "Calm down."

"Move, bitch." The Salem player smacks her right across the face.

Avery is shocked, mouth hanging open, hand on her cheek.

Oh, someone is going to die tonight.

I snap. Without warning, my knees are in the grass and I've got the girl pinned beneath me, my left forearm pressed against her throat. She's gurgling, struggling against my weight. She must have twenty pounds of pure muscle on me. *She's gonna need the strength of an army!* My knuckles collide with her face, make a wet thud noise. There are people all around us screaming: "Oh my God!" "Whoa, whoa!" "Stop!"

Someone grabs the collar of my jacket, yanks me off of her. Once I'm on my feet, I see that it's Mack, blue bangs dangling in her face. "Let's go, let's go," she spits as she hauls me away.

In the distance there's an adult, a coach, helping the girl off the ground. There's blood dribbling from her lip. That's what she gets for hitting my girl. *My girl…* "Where's Avery?" I bark at no one in particular.

"I'm here." She steps to me, presses her palms to my sternum. Her forehead is resting against mine. Her eyes are so bright, glistening with unshed tears. Concern, fear or pain? There's a reddish mark on her face where she was slapped. I run my thumb over it. She winces.

"Are you okay?"

"I'm fine." She puts some space between us. "Are you?"

"If anyone ever puts their hands on you, I'll fucking kill them." I know the words come from my mouth, but I don't recognize my voice.

"Alright." Her tone is soft.

"Take her home," Spence says to her, tense. "Right now."

We shuffle to the car, Avery's arms around my waist the entire way.

We're at the kitchen table, she's sitting next to me, holding an ice pack to my battered knuckles; they're already swollen. The mark on her face has faded. I'm thankful that Cate and Tom are having a date night. "I don't know what happened, I… I blacked out."

"What happened was that bitch hit me, and you stepped in. That's it."

"Did I scare you?" I've witnessed enough people turn violent to know that it can be horrifying for a bystander. I don't ever want to be that violent person, and I don't ever want Avery to be afraid of me. I want to protect her, and I did. But that doesn't make it okay.

"I wasn't scared of you, I was scared for you." She smirks. "Who knew you were such a badass?"

"I'm not." Only for her. She leans in, kisses me—a reward for my rash behavior that she's taken for gallantry. I don't merit it, but

I pucker into it, anyhow. Kissing her does feel right, more so every time. *This is the last time.* It has to be. I'm getting too indulgent.

The front door opens. Cate hollers, "We're home!" Avery stands up quick, takes the ice pack and tosses it in the freezer. She spins around, presses her back to the fridge just as Tom walks into the kitchen, doggie bag in hand. "How was the game?"

"Good," she replies, glances at me. "We won."

*

Things are better between us over the weekend. *All it took was nearly killing someone.* It isn't back to how it was before—not as effortless—but if this is our new normal, I'll have to take it, even if it's not enough. What would be enough still wouldn't be right.

When you feel this way about someone, is it ever really wrong? We're not blood. A few months ago, we were strangers. Perhaps, once we're out on our own, away from her parents and their house, I can consider it. What is it, eight months? No time at all, given any significant lifespan. The future isn't a given for anyone, though. I'm sure Reese thought she had thousands of tomorrows ahead of her. *Not doing yourself any favors with that line of thought.* No, just making myself feel like I'm wasting time trying to escape the inescapable.

CHAPTER TWENTY-SIX

Olivia, Mack, and Hannah have a study group in the library for their chemistry exam. Noah takes advantage of the girlfriend reprieve and has lunch with some of his friends. That leaves Spence and me on our own.

I thought about texting her an apology over the weekend; it warranted a face-to-face conversation. Also, I'm chicken-shit and wanted to give her time to cool off in case she was pissed at me.

The day is unseasonably warm. We decide to eat al fresco, grab our trays and take them out to the courtyard. It's quiet enough around us to have a discussion without garnering undue attention to my brutal attack, which is the last thing I'd want. It was bad enough that a couple of guys brought it up to me in Life Skills this morning. I joked that street fighting was something I wouldn't have to learn in class. It wasn't funny, but they thought it was. That was the only time it's been mentioned to me. "About the crap I pulled at the game," I start. "I hijacked your big moment. I'm really sorry."

She takes a bite of her sandwich, chews, swallows. "Don't apologize, you didn't start it. I was a hot second from swinging on her myself. I can take a lot, but... You did me a favor. Coach would've given me detention until graduation."

Yeah, I'm stunned there were no ramifications for me. I expected to get hit with a suspension first thing this a.m. I guess it's a good thing I'm the new kid in town and nobody knows who the hell I am. "So, we're okay, then?"

"For sure."

We continue with our meal in a tranquil quietness. She keeps looking at me like she has something else to say. It gets unnerving fast. "What's... up?"

"Nothing." She uncaps her green tea, swigs it.

"Bull."

"Are you two together now?"

Losers say 'what?' "What? Who?"

She deadpans. "Which am I, too blind or too stupid?"

"What are you talking about?"

She lowers her volume. "You and Avery."

"Er, I—"

"Bro, I know her. The way she was with you after the fight, all handsy. Either you're already a thing or you're going to be one soon."

I'm done for. My mask has crumbled. *So easy to read, might as well be a library book.*

"You can tell me, I'll keep it QT."

She never told anyone about what happened between her and Avery. The girl can hold a secret like a vice-grip. "We're not a thing. But there are... sentiments? On both ends."

"Gasp! Shocker." She rolls her eyes. "What's stopping you?"

"Come on."

"No, really."

"Uh, for starters, I'm living under her parents' roof."

"Way I see it, that's a bonus."

My turn for an eye roll. "You don't think it's, I don't know, kind of incestuous? She's my foster sister."

"Foster. You're not actually related. It's not like you grew up together or anything. You might as well be roommates, and if I understand porn right, roommates smash all the time."

That makes me laugh. "You're crude."

"Yeah, yeah," she chuckles. "Your situation might be 'unconventional,' but I don't think there's anything wrong with it. You like who you like. It's obvious that you like each other."

There's something else I haven't considered. I can't believe it took me so long to think of it: Dating your friend's ex is against Girl Code, even a garbage friend like me knows that. What's the lesbian equivalent of *Sisters Before Misters, Pals Before Gals*? I could not stand hurting one more person with my stupid, irrational feelings—that goes twofold for Spence. "Would you be okay with it if we got together?"

"Our ship left the harbor a long time ago. Turns out it was the *Titanic*." The faraway look in her eyes. She's not in love with Avery anymore, but she's always going to have love for her. I've heard that can happen, particularly with your first. "You should go for it. She's worth it."

"Maybe someday."

"Don't wait too long. Someone else will scoop her up."

She's a hundred percent correct about that. Girls like Avery can have their choice of anyone they want. I still don't know why she'd choose me.

*

I'm not sure when it happened, but we're all gathered around the dining room table, engrossed in our own work.

Tom's next to me on his laptop, coding something. Cate is scanning over files, comparing what she finds with the words of an open book—*ABA Guide to Family Law*. I'm pretending to be studying my Consumer Mathematics notes, but really I'm replaying my conversation with Spence from earlier, over and over. *You should go for it.* It means a lot coming from her; more than encouragement, she's given her blessing. I didn't realize how important that was to me until now.

I keep thieving glances of Avery from across the table. She's not doing anything special—twirling a pencil as she pores over an equation—nevertheless, she looks beautiful.

Right, she's beautiful. I've determined that as stone-cold fact. I want to swim in the aqua pools of her eyes and play with her long milk-chocolate hair and kiss her perfect lips and cute nose and high cheekbones until humanity's extinction, yadda yadda.

What do I like about her?

I like… That she laughs at the most awkward, inappropriate things. I like it when she smiles, because that means she's giving herself a break from her guilt. I like that she's soft-hearted, even though she tries to hide it, and that she says exactly what she means with a little too much acid or otherwise doesn't say much of anything at all. I like that she's smart and funny and ambitious and supportive of my ambitions. I like that she makes me want to be better—more open, more honest. I like that I want her to be happy and safe.

Whoo boy, you've got it bad for this one. Then I can't let her slip away, can I? "Avery."

"Hmm?" She looks up from her textbook.

I take too long to respond. She drops her pencil and stares at me. I shoot out of my chair as if someone lit a firecracker under my ass. Tom and Cate gawp at me like I'm nuts, but it's brief. "I have to show you something."

She trails me into the hallway. Once I'm sure we're out of her parents' line of vision, I take her by the hand and drag her all the way up to her room. I shove us both inside and slam the door behind me.

She's got her hands up, palms facing the ceiling, like, *What the hell is happening right now?*

Do it if you're gonna. I grab her hips and kiss her hard. When I pull away, she's relieved. Relieved that I kissed her, or that it's over? *Ask her, dumbass.* "What's that look?"

"I was starting to think you weren't—"

That won't do. "I am so into you. I can't control it, and it's bugging me out a little." *Bugged out? Frightened.*

Her mouth is agog. I've stunned her. *Stunned yourself.* "I know what you mean."

Her parents. Their house. I can't dwell on it anymore. I have only ever felt 'right' about one person in my whole life, and it's her. "I want to be with you."

She smiles, seizes the collar of my hoodie, presses her lips to mine—once, twice, three times. "Took you long enough."

I never stood a chance against this girl. Now, the question is... "How do we do this? Is guerrilla-style dating a thing?" It's so absurd, I can't help but laugh. She laughs, too.

No, for real, though. The concept of having to be on the DL is new to me. That's one of the good things about not having parents, no one to potentially be upset with my sexual orientation or choice of partners; I've gotten lucky so far—none of my fosters cared—but I've heard horror stories.

"It can be fun if you think of it like a game. Have you ever played Manhunt?" She reaches for the drawstrings of my hood, gives them a few twirls.

"It's like a mashup of Tag and Hide and Seek, right?"

"Mmhmm. The objective is to be as sneaky as possible." She's wrapping the cords around her fingers. My hood is getting tighter around my neck. And she's pulling me closer. I watch her lick her lips, can't tear my eyes away.

"That does sound like fun."

I assume she's going for my mouth and ready myself. She swerves at the last second and kisses my cheek. "See, I'm good at sneaky." She grins.

"Yes, you are."

CHAPTER TWENTY-SEVEN

There are two things about Manhunt dating that are insufferable. One: the fact that I'm allowed to touch Avery now, but seventy-five percent of the time—when we're at school, when we're with our friends or her parents—I friggin' can't. And two: the straight edginess I carry in the pit of my stomach around Tom and Cate.

It's like I've backslid to how I was when I first moved in, shy and reserved, unsure of how to behave. It's not an awesome sensation, lying to them. Not that I've ever felt good about lying, it's just something that was a necessity, sometimes. I've never had to do it all the time, though; that takes adjusting.

Some evenings, dinner is a nightmare. Yesterday, Avery had the audacity to play footsie with me under the table. We had to have a talk about it afterwards. I told her that it's great at lunch, or at Starbucks, or literally anywhere else, but I can't handle it while having a meal with her parents. She was cool about it—in a sincere way, not that feigned indifference she's so good at.

*

It's been a week, and it has already become obvious to me that she is a seasoned pro at sneaking around. She's been amazing with me. She can sense when I'm getting overwhelmed—it's always in the house when there's little else to concentrate on but our proximity to each other and her parents. In those moments, she signals at the stairs, then climbs them. I wait a minute or two, then follow her up.

When we're alone, she cups my face, or presses her pointer finger to the tip of my nose, reassurance that she understands and that she thinks we're worth all the trouble the cosmos is throwing at us.

Seven and a half months until I can move out of their house. Things will be easier then. *Thinking long term.* It's dangerous, I know, and premature, but I've permitted myself to envision a future with her. I'm afraid of it, yet wishful for it, and the disparity is something I haven't quite reckoned with. If things work out the way I hope, I'll have a long time to get acclimated to it.

*

I've been trying to divide my time between Avery and Spence as fairly as possible, so I decide to have lunch three days a week with Spence and The Squad, and the other two days with Avery and The Brigade. When I floated the idea to Avery, I said, "I don't want to be one of those girls who gets with someone and drops their friends."

She replied, "Good. I can't stand those types of girls."

So far, it's been going to plan.

"You went for it," Spence says as we're queuing up to pay for our chicken fajitas. Just as well I don't have to tell her; my new balancing act is all it takes for her to come to the conclusion.

"Yep."

"Good for you."

She said she'd be okay with it, but that doesn't mean she is. A person can change their mind about anything at any time. I inspect her features for a semblance of affront and find none. "Thanks."

"I have to say, it's pretty dope that you're not ditching us for her, unlike this dude." She pitches a thumb at Noah, who's riveted by whatever Hannah is saying, and whose friends are on the other side of the cafeteria.

"I told you from the start there's enough of me to go around."

"Then, you up for a driving lesson Sunday? You're getting good, might even be ready to take the test soon."

I pull an Avery and laugh. "Yes to the lesson. Hell no to the test."

CHAPTER TWENTY-EIGHT

"Our next project is going to be all about portraiture," Mr. Warren says.

Oh, crap! I blanked. I snatch the PowerShot from my bag and raise my hand.

"Yes, Britton?"

"Sorry. I wanted to return this before I spaced it." My new Nikon is in its branded case on my desk. Mr. Warren and a handful of kids glance at it, at me. That's right, I robbed a bank a few days ago and this is the fruit of my labor.

He motions for me to come up to the front of the class. I pop the camera onto his desk, then mosey back to my seat. Avery's giving me a shit-eating grin.

"I never did give you a proper thank you," I murmur.

"Mmm, I think you did."

Her smugness sets off my stomach thing. I can let myself appreciate it all of a sudden. Nice.

"We're going to take some photos outside today," says Mr. Warren. "Find yourself a partner for test shots."

"You and me?" I don't know why I need to ask.

"Always."

I'm the first test subject, sitting on a bench in the fading sunlight. "Don't look at the camera," she directs.

"What should I—"

"Like, anything else."

I shift my attention to the dead trees and am overcome with gloom. They're as pathetic in real life as they are in Avery's photo of them, sad scraggly things.

I hear her press the camera shutter, click, click, click. "Perfect." She sits next to me, looks at the screen. "You're a knockout."

A knockout? "No, I'm not."

She leans in close to me. "Excuse me, I have impeccable taste."

"So do I."

Lip bite. "We're crazy hot together."

We're in public; I cannot kiss her. I spring to my feet. "I've been dying to use this." I unzip the camera case, pluck out the Nikon and attach the lens to its body. "Ready for that photoshoot?"

She runs her fingers through her hair. "Yup."

The natural light is gorgeous. Correction, Avery haloed by the natural light is gorgeous. She's leaning against a young oak tree, one knee bent, foot propped on its trunk. The grass is littered with orange and crimson leaves, a stark contrast to her light denim skirt and lavender sweater. Snap, snap. Zoom. Snap. Snap. These portraits aren't going to need any editing—not even a spot touchup.

Those big blue eyes. Also, the look she's giving me—smoldering, seductive. *Wit-woo.* My lens is liable to catch fire at any moment. I stop, assess the pics. "Um, can you come here for a second?"

She kicks off the tree, saunters over. I scroll through the photos for her. "Notice anything?"

"The colors."

That and… "You're giving me 'fuck me eyes' in every single picture," I mumble.

She goes red. "I am not!"

I roll through them again.

She concentrates hard. "I didn't even realize I was doing it."

Not that I'm complaining. "I think I'm going to have to use my friends as models for this project."

"That's a good idea," she snickers, then flashes into seriousness. "If any of them give you 'fuck me eyes,' they're dead." I know who she means by "any of them," and that's not something that'll happen. I have to tell her that Spence knows we're together. I've been dodging it. Again, I'm chicken-shit. I resolve to do it as soon as we're alone.

In the meantime, I'm enjoying how adorable she is when she's grappling with the green-eyed monster, even if it is unfounded. "You don't have to worry about that."

She forgets we're outside the school surrounded by classmates. I watch her stifle the impulse to touch me. She pouts, and then it's gone. "I don't know, I don't trust that Mack girl."

I fall to pieces chuckling. "She does have incredible hair."

She gives my arm a playful slap. "Okay, yeah, she does."

After club, we hop into her BMW. She jams the key in the ignition, and I stop her from turning it. She studies me with curious eyes.

Say it, you gutless wonder. Shit. I ready myself to receive livid words, hide my hands in the sleeves of my hoodie and crumple the cuffs into my fists. "Spence knows about us. I didn't tell her, she guessed."

She taps the steering wheel. "I gathered. She's not dumb."

And they used to know each other so well. "She promised to keep it to herself."

"She will."

Even after everything that's happened, all the hurt and all the time that has passed, she still trusts her. Will she ever trust me that way? *Have to prove your worth.*

"Let's go home." She starts the car.

I marvel at her coolness, the earnestness of it, the entire drive.

CHAPTER TWENTY-NINE

For this week's date night, Cate and Tom are going to see the Boston Symphony Orchestra. It's definitely Cate's choice. The most sophisticated stuff I've heard Tom listen to is the Foo Fighters. Nineties alternative rock is excellent, one of my top genres, but it's poles apart from Cate's taste in music. Everything she likes is mellow, airy, steeped in string and brass instruments. Actually, I like all that stuff, too.

Tom appears in the hallway outside of the living room, decked out in a neat charcoal grey suit and a dark blue necktie. My first thought is that he looks like a kid who's been coerced into dressing up for church on Sunday. It's bizarre—he's a jeans and T-shirt kind of dude, the occasional polo if he's feeling fancy. Avery whistles at him from beside me on the couch.

"I clean up nice, huh?" He straightens his tie.

"Very handsome," I say. "You might need a haircut soon, though."

He smooths his greying sideburns. "I need 'em all cut."

Snort. Dad jokes! So corny, yet so delightful. Who knew?

"I'm ready." Cate strolls into the hall. She's in a flowing, floor-length chiffon and lace evening dress—stormy blue—sporting more makeup than she wears to work, yet still understated; classy, as with everything she does. Avery is the perfect combination of her parents, the best of both of them. It's kinda crazy. I wonder what Reese looked like, was like. I wish Avery would talk about her. *Ask her.* No, not tonight.

"Dang, Mom! You're gorge."

"She's right."

Cate tilts her head at us and smiles. Tom helps her into a navy double-breasted pea coat. "Thanks, hun." She kisses his cheek. To us, she singsongs, "You girls have fun."

Oh, we're going to. We've got our own date night planned with Netflix. The 'N' Chill' part is up to Avery. I've been letting her set the tempo. My comfort zone for physical stuff is broad when I'm with someone, all things considered, so it's best left to her to decide what she's good with and when.

"Bye, girls," Tom says. They leave, and we're alone.

It's my turn to pick the movie, a horror film called *The Happening.* As much as for my own enjoyment, I used to choose horror movies for the jump scares and the squeezes they'd earn me. Avery has carbon fiber nerves where films are concerned, so my cunning falls flat. I like it; it means she chooses to touch me, rather than does it involuntarily.

I press play and the opening credits roll. She scoots close to me, takes my hand. It's nice, sitting together on the couch, holding hands. It's not often we get to be this touchy-feely outside of her bedroom. She leans over, pecks me on the cheek. That's nice, too.

Thirty seconds later she climbs onto my lap, cowgirl-style. *Whoa.* "Um, what—" She wraps her arms around my neck, dips her head and kisses me, a first for the living room. Living room! I peel my lips from hers. "Do you realize where we are?"

"Uh huh." She kisses me again. "My parents will be gone for hours. I want to make the most of it while we can." I let out a deep breath. She squinches her eyes at me, brushes her fingers through her ringlets and swoops them to the side. "Unless you're not feeling it." She moves to dismount me.

I'm feeling this and more. I grab her waist, make her stay. "Who said I wasn't?"

She flashes a mischievous grin, then frames my face with her hands. This time I crane my neck and kiss her. I glide my tongue into her mouth. She makes a surprised 'mmm' sound. It's good surprise; her tongue responds to mine.

She is the Best. Kisser. Ever. It's like she's been kissing girls her entire life, none of that gross stuff teenage boys train girls to expect. No poking around for my tonsils, and zero slobber.

Then she does this thing she hasn't done before—sucks in my bottom lip and gives it a tiny bite. My entire body shudders. I moan into her mouth, grip her hips a bit tighter. She pulls back, eyes full of awe. "You liked that?"

She doesn't wait for my answer, just moves her kisses to my neck. I feel the gentle pressure of my skin being drawn into her mouth, her teeth nibbling. Yes, I liked it.

A bit too much. I'm liking this a bit too much, also. "Are you trying to give me a hickey?"

She pauses, looks at me. "Yes. Marking my territory." Another series of nips.

Whew, damn. "And how am I supposed to explain it to people?"

"Tell them you're having a torrid affair with a sexy younger woman," she whispers into my ear. More sucking.

I slink my hands under her shirt, up her spine, relish the litheness of her physique.

The front door whooshes open, then slams closed. Avery tries to clamber off of me, but ends up ass-on-the-rug with a muted thump.

Tom rushes into the kitchen and back out again. He sticks his head into the living room, shoots a questioning look at his daughter: She has scrambled into a split and is stretching sideways, grabbing her ankles. Awks.

Sexy. Her ass should be declared the eighth wonder of the world. "Forgot the tickets?" She frowns at him.

He nods at her. "Don't pull a muscle watching that movie." He scampers out of the house.

My heart is thrashing against my ribcage. I've thrown my hands over my mouth like I've witnessed a kitten wander onto a highway, and she's silent-laughing so hard there are tears streaming down her cheeks. "That was close!"

"No more fooling around on the couch!" I bend down, give her my hand and pull her up.

"Yeah, no." She composes herself beside me. "Is it okay if we cuddle though?"

I've got a girl who'll bite my lip, and in the next breath wants to cuddle with me. Multifaceted. Another thing I like about her. "That we can do."

I put my arm around her and she rests her head on my shoulder. We watch the rest of the movie snuggled together. It's even better than making out.

As we're heading to bed, she stops in front of my room. "I wish we could sleep together." Her eyes bulge and a blush inches up her neck. She's not ready for that, and neither am I. "I mean, I wish I could sleep in your arms."

Her parents aren't home yet. I could hold her until she falls asleep, then tiptoe to my bedroom… It would be risky.

Your thirsty ass also needs to take care of the situation in your pants. Fuck, I hate teenage hormones! I press my lips to her forehead. "Someday."

"You promise?" Her eyes.

I swear on the River Styx. "I promise."

CHAPTER THIRTY

Avery is pacing the floors. Tom, Cate and I gawk at each other across the living room. From their expressions, it's obvious we're all thinking the same thing—she's acting weird. I've never seen her antsy before, and they haven't seen it in a while. That makes me worry. I hope it isn't because of me, although it's entirely possible. She may have been an All-Star Downlow Dater with Spence, but they didn't live in the same house; their bedrooms weren't separated by a paltry slab of sheetrock and some paint. And last night was... sexually frustrating. *She should've rubbed one out, too.*

"Honey, what's with the one-woman waltz?" Tom asks.

Lol.

Avery folds her arms across her chest. "I don't know. I'm bored."

"See, this is why I didn't want you to quit cheerleading. All your friends are at the football game and you don't know what to do with yourself."

Ooh. That's the most Mom Thing Cate's said since I've lived here. Hardline nag. I want to defend Avery, tell Cate that the only reason we're not at the game is because it's forty degrees Fahrenheit out, and raining. Hell, Avery still wanted to go. I told her it wasn't going to happen because three days from now she'll drop dead of pneumonia. Yes, it was a total Mom Thing to say, but when it comes from someone other than your mother apparently it's cute. That's what she called me, anyway. Cute. I'll take it.

*

Okay, so, I fix things. It's who I am. *About to hammer this nail.* The first idea that pops into my head is: *Let's go to the mall.* I hate the mall; so many people, and so much stuff, and everything's oppressively bright and expensive. And why are there so many goddamn different perfume smells everywhere? Ugh. It's sensory overload. Avery likes it, though. Why couldn't she prefer Amazon shopping sprees like every other Zoomer? It doesn't matter. I am so down to go anywhere with her, it's ludicrous. I'd figure out how to get us to the moon if she wanted to pay it a visit.

"Avery, will you take me to the mall?" *Could've done with more enthusiasm.*

If she were a kindergartener and I were Santa Claus, she couldn't be smiling any wider. "Lemme get dressed."

"Um, you're already dressed?"

"Yeah, like a slob."

She's in yoga pants and a long-sleeved Beverly High School Cheer tee, appropriate attire for a shopping trip, but whatever. *Dat ass doe.* "Alright, weirdo, go change. I'll be here."

She jets up to her room.

Tom and Cate are both scoping me. Why? "Thanks for being such a good friend to our little pain-in-the-butt," Tom says.

I am slapped with shame for masturbating to thoughts of his daughter not even twelve hours ago. Oh, Tom, you dear, sweet man, I owe you so many apologies. "It's no big deal."

Tan knee-high boots. Sunburnt-orange mini dress. Off-white knitted cardigan. Full face of makeup. She does not slack off. Me? Vans. Black hip-hugger jeans with holes in the knees. Black Pink Floyd hoodie. Backward Red Sox cap. No makeup—save for a little concealer over my hickey. I am wearing my hair down, though, so that's something. *What a mismatched pair.* How is she not embarrassed to be seen with me? I'm embarrassed for her.

The sheer size of Northshore Mall is intimidating. As I gape at the directory, I do a count: 147 retailers. Overkill. Who needs to go into that many stores? I shop at thrift stores for crying out loud. It suits me fine.

Walking through the place, I can't begin to tell the difference between H&M, Gap and Abercrombie. The clothes displayed in each of their windows are identical.

Avery does not share my point of view—she bypasses all of them. "Can we go to Nordstrom?"

"Whatever you want."

"Whatever I want? You asked me to—Oh." There it is, the look of understanding. And something else; she wants to kiss me. She won't, not when we're out in the world. *Make her promise to, someday. Touché.* "You're so thoughtful," she says instead.

"I try."

"There's seriously nowhere you want to hit up?"

"The food court. After you've dropped mad stacks at thirty-two stores, that is."

She titters. "You got it."

We roam around Nordstrom for about a decade—for real, I've got grey hair, now. The only thing she purchases is a $1,200 Balenci-blah-blah leather tote that looks like someone graffitied all over it. I was googling apartments the other day and found a few hovels for twelve-hundred a month, and she swiped her mom's Amex for that exact amount without a blink. What the hell does she see in me? Is she into slumming it? 'Cuz that's gonna get old for her real quick.

"Hungry yet?" she asks as we're exiting the store.

"Perpetually."

*

We're digging into food court Chinese—the best kind there is. I'm slurping my last lo mein noodle and she's chewing on the straw she popped into her tangerine La Croix, eyeballing me. Am I one of those noisy eaters? I hope not; that's disgusting.

"Do you ever miss your parents?"

That was random. There's no logic to missing people I've never known, and yet… "Sometimes. It would have been nice to meet them, at least."

Her features slip into a guise of total animosity. "Who the fuck gives up their sick baby? Like, how screwed up do you have to be?"

Me being sick might've been the reason they gave me up. I'll always wonder. "They were probably wicked screwed up. Junkies, maybe. I read a study once about my heart condition that said it could've been caused by cocaine abuse during fetal development." If that's the case, it's better that they didn't keep me. Who knows how bad the neglect would've been? I conjure an image of baby me, screaming her head off, sitting in a day-old diaper full of shit. *Damn, that's bleak.*

She rubs her forehead.

I want to change the subject, talk about something less dreary. I still want to know more about Reese. Avery must have good memories of their childhood. Tom and Cate are too incredible not to have given them hundreds. I can go for it, if I handle it with kid gloves. "I wish I'd had a sibling or two. I think it would've been fun." Perhaps I do have brothers and sisters somewhere out there.

Her expression goes from startled to joyous in an instant. "It is, like having a built-in best friend. I was never lonely, that's for sure."

"I bet. And you and Reese were so close in age."

"Yeah, my parents slayed the timing. But two babies at once? No, thank you."

No joke. "What was she like? You said her style was different from yours, but…"

She leans back in her chair. "She was serious, a thinker. She'd get lost in her head all the time. I had to try so hard to make her laugh, but it was hilarious when she would—huge and loud, from her belly, you know?"

"Same as yours."

"Ha! It is."

I love that she's talking about Reese so freely. I want to hear more. "Cheerleading doesn't seem like a sport for serious people. It's too… cheery."

"She switched from basketball when I got to middle school. She was great like that, she knew I wanted to get into it and gave me the push I needed. She was super competitive—always had to be the best at everything she did."

"Was she the best cheerleader?"

She giggles. "She couldn't dance to save her life. Absolutely no rhythm. But she could yell and had real jock muscles, so that made up for it."

"I'm sorry I'll never get the chance to meet her," I let slip, and smother a grimace as I wait for her reaction. She's alright, glad to be talking about her. I wouldn't be surprised if this is the most she's talked about her since she died.

"She would've liked you."

"You think?"

"I like you, so yes."

Would she have told Reese about us? Is her affection for me unwavering enough? *Why it exists at all is beyond comprehension.* "I'm sure I would've liked her, too."

She grins and reaches for my tray. "Finished?" I nod. "Good. I want to take you to Thrash. Their clothes are rocker chic, more your flavor."

I'm not sure my pockets are deep enough for shopping in a high-end mall like this one. But it's not the moon, I can make myself swing it. "You couldn't have told me that before I stuffed my face?" I pat my stomach. "No way I'll fit in anything now."

"Oh, shut up, Scrawny!"

If Scrawny is my nickname, what's hers, Busty? *She does have nice*—Hold it right there. "Okay, take me."

I could go broke in this store on the band tees alone. I manage to rein myself in, but do decide to spend fifty bucks on a BABYMETAL hoodie—the novelty is too good to ignore. Avery tries to swipe Cate's Amex at check out. I prod my fingers into her side and she squeaks. "Looks like I'm not the only one who's ticklish." I press my card to the card reader.

"What a dirty trick!"

"All my tricks are dirty." It sounds more salacious than I intended. She notices, averts her eyes to the floor, purses her lips and goes pink. Right. "Pray you never get to see me hip check anyone."

That gets me a chortle.

I can't stop looking at her as we're walking to the car. Being with her in this oasis of capitalism, our differences have become that much more blatant. I don't want her to see me as some kind of foray into living on the wrong side of the tracks, a leave of absence from the affluence she has known all her life. That would make me an experiment. I've got big feelings for her, and it'll hurt too much when it comes to an end.

The car ride is quiet, until I find the nerve to speak. It's a question I've been mulling over for far too long. Sooner or later, it's going to get in the way if I can't get past it. *She's def flipped your honesty switch.* "I've been wondering about something."

"Mmhmm. What?"

Deep breath. "Why do you like me?"

She doesn't laugh for a change. She takes her eyes off the road, frowns at me. "Are you serious?"

"Deadly."

Back to the road. "Because you're easy to talk to. You're funny, intelligent, and so sweet that you make my teeth hurt. Not to mention you have the cutest ass I've ever seen."

Wow. "Did you practice that answer? Because it was incredible."

"I've had a lot of time to think about it." The lip-bite thing. "When would you say our anniversary would be, like, hypothetically?"

It's a ways in the future. She's thinking long-term, too. "Umm."

"Because, our first kiss was October eleventh, and then all that stupid crap happened. I just... I want every second to count."

That is literally the most romantic thing anyone has ever said to me. Thank God I kissed her, accidentally or not. "Then it would be October eleventh."

She smiles.

CHAPTER THIRTY-ONE

Sunday morning I find her in the bathroom, door wide open, wearing a hot pink Nike sports bra and black leggings. Dear Universe, my sincere gratitude for the invention of Spandex. Her body is bangin'—years of training for the more gymnastic cheerleading routines. In contrast, I'm bones and sinew; I'd probs break a hip if I did any sort of exercise beyond walking everywhere. Scrawny is right. *How you have B-cups is a miracle.* She seems to like my build though, so, it's all good.

Holy crap, she has a tattoo! Tasteful Roman numerals on her right side, a touch below her bra line: VII. XV. MMIII. I didn't notice it that night after her party. It isn't fresh, she's had it for a while. I do the math in my head. It has to be her sister's birthday.

She's pulling her hair into a high pony when she sees my reflection in the mirror. "Good morning."

"Morning." I glance around the hallway, making sure her parents aren't in hearing range. "That outfit. I can die happy."

Her smirk is diabolical. "I'm going for a run. Care to join?"

"By 'running,' do you mean 'strolling at a leisurely pace'?"

"Not even a little bit."

"Better if I stay here, then. Spence is coming to pick me up for a driving lesson soon anyway."

She scrunches her mouth to the side, releases it and shrugs. "Okay." I'm almost certain she means it. "Too bad you're going to miss me glowing with sweat."

No worries, gorgeous, we'll get around to that soon enough. Ba-dum-tss. "I'll catch it next time."

Spence texts me that she's outside at ten o'clock on the dot, as we discussed. She's already sitting on the passenger side, window down. "Yo."

"Yo, yourself." I slide into the driver's seat and start Sweet Caroline down the road.

As I reach the stop sign at the top of the block, I fixate on how she is always on time. I guess that comes with being a disciplined person. I'm kind of envious of her for it. I dislike being late, not because I'm particular about being there for the start of something, but because I don't like to be the center of attention by showing up in the middle of things and interrupting. Outside of school I'm not the best at being punctual, which definitely has something to do with the wonderful commitment issues I have—my tardiness is generally thanks to getting caught in a heated debate with myself over whether or not to go at all.

I'll never forget how mad Paige was that I arrived for dinner with her parents at seven thirty when I was supposed to be there at seven. She reamed me a new asshole for it. Meeting her parents wasn't something I was inclined to do. I thought about skipping it altogether, even as I was jumping off the train at the station a block from her house, and right up until I rang her doorbell. Needless to say, I wasn't dumbfounded—or heartsick—when she dumped me two days later. We were approaching our Best By date, anyhow. According to most of the girls I've been with, I have a three-month shelf life. I hope that's cancelled now; three months with Avery wouldn't be enough.

Spence says, "Bang the right onto the highway."

"The highway?"

"Put your big girl panties on and do it."

Even if I wanted to argue, I would lose, irrespective of the fact that I'm behind the wheel. "Okay, okay."

Route 128 isn't clustered. I'm relieved. If it were a weeknight there'd be a ton of traffic and I'd be frazzled. We're headed south, out of Beverly toward Danvers. "Do you have a destination in mind?"

"Nah."

"You're going to have to tell me where to go, otherwise we'll end up in Providence."

"You want to go to Rhode Island? We can."

She's insane. I don't even have my permit—this is definitely illegal—yet she'd be perfectly fine with me driving eighty miles and crossing state lines. "How are you so chill with letting me drive all the damn time?"

"I feel calm when I'm with you. I dunno why."

She does that for me, too. At first it was jarring. Now that I've gotten used to it, it's nice. We can just be—no pretense necessary.

"I have to know... how is it living with Avery since you hooked up?"

"It's friggin' torture!"

She sniggers. "Thought so. You've got bigger balls than me. I couldn't have survived."

It's weird talking about Avery with her ex, the only other girl she's dated. *Don't think of her as Avery's ex, she's your friend.* "Yeah, either I have a pair of brass ones on me or I'm out of my mind."

"Could be a little of both."

"You're probably right."

We don't end up in Rhode Island, but we do stay on 128 until it turns into Interstate 95. It takes every ounce of courage I have to keep us on the road; the switch from a two-lane mini-highway to a six-lane, sixty-five miles per hour dystopian hellscape is almost enough to make me piss myself.

Spence coos support the entire way. "You got this." And, "You're doing great."

We pull off into Market Street Shopping Center to make a U-turn and I think, *She's my best friend.* It sounds so steadfast and stable, the opposite of everything I'm used to, yet I don't panic over it. It feels natural, easy—something that simply is, like it was destined to happen. Maybe it was. The thing I'm learning about fate is that resisting it is pointless—it has the upper hand of inevitability and will win in the end.

My stomach grumbles. As with everything else, life-changing realizations make me hungry. "Let's stop for something to eat."

She goes, *pssh.* "Dude, your appetite is ridiculous!"

"You ain't kiddin'."

Spence drops me back at the house around one. I've got my hand on the front door, about to twist the knob when I hear Avery shout, "Go put it in her fucking room yourself!"

It's disconcerting. She can be sharp-tongued sometimes, but she doesn't yell at her parents; that's a line she won't cross.

I enter the house very quietly and am relieved to find she's not in my line of sight. The divider wall separating the entryway from the living room affords me some cover; I haven't been spotted. It's not that I'm trying to eavesdrop, it's that whatever's happening here sounds heavy—there is no way in hell I'm going to let my presence interfere.

"You do not get to speak to your father that way, young lady," Cate says, her tone harsher than I've ever heard it. "And I don't understand why you're so angry. It's only laundry."

Then Tom's voice. "Right. What's going on?"

"What's going on is I hate that room! I hate that it isn't Reese's anymore! You just gave it away, like..." Avery huffs away her rage. "You can't replace her, okay? It doesn't make a difference how many girls you foster, or how well we may get along, none of them will ever be my sister."

How long has she been holding that in? Have I helped her or made it worse by coaxing her pain to the surface?

"Is that what you think we're trying to do, replace Reese?" Cate asks.

"Isn't it? There's a hole in our lives now, and—" Her voice trembles, cracks. It's the sound of someone being overcome by tears. "And you're trying to shove someone into it, but it's shaped like Reese. No one else will ever fit."

"You're right, there is a hole and it can't be filled." Cate's voice breaks, too. "You and your sister made my life complete. I love you both so, so much, and I miss her every day. But even when she was here there was enough love, enough space, in this house for someone else."

"Avery, honey," Tom starts, his tenor cool, soothing as a salve. "Don't you remember we talked to you and Reese about us wanting to becoming foster parents? We put in the application months before her accident. We just didn't accept a placement until last winter. It was hard for us. And the only reason we put anyone in Reese's bedroom is because it's so much bigger and nicer than the office. We wanted whoever we brought into our home to feel like they had their own private, safe space."

This is the moment I choose to make my presence known. I step into the threshold between the hall and living room. Avery's eyes are on me, horrified. She knows I've heard everything. Then her gaze drops to the floor. She wipes her tears away with the back of her hand. "Shit. You did tell us. But then nothing ever happened, and—you're right, Reese's room is much better than the office. I'm sorry, I've been stewing about it all this time."

Cate looks at her daughter with such sympathy, she's fit to burst. "I wish you'd said something sooner. You can talk to us about anything." Her attention flutters over to me. "That goes for you, too." Not anything. Not the most important thing.

Avery sucks in a deep lungful of air. "I want the pictures of her, of all of us together, to go up again. I miss seeing her face."

"Oh, sweetheart," Cate says, "we took them down because we thought seeing them every day might upset you."

She shakes her head. "Taking them down upset me."

"Okay," Tom cuts in. He throws his hand up and motions for her to follow him. "Come on, let's do it right now."

I pick up a framed picture of Reese from its new—old? Renewed—spot on the fireplace mantle. It's a school photo; the wavy blue backdrop is universal. She looks about sixteen. Her hair is darker than Avery's—nearly black—and she has Cate's green eyes. "She was really pretty," I tell Avery. "She took after your mom. You look more like your dad."

"Hmm." She beams at the photo. "Oh my God, she hated posing for pictures. She was such a pain in the ass that day. Mom asked her the night before to wear something nice, and that morning she rocked up into the living room in a T-shirt and sweatpants, as usual."

Yes, please, talk about her until you've run out of air! Show me all your feelings, good, bad and in between. "What'd your mom say?"

"'No, ma'am! You march right back up those stairs and change,'" she twitters. "Reese tried to argue her way out of it, but eventually gave up. She knew Mom wasn't going to budge." Her grin vanishes. "You know this had nothing to do with you, right? I'm happy you're here. She's been on my mind a lot lately, that's all."

"Yeah, I know." I touch her arm to send it home. "I know."

"Good." She looks at me and fidgets, apprehensive of whatever thought has popped into her mind. "Do you think—um, forget it."

"Do I think what?" Hit me with your worst; I want it, as long as it's real.

"Will you come with us to the cemetery the next time we go? My parents can't handle being there for very long. They always head back to the car before I'm ready, and it would be nice not to be alone."

I throw my arms around her neck and pull her into a hug, for once not worrying about whether or not we'll get caught being too intimate. It's a huge deal, her wanting me to stand beside her as she grieves over her sister's grave, trusting me enough to let me see her at her most vulnerable. "Of course, I will," I whisper.

She tightens her grip on me.

In my periphery, I see Cate walk into the living room. She smiles at the scene she's stumbled upon. *It's an innocent hug. It's fine.* No, it's not fine. I care so much about her daughter, but in a very different way from what she's thinking. I'm sorry, Cate. I tried to fight it; it was too strong. I let go of Avery. Cate comes over to us. "This place looks much better now."

Avery takes in all the pictures, finally in their rightful places again. "It really does."

I'm about to turn in for the night, reaching to switch off my desk lamp, when there's a faint rapping at the door. My bedside clock lets me know that it's after midnight, too late for it to be either of the adults in the house. They've long been asleep.

I'm right. Avery's on the other side, head bowed and staring at her bare feet. What is she doing, testing her mettle?

I hold out my hand. She snatches onto it. It isn't enough—she can't conquer the inertia on her own. I guide her, inch by inch, inside. I try to leave the door open in case she decides to dash out again. She wants it closed.

I roll the chair away from the desk and motion for her to take a seat. She prefers to stand. She's digging her toes into the carpet, jogging her muscle memory. It's been more than two years since she's stepped foot in this room, as if it were a canyon cordoned off after an avalanche and it's taken that long for the packed snow to melt away.

I watch her glance around at everything—the walls, the ceiling, the rug, the bureau, the bed. Her eyelids are fluttering so fast they rival hummingbird wings. And then she's crying—or rather, weeping—trembling as the salty water splashes down her face.

She's in my arms; I don't give her the option not to be. Her quivering shakes me to my soul. I kiss her forehead, her sodden cheeks. She staggers out of my embrace and leads me to the bed.

We lie down together. Her head is resting half on a pillow, half on the inside of my elbow. She presses her face to my chest and the spot where my T-shirt meets her eyes gets soaked through. We're holding onto one another so tightly that I can't tell where my body ends and hers begins.

I skim my fingers through her ringlets. Soon, the sounds of sobbing transform into the soft, steady breathing of slumber. I don't want to wake her. I don't want us to get caught, either. She wished for this and, albeit under far more somber conditions, happenstance has granted the request. Who am I to argue? The solution to the conundrum is this: I keep her close to me all night, not daring to fall asleep myself.

*

At five forty-five, the burgeoning pink-orange sky peeks through the blinds, and I whisper into her ear, "Avery, it's time to get up."

She stirs, sniffles, wipes at her eyes and looks at me. "You let me sleep here." She shows me a tired smirk.

I swish her bangs away from her eyes. "Well, you were very sleepy. And I promised you someday, didn't I?"

She gives me the gentlest kiss before pushing herself off the mattress.

She opens the door just wide enough to peer into the hall. The coast is clear. "Thank you," she turns around and mouths to me, then heads to her own bedroom.

There's an hour and fifteen minutes before I have to get ready for school. The wakeful night was worth it if it brings Avery some measure of absolution. I climb under the covers and shut my eyes, hopeful that her wounds might, at last, begin to heal.

CHAPTER THIRTY-TWO

My Bio midterm is tomorrow and I am mid-freak out over it. Regular tests get me stressed; tests worth so much of my overall grade are about ten times worse. I had planned to start cramming yesterday when I got home from school, instead I crashed hard—that early morning nap barely got me through the day. Still, I don't regret the sleepless night. Avery's been different since, brighter, more at home in her home.

We're studying together in the living room, a joint decision we came to after we both bombed a quiz in English last week: All homework is to be done in the common areas. Neither of us can concentrate for very long in her room. We always end up talking, laughing, making out—not at all conducive to learning.

I'm going over one of the more confusing parts of biology, dominant and recessive genes. My notes look like this:

BB = brown eyes, dominant.
bb = blue eyes, recessive.
Offspring with a BB + a bb parent can equal BB—brown,
bb—blue, or Bb—green or hazel eyes.

Succinct for such a complex topic.

I'm smacked with a familiar ache, which seems to have ramped itself up over the last little while—that conversation with Avery at the mall, and all the huge, complicated feelings about Reese that the Cahills have finally let out. It's not my favorite subject, my parents, but I can't stop myself from wondering what color irises they have. I've always pictured my father with green eyes, for some reason. I doubt either of them have blue eyes, mine being such a peculiar shade of brown. One or both of them must be blonde, my hair is so light—recessive allele, no brown or black to dominate it.

"You look like you're on another planet. What's happening up there?" Avery reaches out to me, gives my temple a tap.

"I've been thinking a lot about my birth parents. I might try to find them now that I'm eighteen." I don't even have a copy of my birth certificate. That really bothers me. A birth certificate is proof that I wasn't hatched and left to crawl my way to the ocean like a sea turtle; that I'm a person—someone carried me in their body for nine months. *And then left you to crawl.*

She tilts her head and regards me, processing the idea. "You should."

"My social worker doesn't have much information about them, and the law protects their privacy, so she couldn't give it to me, anyway. I'm pretty sure I have to go to court to get my records unsealed, which means I'd need a lawyer and I don't have that kind of cash."

"Really?" She deadpans me. "My mother is a licensed, practicing family lawyer, hello."

"How did I not even think about that?" I feign a stupid face. I did think of it, but no matter how close I may get with them, I'll always hate asking Tom and Cate for favors.

She drops her pen, stands up, takes my hand and pulls me to my feet. "Let's go talk to her about it. She'll know where to start."

Cate is upstairs in the office. The door is slightly ajar. We can hear that she's on the phone and is peeved at the person on the other end. Avery posts up against the wall, folds her arms across her chest. Patiently impatient. That's her to a T.

After a while, it gets quiet. Avery knocks on the doorframe.

"Yep?" Cate says. We both sidle in.

It's my first time being in here. I'm glad that they chose to give me Reese's room. This one is a third the size, and the walls are lined with floating, unfinished wood shelves; it too closely resembles a large closet. I would never have been able to get any sleep. Hooray for PTSD, the gift that keeps on giving!

Avery relays my quandary to her mother.

Cate taps her fingers on the desk. "Let's see. In the Common-wealth of Massachusetts, a judge has to find good cause to unseal adoption records. Although, since you were never legally adopted, the laws are somewhat muddled. I understand that your birth certificate has been lost…" She clicks her tongue. "The Depart-ment of Children and Families is such a nightmare, sometimes. So, we'll have to apply for a pre-adoption birth record, regardless. Your parents would be notified, and they could contest it…" Another series of desk taps. "If a judge wants to try my patience, I'll claim need for access to your family medical history and that'll stuff 'em right up."

Wow. 'We' and 'I.' She's jumping right in. "You must be very good at your job."

"I am." She smiles. "Don't worry, I'll take care of it."

No doubt she's an amazing lawyer, but being a mom is the job she's best at. I stumble toward her, bend over and wrap my arms around her shoulders. "Thanks, Cate."

She gives me a tender squeeze. "My pleasure."

"See how easy that was?" Avery wonders as we're plodding back to the living room.

"Yeah. I just don't like asking—"

She grabs my elbow and spins me toward her. "We get one shot at life, Britton. We have to go for the things we really want, even if we need a little help to get them."

What I want right now is to kiss her, in broad daylight, here in the middle of the hallway. Of course, I am not that dimwitted. "I'll work on that."

"Good." She grins.

CHAPTER THIRTY-THREE

I think I did pretty well on my Bio midterm, but by lunch I'm so fried from fretting over it that I need an extra-large coffee to perk me up.

Over the lid of my paper cup, I watch a blonde guy I've never seen before shuffle up to our table. He's having a terrible time trying to hide his nervousness—he's sort of twitchy, his blue eyes aren't sure what to concentrate on. I comb over his letterman jacket. His sport is Baseball. His name is Mark, and he's a junior. "Sup, Avery?" He rubs his neck.

I take another sip of my java. *Sup, Avery? Bleugh.*

"Hi, Mark." She drops the french fry she was about to chomp on, flicks the salt from her fingers. "What's going on?"

"I was thinking, if you don't already have a date to the Fall Ball, will you go with me?"

I almost spit out my drink, but manage to swallow it before it dribbles out of my mouth. Right, that dumb bootleg-homecoming dance is soon. It shouldn't come as a shock that someone's asking her; nobody's aware that she changed her status from 'Single' to 'In a Relationship.' *'It's Complicated,' at best, you turd.*

Avery is chill as can be. "Wow, I'm so flattered you asked. Thank you," she says, her tone sugary. She gestures to her friends. "We're doing a group thing, you understand. But I'll definitely save a dance for you." She gives him the most natural smile she can muster. No one other than me recognizes how bogus it is.

Man, she is crazy adept at turning guys down. *No duh, she's hotter than a five-alarm fire. She's probs had a hundred boys ask her out.*

He's dejected, but gulps it down. "Oh, cool, it's all good."

That's that. He sulks back to his friends, who jeer him. "Loser!" "Told ya, fool."

Sorry not sorry, Brotein Shake.

"Why'd you curve him?" Kylie asks.

Tasha adds, "Word. I'm shipping it."

Avery peeks at me, contrite. It's a split-second breakdown of her veneer. She twists her lips at Kylie. "He's not my type."

I don't suspect he would be, even if I weren't in the picture. She likes her guys tall, dark and handsome, like Noah. I'm not quite sure how she likes her girls; Spence and I in no way resemble each other. Maybe with girls it's more about personality?

That can't be it, you're a tool. Decent looking enough, however. No, she doesn't just want to get in my pants—our link isn't driven by carnal attraction only. We've connected on a deeper level; it's like we understand each other without really having to try. Now that I've experienced this, I don't know why I ever bothered with dating before. I mean, Paige was cool. Prior to her, Megan... I liked her, and it was almost right, but something never quite fit, like a puzzle piece that was slightly misshapen. I guess I've been going along with it because being with someone is better than being alone. I've never wanted to give anyone all of me, or have all of anyone, until Avery.

Even after the last bell rings, I'm still dazed by how much I wanted to tell off that Mark guy. It's odd. I don't consider myself a possessive person—I've hardly ever had anything to possess—and Avery isn't an object anyway, she doesn't belong to me. Girls aren't chattel for their partners, parents, or anyone else. The political incorrectness of it doesn't stop me from simmering over the fact that someone who wasn't me asked her to the dance. She's chosen me, at least for now. Isn't it okay for me to want to bask in the incredible improbability of that?

I slam my locker closed with too much ferocity. The door vibrates on its hinges.

"That's a mood," Spence says. "Something up?"

I take a gander around, make sure there's no one else in earshot. "This guy asked Avery to the Fall Ball today. Right in front of me."

Her eyes bug. "What'd she say? What'd you say?"

"She told him that she wants to go with her friends. What the hell could I say?"

"Have you asked her?"

I glower at her like she's dense. "Are you out of your mind?"

"You know you have to ask her now, yeah? Otherwise she might think you don't want to go with her."

I hadn't considered that. I want to go with her, but what's the point of proposing it? She'll just shoot me down. "I can't."

"Shit. I forgot how much being on the downlow sucks."

"It does, but the last thing I need is for her parents to know I'm hooking up with their daughter. As for her coming out, you know how personal a decision that is. She'll do it when she's ready."

"What if she's never ready?"

What if she isn't? "Doesn't make a difference. You were right, she's worth it."

"I never thought she would tell anyone that we were a thing. I wasn't even sure whether she was into girls or just me, but she told you, and then you guys got together. Ask her to the dance. She might surprise you."

There is a difference between being out to the people you love and being out to randoms. She's the queen of The Brigade, so it's doubtful her friends would give her shit over it. "You're not going to shut up about it, are you?"

"Nah."

"If I ask her and she says no, I'm going to come crying to you. Relentlessly, until the end of time."

"What are friends for?"

A question hits me like a rockslide. How is it that Spence doesn't have, like, a harem of girls vying for her attention? Forget her looks; she's such a good friend, she's bound to be a great girlfriend. "Are you going to ask anyone?"

"I'll have more fun with the squad… And Noah," she chortles. "If you do end up going with her, make sure you pencil us in for a few dances."

"You bet your ass I will."

*

"About the Fall Ball," Avery says as she's gunning onto Sohier Road. "Are you going with your friends?"

I don't know if I actually want to go at all. I've never gone to a dance before, and I don't see any reason I should start now. *She's a great reason.* This would be the perfect moment to— "School dances are wicked far outside my wheelhouse. I'd rather skip it." Anddd I blew it. What the fuck am I so scared of? She likes me. I like her. We're… In a Complicated Relationship. The hardest part is already out of the way. *Mmm, not at all.*

Cue her inappropriate laughter. "Like I'd let that happen. If you're not going with them, you're coming with me and my friends."

Then technically we would be going together, but it doesn't feel like it counts. Although, it's preferable to sitting alone in my bedroom brooding. "If my presence means that much to you, fine."

She smirks at the road.

CHAPTER THIRTY-FOUR

It turns out, in fact, that no one is ever too old to get excited about Halloween. Kylie, Liz and Tasha were stoked on the idea of going to Salem when Avery brought it up to them at lunch last week, and Amy showed some interest, too. They immediately formed a mini-conclave to coordinate costume ideas, ultimately deciding on sexy versions of the *Sorcerer's Academy* characters—gross, seeing as they're like, nine years old, but whatever. They didn't bother to consult Avery on the matter; they knew she'd opt for something darker, more traditionally ghoulish. They're more accepting of her quirks, these little things that set her apart from them, than I initially thought they'd be. It further solidifies the idea that they wouldn't give a shit if they knew she's into girls, or that we're seeing each other. Pushing the issue is not something I'm prepared to do though. I don't want to cause friction. It wouldn't be fair to either of us. I'm not eager to tell Cate and Tom about us anytime soon either.

The sun's gone down and we're both getting ready for the night's revelries. I settled on a simple getup: a pair of black pants and a zip-up hoodie I already owned with a graphic of a life-size skeleton on its front and back. I splurged on a realistic-looking skull jaw half-mask when Avery and I went to buy her special effects supplies at Party Planet.

She's in the bathroom in front of the mirror, applying the finishing touches to her makeup, and I'm propped against the doorframe ogling her, my mask dangling around my throat. She is looking awesome as a School Girl Zombie, chosen to complement the theme agreed on by The Brigade—short grey and red plaid skirt, grey V-neck cardigan, black knee-high socks and flat, black Mary Janes to complete the outfit. She's applied patches of gnarled skin and bite wounds oozing with sticky blood to her face. I step inside, close the door behind me, then slink over to her. I encircle her torso and rest my chin on her shoulder.

"Careful," she warns.

"Gotcha." I kiss her neck, watch for her reaction in the mirror. It's a smile.

Here we go. "How would you feel if Spence met up with us?"

"I was really hoping to have some silly fun tonight." She glares at my reflection. "You already invited her, didn't you?"

She got yo' ass. It was selfish of me, I know. I wanted to celebrate my first Halloween in a decade with both of them. "We talked it over. I told her that I'd have to get the okay from you and get back to her."

"You can't un-invite her, you're not douchey like that. And I'm trying to be less douchey, so I'm not going to ask you to."

She's not douchey, she's sensitive—massive distinction. "You sure?"

She nods. "I can't promise you that I'll be all smiles, but I'll do my best."

"Thank you."

"Uh huh. Now get out so I can finish. You're distracting me."

"You're sexy when you're bossy." I place a kiss on another cosmetics-free part of her neck and bounce out of the room.

She borrows her dad's SUV, and we pick up The Brigade at Kylie's house—it's on the way to Salem. We take the backroads to avoid the tourist traffic on the highway.

If parking was difficult on a normal Saturday afternoon in September, tonight it is downright nightmarish. After circling the surface roads for fifteen minutes, Avery gives up and pays for valet in the Museum Place garage. It's a convenient location, steps from the Essex Street pedestrian mall.

The cobblestone pathways are overcrowded, and we're forced to walk in pairs—Amy and Liz, Kylie and Tasha, Avery and me. It gets me wondering if her friends are oblivious to everything besides their own tits. We're together all of the time now, how could they not know we're dating? Then again, outside of Spence, who only twigged because she's been there, The Squad hasn't figured it out, either. Most teenage girls are too wrapped up in their own stuff to notice other people's. I'd love to be more like that, but once it's ingrained, alertness is hard to shake. As with a feral animal, vigilance has always been key to my continued safety.

My phone chimes, dislodging the thought from my head.

Spence: I'm outside Wicked Ink.

I remember where that is from the last time. *We're a block away.* I write back to her.

Be there soon.

"Spence is here."

"You started hanging out with her again?" Tasha shoots to Avery. She's taken aback, though not judging. When Avery was part of The Three Amigos, was she not friends with The Brigade—no overlap? There are still things about their situation I don't know, and it isn't my place to ask. It's not like it makes a difference. What matters is if and how they can move forward.

"Britton wanted her to come. Tonight, we're all hanging out with her."

"I think she's cool," Liz adds, shrugging. As she says it, I decide that, out of all of Avery's friends, I like her the most.

No one else has anything to say about it. If they do, they won't voice it after Avery's declaration. To have that kind of sway over people… It's like her superpower.

We find Spence standing with her back against the building's brick façade. She's dressed as a pirate, hair draped over her shoulder in a long French braid and topped with a tricorn hat. Purple corset top. Jagged black skirt. Fishnets and leather knee-high boots. I didn't expect to see her in something so girly. Ever.

Without thinking, I give her a wolf whistle through my mask. "Damn, you brought your A-game."

Avery nails me with a scowl that makes my freaking rectum prolapse. It's much scarier than the last time she let her jealousy show, yet in a weird way I'm happy about it. She wants to be the only girl I look at. I can't imagine how she doesn't realize that she is.

"Thanks. Hey!" Spence says to the group. Then, to Avery, "Dope getup."

"You, too," she replies coolly.

"Let's do a lap, see what's good," Tasha says.

We head for Washington Street.

I'm glad I brought my Nikon—it's strapped around my neck, but isn't getting much rest. Every few seconds there's something else to photograph.

We're passing a pair of women who've turned clear umbrellas, tendrils of white ribbon and LED string lights into bioluminescent jellyfish costumes. I stop them for a photo. They ham it up for the camera as I snap, snap, snap.

A few minutes later we come upon six people dressed as the original nineties Power Rangers. Spence and I—and shockingly, Kylie—geek out over them. I take some pics of them posing together in fight stances, and then get a few of our two groups combined. Avery is funny, limbs outstretched and wrists limp, calling for the Pink Ranger's brains. Pink Ranger is into it, pretending to karate kick and chop her away. The shots are hilarious. I'll have to print and frame them. Avery having 'silly fun' is the greatest thing I've ever seen. Every picture I've taken tonight is being submitted for my Photography Club portraiture project— I'll hear no objections from Avery or anyone else.

Spence is friendly enough with the other girls, Liz in particular since she's so receptive, but she mostly sticks with me. I've been hyper-focused on balancing my attention between her and Avery. Based on Avery's displeasure at my reaction to Pirate Head Bitch in Charge, if I don't get it right there's a good chance the night will go to hell. I'm managing it well so far.

The atmosphere around us is helpful; it's so light and jovial that Avery and Spence engage in short bursts of unflustered conversation about all the ingeniously costumed carousers we encounter. I fall a step behind them, observe with a satisfied heart as they stroll side by side.

I don't get to bask in it for long. Avery notices that I'm no longer keeping stride and looks over her shoulder to find me. She slides her arm behind her back, wiggles her fingers. I brush my fingertips against hers and she captures my hand. She tugs me in between her and Spence, then lets me go.

"Yo, let's go to the Common!" Amy yells to us from the front of the pack. "The Rock 92.9 stage is there."

Avery gives her the go-ahead with a nod.

The Common is fire. There's a huge stage set up in the center of it, and an expansive Oktoberfest Biergarten tent next to it. There's gotta be close to a thousand people rocking out to a female-fronted band called Friday Night Fistfight and enjoying some hoppy beverages. We push through the crowd, closer to the stage. By the fourth song—a pop-punk cover of CHVRCHES'

"Miracle"—we've all gotten very into the music. Spence is to my right, Avery to my left. Both of them are singing, moving to the rhythm. It occurs to me that these two girls are my favorite people on Earth, and considering they've put their painful history aside to be with me tonight, I might be one of theirs, too. *How TF did you get so blessed?*

"What's that goofy grin about?" Avery asks.

"I'm having a wicked good time, that's all."

I understand her expression. Despite itching to wrap her arms around me, she won't let herself. She doesn't do anything she doesn't want to do, but she doesn't do everything she wants to do, either.

Spence nudges me with her elbow. She's goggling a tall guy dressed like the Grim Reaper who has a drink in his hand. "I'd murder for a beer right now, wouldn't you?" she shouts.

"I don't actually like beer. It's better than spirits, and I'll drink it if it's there, but…" Without a word, Avery takes off for the Biergarten. I'm so stunned, I wonder aloud, "Where the hell is she going?"

Spence does this half-snicker half-outbreath thing, "She must still have her fake ID."

I can feel my eyebrows climbing my skull. "Her what now?" Naturally, she has a fake ID. The entire Brigade probably has fake IDs. They're the Cool Girls, and that's such a quintessential Cool Girl thing.

The Large Hadron Collider must've malfunctioned and sent me to an alternate dimension, because I never imagined I'd end up with a popular cheerleader type; they don't date girls. *Not openly.* There's the catch. And so, her happiness remains elusive, buried beneath her guilt. And mine, captive within the walls of her parent's home. Someday we'll be free, we just have to hang on.

Spence smirks. "It's a really good fake, too, scans and everything. Never fails." She nods at Avery, who's already gotten past the burly bouncer. My gaze is on her as she gives one of the bartenders her order and then pays.

She strolls back to us with a beer in each hand, all unruffled confidence, boasting a simper at everyone she passes—including two cops. It's astonishing how she can be so audacious at times, yet so timid at others. And it's astonishing how much I like both sides—every side—of her.

"Here." She hands one of the blue plastic cups to Spence and takes a sip of the other. Spence digs into the top of her corset, pulls out a bundle of folded bills. Neat trick. Avery scoffs at the money. "Don't insult me." She doesn't wait for Spence to thank her before joining her friends, who've separated from us a bit.

Spence swills her beer. "She hasn't changed at all."

She has changed. A lot. The shiny Avery that Spence knew is locked away inside of her. Still, there are pieces of the girl she used to be shimmering through the darkness; I'll keep prying them into the light for as long as it takes. She will be happy again. What she did just now… that's significant progress.

We watch a few more bands and Avery imbibes a couple more beers before everyone agrees that we need food.

We take off for the center of downtown. There are long lines to get into every place we pass, but we jump on one outside a restaurant called The Village Tavern, Avery insisting that the food is phenomenal and that I would die over their fried chicken.

Standing in front of us is a mixed group of guys and girls around our age, some in plain clothes, others dressed up, and one girl keeps looking at me. She's in an elaborate witch costume, thick layers of greasepaint on her face, features distorted by FX appliances. I'm not sure if I know her; she may know me from somewhere. I take my mask off, let it drape around my neck.

"Sick camera." She smiles and points to my Nikon. Okay, she doesn't know me. So, what's with the leering? "Where'd you get it?"

"Thanks. Uh, I'm not sure. It was a gift."

"Chroma, in Beverly," Avery chimes in.

I snap, "Right, it's from there."

"Oh, cool." She disregards Avery, concentrates on me. "Are you from Beverly?"

Nope. "Yeah." I squint at her. Her irises are purple, pupils vertical like a cat's. "Those are some wild contacts."

She giggles, "Like them?"

"I do."

Avery thrusts her hands into her pockets, pulls her jacket tight around her and announces to our friends, "I gotta pee."

"Me, too," I say. "You guys?" A collective headshake *no*. I spy a row of green chemical toilets a little way down Essex Street. There's not too long a wait to use them. "Avery..." I point them out to her.

She gives me a headshake. "We'll be back."

We're queuing for the toilets and she turns to me, arms folded. "That girl was flirting with you, and you were flirting back."

"What? No! We were just talking."

"She was creepin' on you the whole time we were in line!" She twitters. "You're so bad at recognizing when someone's feeling you."

"Because I don't get what it is they could possibly be feeling," I admit.

"I wish you could see yourself through my eyes for even a minute, then maybe nothing that ridiculous would come out of your beautiful mouth ever again."

Ah, shit. If I don't change the subject this instant, I'm going to lose control of myself and kiss her in front of a hundred thousand people. "Hey, uh, that was cool of you, to get Spence a beer."

"It wasn't the first time."

"Will it be the last?"

"I don't know. Maybe not. It's starting to hurt less."

"That's something."

"Yeah."

A stall becomes vacant and she signals that I should go first. I step in. As I'm about to close the door, she scurries in after me. It's cramped, and it stinks of piss, but that doesn't affect her; she grabs me by my belt, jerks me to her. She plants her lips on mine, shoves her tongue into my mouth. My surprise doesn't keep me from savoring her. I run my hand up the nape of her neck, into her hair.

It's different than all of our other make-out sessions, hurried and more needful, as though she has something to prove—I don't know if it's because of the beer or that girl flirting with me, or even my stupid whistle at Spence earlier. Is it alright not to care about the reason?

She pulls back and flashes a sly grin. "I didn't actually have to pee. I wanted to see if I could get you alone."

Again with the mind-reading! "Same."

She smashes her lips into mine once more, gives me a bite. She unzips my hoodie and slides her hand under my shirt, below my bra. Her warm fingers, rubbing, pinching. She sure as shit knows how to turn me on.

She takes my right wrist with her free hand, presses my palm to her inner thigh, guides me up her skirt. My fingers move on their own accord, slip the crotch of her lace panties to the side.

No!

I yank my hand away. "Hold up." Sex is the one thing I let myself be impulsive about, because it's mind-blowing and I know I'm good at it, but I am not going to allow this to happen with her in a fucking porta-potty. And definitely not when there could be so many negative motives behind her wanting it. She shrinks away from me, embarrassed, slighted. I have to fix this.

"Avery." I step to her, cup her cheeks. "You deserve a bed, and like, candles and rose petals. I want to do it right, when you're sure."

Her eyes are softer than I have ever seen them. "I—"

A loud banging kills the mood; the shoddy plastic door rattles beneath an angry fist. "Fucking hell, get a room!" a woman shouts.

We disintegrate into laughter. She unlocks the door, takes my hand and pulls me into the busy world. The Banging Woman glowers at us. Avery spits, "Fuck off," and leads me back toward the restaurant.

Our fingers are still intertwined, and I'm dazed. It could be she's feeling bold because her costume gives her a measure of anonymity, or maybe it's the fact that there are so many other spectacular things going on around us that it's unlikely anyone would pay attention to something as banal as two girls holding hands.

When we get closer to our friends, she does try to let go of me. I hang onto her a millisecond longer than I should. She looks at me with remorseful eyes. "I'll get there soon."

I can see how much she means it, how much she wishes she were already there. "I know, Babygirl." Babygirl! *Damn near fingered her in a porta-john and you're freaking out about giving her a cutesy pet name?* "Um, I, not—"

"Babygirl is good. I like it." She smiles.

I smile, too.

The food is great. The conversation is better. We chuckle a lot about stupid stuff, bad fashion trends and dumb shit kids have done at school—getting caught vaping in the bathroom, pulling fire alarms to get out of tests, streaking at the Spring Pep Rally last year—and it's the most ordinary, yet most sensational occurrence, just being a normal teenager. I didn't realize it was supposed to be this way, a celebratory, carefree period in a person's life. They've inspired me: I'm going to try to enjoy the remainder of my high school career as much as I can.

Throughout, Avery holds my hand under the table. It's a good place to start. I like the sensation of her skin on mine. I don't much care how or where it happens, as long as it does.

We overstay our welcome—an hour and a half on the busiest day of the year—until Tasha goes, "Shit, it's eleven thirty. My parents are going to flip."

"Time flies," Spence says, and hails the waitress for our check.

The server places the bill presenter in the center of the table and Kylie grabs it. She's the math whiz of The Brigade, though I suspect she's not as good at it as Spence. I have cash at the ready. Avery slides a hundo-note from her phone case. "I've got this," she says to me.

Uh, no. I slap seventy bucks on the table. "Not tonight you don't." My face must give away that I'm not going to sway on this one, because she doesn't try to argue. In my mind, I've taken her to dinner, which means I pay; I won't have it any other way.

"You can be stubborn when you want to be."

Once in a while. About etiquette, always. It's something Eddie, one of the friendlier counselors at the group home I was at a few years ago, taught all the boys—how to be a gentleman. I remember he started including me in his lessons after I came out to him. He was the first adult I told, and that was his reaction: "Then you have to learn how to treat a lady, too." Simple, easy. He was a nice guy.

Kylie stuffs the collected cash into the check presenter. "Alright, we out." And with that, the evening's merrymaking comes to a close.

We walk Spence to the Klop Alley parking lot. She says goodbye to The Brigade first, then turns to Avery. "Thanks for letting me hang out with you guys tonight. It was fun."

"Yeah, it was."

Spence and I are both aware that Avery's gaze is on her. Regardless, she throws a loose arm around my shoulders. "I'll see you at lunch tomorrow?"

"Yep. Text me when you get home, okay?"

"Okay." She slides into Sweet Caroline.

My eyes are all over Avery as Sweet Caroline disappears down the road. She notices. "Why are you looking at me like that?"

"Like what?"

"Like... that!"

This warmth in my chest, in my stomach, in every part of me... This is me proving the theory; I'm in lo—*Whoa, calm your tits! It's been like, a few weeks.* No, it's been since the second I saw her, that very first moment our eyes met as she was jostling down the porch steps. I didn't believe *coup de foudre* existed, then it happened to me, faster than a heartbeat. Everything that's taken place since then has only made me more certain of it. *Unless you're trying to get dumped, let her say it first. If she feels the same.* "Because you're awesome."

She does her signature lip bite. "You, too."

"Guys, come on! It's cold," Liz calls to us from the sidewalk.

She loops her arm through mine, something I've seen her do countless times with Tasha or Kylie or whoever else—acceptable contact. "Let's go."

CHAPTER THIRTY-FIVE

Cate's car is in the driveway and Tom's is not—odd for a Thursday afternoon. Tom usually ends the week working from home. He was here when Avery and I left for school this morning. Cate headed out around the same time we did, but we didn't stick around to watch her drive away in her Mercedes. Tom could have driven her to work, although I have no idea why he would. Avery is as confused as I am. She calls into the kitchen, "Mom?" No reply. She saunters to the staircase landing and hollers up the steps, "Yo, parental units!" Nothing. "Weird."

"Did they have something scheduled?"

"Not that I know of."

This could be bad. Something with her grandparents? "They would've let us know if there was an emergency, right?"

"Have you met my parents? One of them would've picked us up from school."

"True." Everything's fine, nothing to worry about. I open my messenger bag, grab *A Tale of Two Cities* and park my ass on the recliner.

Avery tosses her backpack onto the floor near the coffee table. "Straight to homework. Such a diligent student."

"Gotta keep my grades up. I need as much scholarship money as I can get for MassArt." I flip to the first chapter and start reading.

"Hey." She slips her hand under my chin, bends over and kisses me—a reckless violation of the ground rules.

Kissed her back, though. "What brought that on?"

She falls onto the couch. "I'm happy you're taking our pact so seriously."

"Aren't you?"

She decides to dive into *Two Cities*, as well. "I've already started my application for early decision. It's due December first."

That's also MassArt's early action deadline. Today is the first of November; time is running out. Time is such a weird concept. It has always felt arbitrary, long stretches of it go by without any change until *bam*, the universe throws everything into chaotic upheaval. "I should get on top of that, too."

"Yes, you should."

"I will this weekend. I promise."

I'm halfway through the third chapter when I glance over at Avery. She's lounging on her stomach and her feet are doing little kicks in the air. How can someone be so cute while reading? I could spend the rest of my life watching her read. Minutes, hours, days, forever.

The Fall Ball. Tick tock, bitch! It's two weeks from Saturday. I wouldn't mind going, if it's with her—legitimately. Avery's words reverberate in my brain: *We have to go for the things we really want.* Taking her to the dance is what I really want. I have to make myself clear about it. *Quit dicking around and ask her.*

"Will you go to the Fall Ball with me?" It comes out sounding like one word. *Idiot.*

She places the book on the arm of the couch like a little paper tent. "Was that not the plan?"

"I meant *with* me, as my date. We could still go in a group with your friends, and we could sit out the slow songs." Baby steps.

"Can I think about it?" *Ouch.* It's better than a flat-out rejection, but I can't keep my features from betraying my disappointment. "No, listen." She pushes herself up into a seated position, reaches out and caresses my cheek. I nestle into it. For the second time today, we break the first commandment of Manhunt dating. The kiss is soft and sweet. "It's not that I don't want to. I just need to let the idea… marinate."

"I get that. It's okay if it's too much. I wanted to ask you, that's all."

"I won't leave you hanging."

"Okay."

"Girls, we're home!" Cate says as the front door opens. I smell the pizza before I see it. She and Tom come into the living room.

"Where have you two been?" Avery goes into Adult Mode, crossing her arms and shooting daggers at her parents. It's adorable, and a tad intimidating.

Tom sets the pizza box on the coffee table and raises his hands as if he were being mugged. "Peace offering." He and Cate sit together on the loveseat.

Cate focuses on me. "We had an appointment with your social worker."

A what? Why? Sometimes Joanne does home safety checks, but it's been years and multiple foster families since the last one. Younger kids take priority, as they should—they haven't honed their survival skills yet, don't know how to keep themselves out of danger.

Pizza. A few foster parents brought me special treats in the past when they sat me down for the 'you're being re-homed' talk, a way to soften the blow and quiet their consciences. No, please don't make me leave! I'll be better, perfect! "Did I do something wrong?" *So many things.*

"Not at all, kiddo," Tom says.

Cate's mouth droops open. "Don't be silly. You're a great kid and we're glad to have you with us."

"Then what's happening?" Avery's defensive. She's on the edge of her seat. Her furrowed brow, tight lips...

Avery posed the question, but Cate directs her response to me. "I needed her to sign off on your records request. I didn't want to fax or e-mail it to her; Lord knows how long it would've taken her to get it back to me."

Whew. "I'm sorry. You shouldn't have gone out of your way."

"Nonsense."

Tom thumbs at his wife. "She's had to hire private investigators to find folks who were dodging divorce papers. This was a cinch."

Cate agrees. "Everything's sorted. I've spoken to a friend who's a clerk at the Registry of Vital Records and Statistics and sent him the paperwork; he's going to expedite your application. Once they've received notification of inquiry, your birth parents will have fifteen days to respond with an objection. We'll know in a few weeks if we have to go to court."

She's putting in so much effort for me without expecting anything in return. I don't know what to say. There is no expression in the English language to convey the magnitude of my gratefulness. "That's great. Thank you so much."

"You're very welcome. Now, the two of you dig into that pizza before it gets cold."

"Don't we need plates?" Avery examines her mother.

Tom shoos the issue away. "Take a walk on the wild side."

CHAPTER THIRTY-SIX

"Britton, is there something bothering you?" Cate asks from the couch, putting down the manila file-folder she's been reading.

I made a mistake, couldn't keep my face neutral while mooning over Avery's *Can I think about it?* from last night. I honestly do understand where she's coming from—going to the dance with me, lowkey or not, is a grand gesture—but that doesn't change the fact that it stung. I want to do couple-y things with her, even if we keep them confidential. Isn't that what we are, a couple? "No, I'm cool. Kinda bored." I hold up the cable remote. "There's nothing on TV." I can't concentrate on reading. The Squad is going to The 99 restaurant for dinner, but I'm not in the mood for a kiki or whatever-the-frig Olivia called it. Avery's in her room. She said she needed silence to write her entrance essay. It's a good thing; she shouldn't have to witness me moping like a spoiled brat, and that's the sight she'd get if she were here. It's useless to pretend otherwise; she knows I'm bummed.

"I was going to get dinner started. Would you like to help me cook?"

It's Friday. "Aren't you and Tom going out tonight?"

"Date night this week has been pushed to tomorrow. We have tickets for the Bruins game in the afternoon. I asked Avery if the two of you would like to come, but she said you had other plans."

We do? "Ah, right. I blanked for a sec. Sorry."

"How about giving me a hand in the kitchen?"

I like cooking. It's something I've gotten good at over the years. I've had a lot of practice. Being able to prepare meals for yourself is essential for foster kids; sometimes it was the only way I got to eat. "Why not?"

Making dinner with Cate is fun. I didn't expect it to be, but she has the radio blasting and she's singing along with the songs. I get a bit carried away and foot it to the beat of one or two, myself. We stuff the last mushroom with chopped Italian sausage, garlic, cheese and breadcrumbs, and she slides the tray into the oven. "Nice job." She wipes her hand on her apron and holds it up for a high five. I'm happy to oblige her. "Can you do me a favor?"

I nod.

"Please go tell my daughter that dinner will be ready in twenty and she needs to get her butt down here to set the table."

"Will do."

I'm a second away from knocking on Avery's door when the sound of her voice stops me. "Like, what should I do?"

And then I hear Spence, kinda crackly, as though they're FaceTiming. "If you don't take that girl to the dance, I swear to God I'm going to."

"You will not!" Avery brays.

"I will, too! Sorry, but, she's hot."

"She is hot. That's not even what it's about. She's so endearing."

I should not be listening in on a private conversation she's having in the sanctuary of her bedroom. *Forget that, they're talking about you.*

"You said it. So then, what's your malfunction?"

"I'm a candy-ass little bitch," Avery sighs. "It's a lot, going from Netflix and Chill to full on PDA."

"What PDA? You're going to eat dinner and shake your ass to some music. Don't fingerblast her on the dance floor and you'll be golden."

More laughter from Avery.

"For real, though, she shouldn't be your dirty secret. I was, and I only ended up getting hurt. And you did, too. So, if you like her—and I think you more than like her, because you called me to talk about her—don't screw it up, okay?"

Ah, enough. Knock, knock. "Avery?"

"I have to run. Thanks for the pep talk."

"You're welcome. Bye."

"Come in." I open the door. She sits up, scoots to the edge of her bed. "What's up?"

Be cool. "Sorry. Were you on the phone?" I sit down beside her.

"Uh huh. With Spence, actually. I gave her the super overdue apology I owed her."

"That's great. I was hoping you guys would reconnect."

"*Nooo.*" She grins.

"What changed your mind?"

"You did, obviously. You became friends with her, which forced her back into my life. Then you yelled at me, and kept pushing. It helped me see that I was being really unfair to her. She wasn't responsible for what happened to Reese."

"Now all you have to do is stop blaming yourself for something that wasn't your fault, either."

"I'm trying. Besides, I needed girlfriend advice, and since no one else knows I'm bi yet, she was option A through Z."

Did she just say... "Girlfriend?"

Her brows arch. "Too soon?"

It's not that it's too soon, it's that I like the sound of it too much. I don't know that anyone's ever made such a straightforward declaration of it. I am Avery Cahill's girlfriend, and she is mine. Unreal! "I am totally your girlfriend."

"Then, can I get a kiss from my girlfriend?"

I peck her on the forehead.

"Not the kind of kiss I was looking for, but I'll accept it. Oh, my bad, I got sidetracked, did you need something?"

"Your mom told me to tell you to get your cute butt downstairs and set the table. She didn't say 'cute,' that was me."

Pfft. "Fine."

"By the way, what are we doing tomorrow afternoon?"

"Huh?"

"Cate mentioned the Bruins game and—"

"I made something up to get out of it. I wasn't interested in a double date with my parents, and I didn't think you would be either. Was I wrong?"

A double date with—Gross. I hadn't thought about the implications of our relationship on family outings. They seem impossible, now. The whole dynamic is messed up, but it's too late to go back. I wouldn't even if I could. "You were not wrong."

"Do you even like hockey?"

"I can't follow it. The puck is too small to see. Do you?"

"No. Ice rinks are cold. Shivering for two hours isn't my idea of fun."

"We can go to the football game, that way if your parents ask, we'll have something to report." I've told her how much I can't stand football; she's aware I'll only go because she wants to.

"Or we can watch the girls' soccer team crush Masconomet. It's their last match of the season, right?" Okay, they're getting along better, but Avery volunteering to be around Spence for an extended period? She crows at my awe. "I've got a handle on reading you, Scrawny, you know that?"

Yes, I do. I haven't been trying to hide my feelings from her as much, of late. I want her to know me. I want her to love me, even the least endearing parts. "I'd rather cheer on a team that has a chance of winning."

"Soccer it is."

"Cool. You still have to set the table." I stand up.

"Ugh!"

"Come on, I'll help you." I heave her off the mattress. She drapes her arms around my neck and rubs her nose against mine. I've heard this called a 'kunik'; they were never my favorite thing, but she has me rethinking that position.

*

We meet Mack and Hannah on our way to the bleachers and decide to sit together. Once again, the stands are overflowing, which is to be expected for a home game: Aside from the volleyball and boys' lacrosse teams, the girls' soccer team is the only Beverly High School fall sport with a winning record.

Beverly dominates Masco in the first half, scoring three goals to none. In the second, Spence, Erin and the two midfielders kick the ball around to each other as if they're running passing drills instead of competing against another side. It's like watching the US Women's National Team play an under-15 team; they manage to score two more goals despite easing up on the gas. Erin earns a brace, and in the seventy-second minute, Spence gets the hat trick. She downplays her elation for the sake of sportsmanship, gives Erin a high five and then goes dead-serious.

The ref whistles the end of the match, result five to nil. Spence drops to her knees and covers her face with her hands. I can tell by the way her body is shaking that she's crying—happy tears this time. In the twenty-five years since its establishment, no Beverly girls' soccer team has had an undefeated season or clinched the division championship. These girls have made history, are the pride of the city, and Spence led them there. Olivia dashes up the pitch, slides into the grass and embraces her, knocking her flat on her back. The field players pile on top of them, and the team bench clears to join in. Mack and Hannah rush down the bleachers, onto the turf, intent to add their bodies to the heap. I'm on my feet ready to run, too, but I stop to inspect Avery. She's out of her seat, and is excited, but won't be throwing herself at Spence—fine by me. I want them to be cool, but yeah, no touching. "What are you waiting for?" she asks with a chuckle and gestures at the field.

For that. "Meet you down there."

There's an impromptu party at Erin's house. Spence invites us. Avery is sincere in her congratulations, however, isn't in the head space to attend another bash with her. Parties in general won't ever be her bag, again. "Thanks, I'm gonna pass." She tugs my sleeve. "You should go, though."

Really? "Are you—"

"Yes. Celebrate with your friends."

"Bitch, yas!" Olivia says.

"I'll give you a ride home after," Hannah adds. "It's close to my place, anyway."

"Seriously. I want you to go and have fun." Avery's smile. She means it.

"Okay, I will."

"Don't worry, sis, we'll take good care of her." Olivia winks at Avery as we drop her off at her BMW.

"Don't get too drunk," she says to me with a smirk.

She knows full well that won't happen. Losing control of myself isn't my style. And anyway, Erin's parents will be there; so there probably won't be any booze.

"Harhar. I'll see ya later," I reply.

"Bye, guys. Congrats, again."

The rest of us continue on to Hannah's Mitsu, and I realize she's studying me. "You guys have gotten pretty close, huh?"

Finally, someone's noticed! "We have."

"It must be strange for her after, you know, losing her sister. Probably nice, too, to have that kind of relationship with someone again."

Eww, no. "It's really not like that with us." I watch Spence suck her lips into her mouth, uncomfortable because she's the sole member of The Squad who's clued in.

"Well, you're getting along. That's what's important, right?"

"Right." I have to remind myself that secrets aren't the same as lies.

CHAPTER THIRTY-SEVEN

I promised Avery I would start working on my college application this weekend. It's already Sunday afternoon. I get comfortable in my desk chair and plunge headlong into it. I've visited the MassArt website before and it is everything I anticipated from a fine arts school—bright hues, bold fonts, dramatic video intros on every page. This visit, I click the Apply link. Undergraduate. There are fifty-two friggin' sub-links below it: Applicant Types, Deadlines, Standards, Financial Aid, Portfolio Tips. I know the deadlines. My grades meet the standards. Financial aid comes later. Portfolio tips are what I'm here for—I decided against e-mailing Sara Roscoe. It felt wrong to ask her for advice when I have no intention of applying to BU. If I'm not accepted to MassArt, I'll stick with my original plan—community college. Two years at North Shore or Bunker Hill cost a fifth of one semester at most of the universities in Boston. I could always re-apply to MassArt after I earn an associate's degree elsewhere.

The portfolio requirement is fifteen to twenty pieces that demonstrate my 'strength and uniqueness as an artist.' They want me to show them the world from my perspective. Hahaha. How do I see this place mankind calls home? It can be ugly—violent, unfair and unforgiving, which makes the beauty in it stand out so ferociously, streaks of color in an achromatic mural. What makes it beautiful? Happiness. Sadness. Tenacity. Vulnerability. Kindness. Friendship. Love. Avery. I have to include photos of her in my collection. She's transformed my point of view. My favorite color isn't grey anymore; I have two new ones: the blue topaz of her irises and the soft pink of her aura when she smiles.

Very soon it's going to become very difficult for me to keep myself from dropping the L word first, in spite of how terrified I am to be feeling it at all. Why wouldn't I be terrified? The people who were supposed to love me never did, so how could I begin to know how to do it properly? Love really is a volcano, and lava destroys everything it touches. I couldn't stomach it if I destroyed this.

Focus. Application form. Click. Here we go.

Avery corners me in the bathroom as I'm in the middle of my post-dinner teeth-cleaning routine. She observes me in silence for the longest time.

I hold the toothbrush in my left cheek, chomp down on the bristles. "Whrt?"

"Did you finish your application?"

"Nrp. Pics ned wrk."

"Okay. Another thing."

"Hmm?"

"The Fall Ball."

It's been three freaking days since I asked… my anxiety over it hasn't been killing me or anything. How sneaky of her to bring it up now. I can't reply with a mouthful of toothpaste and saliva. "Urnhurh?"

She lets out a gusty breath. "We're going."

I don't care that she'll see me being gross; I remove the toothbrush from my gob and spit the foamy mess into the sink. "Duh." Spell it out for me like I've only got two living brain cells. I need to hear it in no uncertain terms.

"We're going together."

"I see. You mean like on a date?"

"Omg." She rolls her eyes and wipes a bit of gunk from the side of my mouth. "Yes, like on a date." Her vibe changes in an instant. "If it's seriously okay with you, I might take you up on the offer to sit out the slow songs." She's shamefaced. She shouldn't be. It was my brainwave to begin with. It seems to me that slow dancing is overly affectionate—something people do at weddings to exhibit the seriousness of their relationships. A high school dance could do without them; there's no need for kids our age to be that ostentatious.

"I don't like the idea of slow dancing, anyway." *Not that you've ever tried it.* I will. In the future. Possibly. When she's open to it.

"I shouldn't have made you wait so long. I was being selfish, pretending that I didn't understand why it mattered whether or not it was an official date. I know it's special, your first dance. It's natural that you'd want to go with your girlfriend. I'm sorry I'm such a shitty one."

"You are not a shitty girlfriend, you've got stuff. Complex emotional stuff. I don't mind being in the closet so much. It's not bad in here, as long as you're with me."

"God, I really… mmm." She wraps her arms around my torso and kisses me. Her lips are plump with tenderness and some other unnamable thing. Whatever it is, I like it a lot. It's an extra bit of warmth, another log on the fire we're stoking. She follows it up with a broad smile.

I push her bangs behind her ears. "While you're in such a good mood, I should tell you that I plan to use some of the photos I took of you for my MassArt submission."

"The ones in the park?" She looks okay with it, natural. It's not a strained attempt at stoicism. She was wrong the other day—neither one of us has a handle on reading the other; both of our walls are coming down, brick by brick. There are still a few layers left to dismantle.

"Yes. Is that alright with you?"

"Will they help you get in?"

I was already in love with her then—the camera knew before I did, captured the truth without my consent. The sheer candor of those portraits... They'll be the reason I get in. "I think they will."

"Well then, you had better use them." She strokes my cheek.

"Yes, ma'am."

CHAPTER THIRTY-EIGHT

"It's mad cute. He jumps up and does karate moves whenever Michelangelo is on screen," Olivia tells us between bites of her sandwich. Her eight-year-old brother, Mikey, has formed an obsession with the Teenage Mutant Ninja Turtles; the orange-masked character is his favorite due to their shared name. "He knows every word of the theme song and sings it all the time. He's driving my parents batshit."

"The 'heroes in a half shell' line is weird," I blurt. "That's not unique to fictional mutant turtles; real turtles have half shells. Also, they're not turtles, they're tortoises—they're always on land."

Mack goes, "*Umm?* Arguable. They live in a sewer. Lots of water around."

"There's that, too! Neither turtles nor tortoises inhabit the underground of New York City, rats do—it's only a logical home for Splinter."

"Should they rent an apartment?"

Hannah's entertained by the back-and-forth. Olivia's chortling. Spence smacks her lips together. "You're debating the realism of a cartoon about giant talking reptiles who were raised by a giant talking rodent and are experts in martial arts. Are you guys high?" She giggles.

"I may have toked up before class this morning," Mack replies, straight-faced.

"Gimme a break. I want to be a wildlife photographer, okay? I'm clearly very into animals."

"Quick question, ladies," Noah interjects. He's got his phone in his hand. "The limo company e-mailed me. They wanna know how many stops the driver's gotta make. Are we all gonna meet up at Hannah's?"

The dance... We've hardly discussed it. That's why I'm certain my friends are different from all the other girls at school, who won't shut up about it and it's still a week and a half away.

I seek out Avery across the cafeteria. She's mid-chat with Amy and Jason, but it's like she intuits that I'm scoping her. We catch each other's eyes. She's a hundred feet away from me, but her smile has me seeing stars.

"Ground control to Brit," says Hannah.

"Huh?"

Noah scratches his scruffy chin. "Are you bringing a date?"

"I'm going with Avery."

Spence side-eyes me.

"And her friends. Sorry, I should've said something sooner. I'll still chip in my share for the limo." It's going to be murder on my bank account; nonetheless it's the right thing to do.

"No worries." He waves me off. "We were expecting twelve, but they only had a ten-seater, so we're chill."

He's not the most talkative, or the sharpest, but he is nice. I can see why Avery liked him.

The whole 'conversation over dinner around the dining room table' thing is actually pretty great. Tom and Cate are always attentive. They care about how our days went, about how each other's days went. I missed it that week Tom was in Japan. When he got home, we fell right back into it, like a family.

Tonight's discussion is heavier than an average Wednesday's; there are a bunch of topics to cover. Cate's firm is taking on a high-profile case—some pro footballer got caught cheating on his wife with a porn star. There was photo evidence of the affair slapped all over the tabloids. The wife, Cate's client, is petitioning for divorce and aiming to suck every last drop of blood from her husband's body; we unanimously support this endeavor. Cheaters are the worst.

Tom's new game, *Terror in the Streets*, a zombie-hunting first-person shooter, is going live on Black Friday. It tested well, especially in the Asian and European markets, but there are still glitches to iron out. His staff is in a frenzy.

Avery and I received the results of all of our midterms. Her GPA went up to 3.9. Mine dropped to 3.75, brought down by a B in Tennis, which I'm lucky to have gotten as I am a bumbling oaf who can barely get the ball over the net.

She has completed and submitted her application to Northeastern. My MassArt app is almost finished. I'm still trying to choose the last five photos for my portfolio. I'm leaning toward a few that I took of Salem's various historic graveyards on Halloween; the eeriness of them stands out from the ordinariness of the rest—a touch of pretty-ugly to counterbalance the conventional beauty. "It's weird, this year feels like it's flying and dragging simultaneously," I comment.

Cate gets it. "That happens when there are big changes on the horizon. It's excitement mixed with a hint of fear."

"Damn, Mom, you're like a philosopher," Avery sniggers.

"Hey! Your Fall Ball is next weekend, isn't it?" Tom questions.

Avery pushes some string beans around her plate with her fork. "Yup."

"Are you excited?" He elbows his daughter in the teasing way dads in movies do.

"I don't have anything to wear!" Avery's tone is whinier than I'm used to, and it's such a stereotypical teenage girl thing to say. It's darling coming from her.

Cate's amused by it, too. "There's an easy fix for that. I'll give you my credit card and you two can go shopping this weekend. Take your friends, have a girls' day!" To me she says, "I'd offer to come with you, but she gets flustered when I gush over dresses."

"We'll go on our own. I don't want anyone to see my dress until the day of the dance."

Smart. Girls at our school live by the credo 'imitation is the sincerest form of flattery.' Everyone wants to copy the Queen Bee. Their efforts are fruitless; no one measures up to Avery.

Tom's eyes bug out as if he was smashed in the head with a baseball bat. "Are you going with boys? Because I'll need to meet them first." He flexes his right bicep. "Fatherly duties and such." He's joking, and sort of isn't.

It's awesome that someone's eager to take on fatherly duties for me. *And you wanna bang his daughter.* Fuck a duck…

Avery cracks. It's a miniscule wince, imperceptible unless you were watching for it. Unlucky for her, I was watching for it. "There will be boys at the dance. Neither of us is going with one." She glances my way.

I never did get around to coming out to Tom and Cate. Here's my opportunity. How to phrase it? *'I'm a vagitarian.'* "I'm a va—lesbian!"

Cate is unbothered. "I sussed that out. Kudos for telling us."

Tom feigns dejection. "I can't have a fatherly man-to-man talk with a girl." He looks to his wife. "It's up to you, hun."

Cate reaches across the table and pats his hand. "I think we already know her girlfriend."

Avery's soul vaults out of her body, and I'm pretty sure I'm having a stroke.

"Who, who?" Tom prods his wife, giddy as a schoolgirl.

"Valerie Spencer."

The name is a defibrillator for Avery's stopped heart. She's relieved Cate didn't say, *Our daughter*—as am I—though annoyed that she said Spence.

It makes sense. Spence is the only person Cate's seen me hang out with. If I let her stand uncorrected, Avery will not be pleased. "I'm not, we're, she's… no. She's a girl and she's my friend. Regular friend." *Brain is damaged, send help!*

Cate shows a pout. "That's too bad. You'd make a cute couple."

Oh God, that's just going to make it worse. Avery's anger is rising. What a raw nerve to poke! She pushes her chair away from the table and snatches her plate. "Thanks for the nosh, Mom."

I do the same. "Yeah, thanks, Cate." We don't thank her enough.

I shadow Avery into the kitchen. The saloon-style panel doors swing open and closed.

"That blew." She tosses her silverware into the sink.

I misinterpreted her reaction. She wasn't angry, she was upset. A smidge green, but more covetous of my openness, of Spence's, that led her parents to assume we were dating.

You could have come clean. Oh my God, what? Why would I suggest that? I like being close to her; I like having a warm place to sleep and adults who give a shit about me. They're fine with me being gay, but me seducing their kid is an altogether different thing. Who knows how that would go over? Set aside the violation of their trust; I'm a mudlark with nothing to my name and an uncertain future. They have a kingdom, and she is their heir—what if they find me unsuitable?

I can't worry about this now. I have to say something comforting. *Better make it good.* 'I love you' would be good. *Not that!* "You don't ever have to be jealous of anyone. I'm yours. Entirely. You know that, right?"

"I do now."

She should've known it ages ago. She isn't clairvoyant, after all. I have to use my words more often. "I'm happy exactly as we are. I don't need anything or anyone else but you."

The Lip Bite™. "You have to go upstairs. Double-time." She steps closer to me, whispers in my ear, "I want to kiss you."

I scramble out of the kitchen and jet up to her room.

CHAPTER THIRTY-NINE

Dress shopping comes in third on the 'Top 10 Ways to Torture Britton' list. Having to spend more than half a minute in a small space comes first, and root canals are second.

On the flip side, Avery is thrilled. Moreover, she's basking in it. We killed an hour in Nordstrom, another hour in Neiman Marcus—she did find a Versace cocktail dress she really liked there, but it was $2,700, and she scoffed at that price tag. She made an adorable *gah!* noise and said, "Not for something I'm going to wear once."

She decides to stray from the department stores and take a stab at the handful of smaller shops. Jessica Sereja Designs is the third store we visit. The instant we stroll in, she gasps and gravitates toward a fuchsia-to-rose gold ombre sequined mini dress; it's singular, one of a kind. She inspects it, front and back, checks the price tag and beams. "This is it." It's dress number four of the day, although she wasn't this certain about any of the others.

"Try it on." I don't have to see her in it to know it's going to make her blue eyes pop like whoa.

She steps out of the dressing room and strikes a pose, hand on her hip, elbow bent—straight out of a fashion magazine. "What do you think?"

The dress was pretty on the hanger; it is breathtaking on her. It hugs her curves in all the right places. The plunging neckline shows enough cleavage to qualify as scandalous. She's got C-cups, at minimum. Argh. The short hemline is also something to behold. I lean forward in my chair. "I think that is a dangerous dress."

A suggestive grin. "Does it make you want to get me out of it?"

Yep, right here, if I'm honest.

"Your face right now!" She points at me, doubles over laughing. "This is definitely the one."

I'm carrying her garment bag. And the bag containing her sparkly new Jimmy Choo pumps. This is what the boyfriend in hetero couples must feel like—a pack mule. *Please, you love it.*

"You haven't looked at any dresses yet and I know why," she says.

"Let's hear it."

"At first I thought it was because you didn't want to use my mom's credit card, but you're also not a dress kind of girl."

Nailed it. The whole damn thing. "Correct on both counts."

"My mom will be pissed if you don't let her pay for your outfit, so that's settled." Her mouth twists like it does sometimes when she's working on logarithms. "I have a solution to the dress problem!" She takes my hand, entwines our fingers and drags me to the nearest escalator. We're in a congested-ass mall, in the middle of the afternoon on a Saturday. Does she realize that she's holding onto me, or was it a spur of the moment reaction to her excitement? *She knows her friends won't be here. Football.* And mine aren't the type to hang out in a place like this.

"Where are you taking me?" It could be to the seventh layer of hell; I don't care as long as her hand is in mine.

"You'll see when we get there."

*

We go into a store called Spruce. It's way more my style. The clothes here are dapper, tailored for women who prefer a more masculine approach to formalwear.

We're greeted by an employee who gives us a chipper, "Hi! Can I help you ladies find something?" She ogles us, spends a significant amount of time on our clasped hands. Heat rises in my chest as I steal a glimpse of Avery. She understands that this woman has us pegged and still does not let go of me. *Is this... Are you Winning?*

Avery goes, "She needs a three-piece, Mandarin collar on the blazer if you have it, and"—she takes a gander around the store, points to a collarless button-down—"that shirt."

The woman and I share a look. We're both flabbergasted. "Dang, girl, you want an application?" she asks.

I chuckle.

"What color suit are you looking for?"

Avery leaves that up to me. I consult her anyway. "You want me to say white, don't you?"

Now she's flabbergasted. "How did you know that?"

"It complements fuchsia." I wink at her, make a *click* with my tongue.

"You guys are too cute. What size are you?"

"Four," Avery and I reply in unison. I am agog. She shrugs. "I've spent months checking you out."

Holy shit, she said that aloud, clear as water! All I can manage to stammer out is, "As long as I don't have to wear a tie."

"No collar, no tie," Avery responds with a smile.

My blazer, shirt—both collarless per Avery's request—and pants are a crisp ivory. I've chosen a silk mint waistcoat for a splash of color; I could've picked a fuchsia one, but didn't want to match her—too obvious for a school function. I'm standing in front of the full-length mirror in the fitting room, tugging on the jacket, checking myself out from different angles. *Not bad.* Not bad, hell! This thing was made for me.

"Come on, I wanna see!" Avery calls through the curtain.

I step out into the waiting area, hands in my pants-pockets.

Her stare is penetrating—pupils dilated, mouth ever-so-slightly open. I've seen this look from her before—lust. We're humming the same tune. "You like?"

She gives me a slow nod. "Mmhmm. A lot."

"I'll take it," I call to the clerk. I don't give a good goddamn what it costs, wrap this bitch up, it's mine.

As we're leaving the store, I take her hand. She allows it without a balk. We walk, digits laced together, all the way to the car. "I'm a little surprised by this..." I tap my pointer finger against her knuckle.

"Girls hold hands with their friends all the time."

Girls like us are rarely friends—a girl as femme as her and one who's so noticeably... Olivia said it best: full homo. When we hold hands, we look like a lesbian couple. I know she knows that. "The woman at Spruce probably isn't the only person who guessed that we're more than friends today."

"You're more important to me than the opinions of strangers. I have to show you that."

"I l—" *Nope.* "I like that. Thank you."

"Me, too. And you're welcome."

CHAPTER FORTY

The week is a blur. It's already Friday afternoon. I'm thankful that my midterm exams are over. If they'd have been this week, I'd have flunked every one of them. I did manage to finish up my college app. I submitted it about two minutes ago; it's whirring its way across the interwebs to some admission rep's inbox. *Ever the plucky conqueror.* Nothing left to do but wait. Here's to dreaming big! It's the sole productive thing I've done in the past six days. I was useless in Photography Club yesterday. We went around the room showcasing some of our portraits, and I couldn't come up with anything to say about mine—the pics of the jellyfish women from Halloween night.

The buzz about the Fall Ball has been all-consuming; none of my teachers managed to friggin' teach anything because none of the senior girls were interested in learning anything. Christ, how bad is it going to be come May when Prom rolls around? The literal Last Dance for us. If I'm this nervous about a semi-formal, I'll flatline over Prom.

I am stupid nervous. It's preposterous. I survived an emotionally abusive foster home where I virtually lived in a cupboard, another foster home where the mom doled out slaps like she was the Tooth Fairy's evil cousin the Smack Fairy, a psycho foster sister who kicked puppies and despised me so much that I was afraid to sleep in our shared bedroom, and a group home where I was the lone resident who didn't have a juvenile criminal record for assault… yet here I am, shitting myself because I'm going to a dance tomorrow. It's made me realize that I am incapable of being normal. I've taught myself to believe that normalcy is overrated, that because I had an atypical childhood, I'll be better prepared than my peers to deal with real world grown-up stuff. Who'd have thought that something as natural and grown-up as falling in love would screw me up?

The problem is that I want the night to be perfect, but I know nothing ever is. Perfection doesn't exist.

Isn't there something about flowers that I'm supposed to take care of? Eddie covered it in a tutorial. *Corsage, dingus.* That's it! Corsage, or wristlet. Corsages are the things that get pinned to the gown, right? No, that'll leave holes in her pretty, pretty dress. Wristlet, then. Fuck, will I even be able to get one this late? Why didn't I think of this sooner?

I check the time—four twenty-two—and get to googling. The nearest florist, Sweet Somethings, is half a mile away. It closes at five. *Run your ass.*

I fly down the steps, nearly ram into Avery at the bottom and cause her to spill a bit of the drink she has in her hand. "Shit, Scrawny! Where's the fire?"

"Sorry!" Her parents aren't home. I give her a kiss. Screw the undercover protocol, I almost killed her. "I'm... going for a jog." *In a pair of jeans?*

"Oh-kay." She doesn't call shenanigans even though she knows she could.

I'm sweaty and winded. *Compose yourself, you have business to conduct.* I strip off my hoodie, tie it around my waist and rest my arms on my head to catch my breath. I gotta start working out, this is pathetic.

Sweet Somethings' automated glass doors swish open. A middle-aged blonde woman in a blue apron holding a tall exotic potted plant appears before me. "Hello," she greets me as she places the pot down on a tiered display riser. "Are you picking up an order?"

I read her name tag: Andy. "No. I need to place one. It's last minute."

"I'll see what I can do for you. Come on in." The shop is teeming with flowers and plants. I feel like I've stepped into the Secret Garden; it's otherworldly. "What is it you're looking for?"

"A wrist corsage."

"Ah. You must go to Beverly High. We've been taking corsage and boutonniere orders for weeks."

"Yeah. I'm new at this. I, uh, forgot to get one for my girl-friend." Huh. That's the first time I've referred to Avery that way to anyone.

"Oh, dear. You'll be single by tomorrow night!"

Lol. "You see my problem."

"What's her favorite flower?"

I know this! She's mentioned it before. "Stargazer lilies."

"And what color is she wearing?"

"An offensively bright pink."

She chuckles. "A stargazer will pair beautifully." She opens the door of a refrigerated case, plucks out a large lily, two small white roses, a sprig of greenery and a handful of baby's breath, then arranges them. "How's this? Wrapped in pink and white ribbon."

It's very Avery. "She'll love it."

"Great. I'll set it. Give me a few minutes." She vanishes behind the counter into a back room where another woman is putting together a colorful bouquet.

"Here you are. Keep it somewhere cool until you give it to her." She hands me the wristlet in a plastic container.

I stare at it. *Elegant.* "How much do I owe you?"

"Nothing. Don't tell my wife." She winks, signals at the back room.

I get it; she sees her younger self in me. I see an older version of myself in her. Someday I'm going to be a blonde middle-aged woman who has a wife. Whoa, that's gonna be wicked. "Thank you."

"You're welcome. Enjoy your dance."

I turn to leave, then pause. "Um, actually, can I get a bag for this, please?"

It must be an odd request; her brow furrows. Flowers are meant to be seen.

Whatcha gonna say, 'I'm fucking my foster sister so I have to hide it if I wanna surprise her?' I'm not fucking her. I'll never 'fuck' her; that implies sex without emotional attachment, which would not be possible with Avery. "If you have a bag, that is."

She reaches under the counter and presents me with a plain brown paper sack. "Good luck."

CHAPTER FORTY-ONE

Avery and her mom are getting their nails done. Afterward, they're going to a salon. Avery refused to tell me what hairstyle she's chosen. I know she'll be stunning however she wears it. Cate asked me weeks ago when she made the appointments if I wanted to join them. Avery knew my answer before I gave it.

I should've gone. Waiting around the house has me anxious as hell. *It's gonna be a long afternoon.* Tom detects it—for a man, he's remarkably in tune with women; he was meant to be a father of daughters. He's on the couch, working on his laptop. He slips his headphones down around his neck. "Hey, kiddo, mind giving this sequence a play-through and letting me know about any glitches? I've been looking at it too damn long."

It's bullshit, but I adore him for it. "No problem."

He takes his headphones off, hands them to me and shifts the laptop onto my knees. "Use the arrow keys to run, the trackpad to aim the gun and tap it to fire."

"Cool."

I'm no gamer. Still, I welcome the distraction. The graphics are high definition—buildings on fire, plumes of smoke stretching toward the sky, horrified people fleeing the city, gnarly zombies zooming at you from every direction. The scenes are immersive, intensified by the soundtrack of dissonant string instruments and heart-pounding beats. The gameplay is smooth, good for a novice. No glitches whatsoever. He might be a genius. *He's going to make a shitload of money on this.* Good for him, doing what he loves and making bank for it. I can only hope to be so fortunate.

Avery and Cate arrive home around four. She manages to dodge me; I don't get to see her until she's all dolled up. She yells to me from the top of the stairs, "We're leaving at seven!"

Three. Whole. Hours.

We meet in the hallway outside our bedrooms. The first thing I focus on is her hair—a rose gold and diamond headband, loose curls flowing down her shoulders and her back, like a caramel waterfall. Next is her makeup: glittery, bright-pink smoky eye, black mascara, a hint of wing to her eyeliner. *Her eyes are unbelievable.* Soft pink cheeks and a slick, neutral lipstick. Draped around her neck is a simple laureate necklace with a pink teardrop-shaped pearl resting in her cleavage, and the shorter chain with Reese's crown ring on it. Then, the dress… "I'm calling the police. You're trying to kill me."

Her left eyebrow arches. "Have you seen yourself?"

I'm wearing a little makeup. My hair is straightened and slicked back in a low ponytail, a gender-bended Prince Charming. From the way she's gawping at me, I know all of it was the right decision. She steps to me, fingers the top button of my waistcoat. "I'm in trouble."

"You might be." *Forgetting something?* "Oh! Wait." I dip back into my room, grab the plastic clamshell container from the bag on my desk.

Her eyes bulge at the sight of the corsage. "When did you get—"

"Last night, that 'jog' I took." She's getting teary-eyed. "Don't cry, Babygirl, you'll ruin your makeup." I slide the band onto her left wrist.

She gambles on a kiss. I can't—don't—stop her. "I love it."

"I knew you would."

"Avery, Britton, it's getting late!" Cate hollers from below. "Ready?"

"Yes," she replies.

"You're both so beautiful!" Cate squeals as we reach the landing.

Tom is in hyper-dad mode, snapping picture after picture of us with his cell phone.

"Dad, please."

"Just a few! For posterity."

Avery rolls her eyes at his dorkiness, but complies. We pose beside each other, smiling.

"Let's get one with all of us together," Tom says. He sets the autotimer and props the phone up on the console table, then rushes to the stairs. We all cram in close to each other, Tom next to Avery and Cate next to me. A red light blinks three times. "Everybody smile!" The flash goes off. He hurries back to the table, scoops up the phone and examines the photo. "Looks great!" He shows it to me. It does. We look like a family.

"I wish Reese were here," Avery says, not melancholic, simply conscious of her absence.

Tom squeezes her shoulder. "She is, honey. In our hearts."

The moment is ruined when Cate notices the corsage on Avery's wrist. "That's lovely."

Major oversight! I was so excited about the prospect of buying her flowers—I've never done that for anyone—that I didn't stop to think about appearances.

Avery covers my ass. "I figured I deserved it, even if I'm going solo." She is damn clever. It smarts: People buy flowers for their significant others all the time, a proud display of affection, yet I can't. Another 'maybe someday.'

A car horn blares outside. Cate and Tom see us out.

*

There's a long white stretch Hummer limo at the curb. I goggle Avery. "You didn't leave anything for Prom."

"This wasn't me, it was Amy. It's the squad's last Fall Ball."

I didn't realize how much this not-quite-Homecoming dance means to the jocks. On a scale of one to ten, Spence's enthusiasm over it comes in at a solid six. Then again, she's more levelheaded than most. "I understand that." I open the door, usher her inside, and climb in after her.

"Have a good time!" Cate calls to us. Tom waves.

The inside of the Hummer might as well be a night club. There are blacklights built into the interior roof and floor, and the music is pumping through the speakers at a deafening volume. It's Amy and Jason, Liz, Kylie, Tasha and her 'Bae' whose name I can't remember, Kevin, and another cheerleader, Isabelle.

The drive to Carriage House takes fifteen minutes, though feels much longer. All I want to do is hold Avery's hand, like Amy and Jason, and Tasha and 'Bae' are doing. I won't reach for her in front of her friends. I beam, make small talk and laugh to keep myself preoccupied.

Carriage House is, in a word, grandiose. It's a château-style building surrounded by a tall iron fence. There's a gilded fountain near its entrance. Lots of kids are already clambering for photos. Any other time I'd be among them, but I left my Nikon at home. Avery is too exquisite to keep looking at through a viewfinder. I want my eyes to capture her, burn the memory of her and this night into my mind.

We pile inside the grand lobby—there's a four-tiered crystal chandelier hanging from the ceiling between two winding, marble staircases. A maître d' in full penguin suit greets us, "Welcome to Carriage House. Upstairs to the Great Hall, please."

The lights in the Great Hall are low, and the whole room is decorated in our school colors—fabric streamers extending from the chandelier in the center of the room to all the corners, four intricately braided balloon arches, one on each side of the square dancefloor. The round tables are adorned with layered black and orange cloths and topped with towering centerpieces of bright, exotic flowers. There are laser lights flashing. The music is blaring. It's like something out of a movie. I'm overwhelmed by it.

"You okay?" Avery asks.

"This is surreal." I hear the astonishment in my voice.

She gives my arm a rub, then says to everyone, "Let's find a table."

Half an hour or so into the evening, Avery suggests I go find Spence and say hi. I was going to do that anyway, but it makes me happy that she says it. They're becoming more comfortable with each other day by day, and I'm relieved. I love both of them. Platonic love is another new concept for me; less scary, just as brilliant. I've been missing out.

I spot Spence at a table on the other side of the room with Mack, Olivia, Hannah and Noah. She's wearing a black suit with an electric blue shirt and a black skinny tie—very debonair, and she knows it. "You look fly," she says to me as I take a seat in a vacant chair beside her.

"Thanks. You're not bad yourself." Then to the others, "You all look amazing."

A round of thanks.

"Having fun?" Spence asks.

"Yep. You?"

"Yeah." She gets close to me so she can keep her voice low. "I'm glad you didn't have to come crying to me"

"So am I."

She scans the room, finds Avery on the dancefloor with Amy, Jason, and Tasha. "You're lucky. She always told me to fuck right off with my nonsense whenever I asked her to do anything date-ish. She's surer about you than she was about me."

"I'm sorry things didn't work out for you two. Mmm. Not *that* sorry."

She snickers, palms my shoulder. "Go dance with your girl."

"See you out there?"

"Definitely."

We dance and dance for what seems like hours—sometimes just the two of us, sometimes with her friends, and sometimes with mine. Every song is catchier, more infectious than the last. It occurs to me for the first time ever that I really like to dance. And I've got some pretty sick moves. At the moment, our two friend groups are mingling together on the floor—all of us having fun, no cliquey garbage getting in the way. Olivia and Kylie are werking it, and it is a spectacle. Spence and I are facing each other and Avery's behind me. I take a chance, lean my head back against her shoulder. She puts her hands on my hips! Spence gives me an eyebrow waggle. She throws her finger up, makes a little circle in the air and mouths, "Turn around."

Thanks for the hint, buddy. I got this.

I do a quick spin and am eye to eye with Avery. We sway together, our bodies obeying the push and pull of the pulsing beat. It feels like we're alone in the room. My God, the way she moves—sensual undulations, as if she was born for this. She's glimmering under the laser lights, dewy with sweat. I'm the one who's in trouble; her hips, stomach, shoulders, neck… I want to touch her, kiss her, everywhere.

The tempo shifts and throws me way off. The tune is a ballad, Christina Perri's "A Thousand Years." It's too slow for us to dance to. Shame. This is a great song.

All the groups that have been dancing together break into couples. The kids who are here stag move off the floor—it's not even a thing to second-guess for any of them. Not so much for me. I side-step in the direction of our table.

Avery clutches my elbow. "No."

"It's a slow song."

"I'm aware." That grin! Coy. She slinks her arms around my neck, holds me so close to her that I can feel the rise and fall of her chest as she breathes. I'm a train wreck; I have no idea what to do with myself. "This is the part where you put your arms around my waist." I do. She leads and I follow, step for step. *Totally her puppet.* Yes, I am. It's fantastic.

I can't stop looking at her. She doesn't take her eyes off of me, either. This is what I wanted, the most socially acceptable thing a couple can do in public. So why is there a knot in my gut—not the good kind?

A blink is all it takes; I see that every person in the room—students, teachers, wait staff—has their gaze glued to us. Spence, sitting at her table with Olivia and Mack, pumps a triumphant fist at me. Olivia's impressed. Mack is stupefied. Dancing beside us, Hannah and Noah are trying to stifle their curiosity and are failing.

"People are staring." I hitch my chin at the tables.

Avery's attention does not leave me for a millisecond. She brings her lips close to my ear. "Let them stare."

I can feel the wonderment in my eyes as I look at her again. The expression on her face; it's the same one she had on Halloween, when I stopped myself from *going there* and had to explain why.

I wish I knew how to describe it, what to call it. I'm overcome with the most intense ache to kiss her. That would be too much.

The song approaches its end, piano and violins hanging in the ether. No, not yet! I worry that its fading will make her regret her decision. It doesn't. She takes my hand, places her fingers in the spaces between mine. How seamlessly our hands fit together, as though they were made for one another, Nature's grand design. *Don't get sentimental.* Screw that. This isn't a mall full of strangers; she's declaring to the entire school that I am hers and she is mine. This is massive for me. I'm going to enjoy it.

"Ladies and gentlemen," the DJ's voice streams through the sound system, "kindly make your way to your seats; dinner is being served."

The Brigade is silent as we gather in our chairs. Liz has her elbow on the table, hand up, chin resting in her palm with her mouth hidden behind her fingers. It doesn't do much to conceal her smirk. Jason nods at me, Secret Bro Cipher for 'Respect, homie.' Tasha reaches over to Kylie and gives her shoulder a light smack. "You owe me twenty bucks, bitch!" All of Avery's friends fall into hysterics. They've known this whole damn time! An open secret. Hard to believe with this group of girls that nobody dared to inquire about it.

Avery brings my hand up to her lips, gives it a gentle kiss. And for a moment, everything in the universe is perfect.

CHAPTER FORTY-TWO

The limo ride at the end of the night is glorious. I have my arm around Avery's shoulder, and she's snuggling into me. I spy Tasha and Liz ogling us in a way that tells me they think we're sweet. They exchange quiet words and end up coming off like smug parents who've been paying too much attention to their kid and figured out something they were trying to keep hush-hush.

The Hummer drops us off around half-past midnight. I hop onto the curb first and help Avery out of the car. Amy calls after her, "Get it, you thirsty bitch!"

"Shut-the-fuck-up," she blurts, and slams the door. Even in the darkness, I can see her skin flushing.

I have no expectations. "Hey…" I snake my arm around her waist and peck her on the forehead. "No pressure."

"I know."

The lights inside the house are off, save for the nightlight at the top of the stairwell. All around us is stillness and shadow. She takes off her heels, places them near the shoe rack in the foyer. I slip my white flats from my feet and leave them next to hers.

We creep up the stairs. "Thanks for tonight," I mutter when we reach my room. "I enjoyed every minute."

"Thank you."

I give her a kiss. "Goodnight."

She lets out a low, disbelieving breath. "Seriously, that's all I get?"

"How much do you want?"

"Everything." Her hand shoots out through the dimness and she tugs me to her by my jacket. I envelop her. Her mouth is on my mouth, our tongues tangling in a graceful polonaise.

Not in my—Reese's—bedroom. *Should've booked a hotel.* Presumptuous. I push us away from my door and we shuffle, still kissing, to her room.

She closes the door behind her, presses her back to it.

If we're going to do this, I want to see her. Every. Last. Inch. I switch on the desk lamp. That lustful glare has returned. *Alright then.* I beckon her with my finger.

She's in my arms and we're kissing again. Her lips are frenzied, starving for mine. I couldn't slow her down if I wanted to.

She unbuttons my vest, my shirt, relieves me of both, and then unclasps my bra and strips that away, too. She combs over me, homes in on the long, thin scar over my heart. She goes to run her finger across it. I encircle her wrist. "Don't…"

She's surprised, but doesn't falter. "You're perfect, you hear me?"

I kiss her so hard it knocks the wind from both of us.

I shed the rest of my clothes, pull her close, unzip the back of her dress; it falls down around her feet and she kicks out of it. I'm staring at her. Perky breasts, toned abs. "You are gorgeous."

She smiles, kisses me again.

I walk her backwards to the bed. We collapse onto it. I'm on top of her, reveling in her lips, running my hands over her breasts, her stomach. My fingers creep beneath the elastic band of her panties. She tenses up.

"Maybe we should stop." I try to push myself away. She doesn't let me go.

"I don't want to stop."

I search her eyes. She means it, although there is something… "Aww, sweetie, you're nervous." I kiss her cheek.

"I'm clueless and you're so… not."

Yes, I'm experienced, but none of the other times felt this meaningful. It's like they were dress rehearsals, and it's finally opening night. "We just have to let each other know what feels good, okay?"

She nods and raises her hips, allowing me to get her fully naked.

I kiss her lips, nuzzle her cheek, nibble on her earlobe. She gasps. I lick a trail down her neck, her clavicles; brush my tongue over her nipples, her ribs, her flawless abs.

She's already breathing heavy.

I slither down her body and spread her legs. I kiss, then nip, the insides of her thighs. Closer, closer. I taste her. She's ready.

My tongue finds her sensitive spot. I tease her at first, give her time to get into it. Her muscles go taut. I go harder. Tighter, and tighter still. I start to suck.

"Harder," she murmurs. I oblige her, increase the pressure. She paws at the back of my head, pushes down a little. That's it, beautiful, show me how you like it.

She's rocking against me. Her soft moans grow more and more constant. "Don't stop. Please, Britton."

My name… Her voice, begging me. I'm not stopping; I'm gonna make damn sure she finishes.

I glide my fingers into her, work her insides to the rhythm of my tongue. I feel her throbbing. *Almost.* "Oh God. Oh my God." Her legs quiver. She pulls my hair. Clenching. *So close.* I pick up the pace. *Come on, Babygirl.* She bucks up to my mouth and her back arches. "Aaahh!" *There it is.*

She collapses, her whole body shaking. I crawl up the bed, flop down beside her—wipe the sweaty bangs out of her eyes, and then my own.

Gradually, her breathing returns to normal.

I grin. "That was the best orgasm of my life, and it wasn't even mine." A cackle charges out of her and I quickly cover her mouth. "Shhh. Your parents!" I say through my own tittering.

She quiets down, pulls my hand away. She kisses me and wicks the remnants of herself from my lips. "There's something I want to try."

"What it is?"

She whispers it into my ear as though the walls might overhear her.

I'm impressed. "That's advanced."

"I saw it in a porn once. It got me so turned on…" She blushes. No reason for that anymore. "Let's do it."

"Yeah?" Her eyes sparkle with anticipation. She scooches up the mattress, plumps a pillow under her head.

I get on my knees, straddle her shoulders and steady myself against the wire headboard. "You're sure?" I look down at her.

She's glaring at my pelvis, biting her lip. "Hell yes, I am." She wraps her arms around my thighs and thrusts her face into me.

My body doesn't wait for my brain to give it directions, just starts grinding against her. She releases my legs, reaches up, cups my breasts, massages me. Pinches. *God!*

She's making circles with her tongue on the most incredible spot. "Right there." I'm about to say, 'a little faster,' but she speeds the cadence—just a touch—on her own. It's as if we've done this a thousand times before, like she already knows exactly what it takes to get me off. "Yes, like that!"

She has me panting. My knuckles are white, wrapped so tightly around the bedrail. I'm not going to last much longer. The tension inside me is building and building. All of my muscles feel ready to snap. I'm starting to quake. Heat spreads to every corner of my being. *Oh shit, I'm gonna…* "Fuck, Avery!"

That's it. I'm spent. My breath is ragged. I fall sideways off of her.

She turns to me. I watch her lick her lips. She slings her arm across my torso and wrenches me to her. "That was intense."

"I'll say, Jesus."

"Did you really co—"

"Yes!"

She looks so proud of herself. She should be. I kiss her shoulder.

We're quiet for a long time, folded around each other. I play with her hair, wrap wispy tresses of it round my fingers. I am so content. Sex is different—better—when you're in love. I don't think I'll ever get enough of her. "Ready for round two?"

Her eyes go wide. "Ro—round two?"

"Unless you don't have the stamina." *Challenge proposed.*

She pushes herself up on her elbow and squints at me. "Oh, you gonna learn today."

Challenge accepted! I kiss her, whisper into her mouth, "Show me what you got."

CHAPTER FORTY-THREE

I jolt awake. My body is hot, even though I am bare-ass nude. Last night we... Twice. *And you're still in her bed.* Shit! We fell asleep! I throw the covers off, attempt to get up, but she grabs my forearm.

"Don't panic. It's still early." She motions to her nightstand. The digital clock reads *6:19.* "Good morning." She leans in, kisses me. It is a very good morning. She rakes her fingers through my tousled hair. "You're precious when you're sleeping, all curled up in a tiny ball."

I have to smile at that. "How long have you been awake?"

"Not long." She sucks in her bottom lip.

"Are you—" *Regretting it?* "Alright?" She was so into it last night, but...

"I'm great. I was—could you hold me? Just for a little bit."

It's Sunday morning. We have at least an hour before Tom and Cate get up. I lie flat on my back, open my arms wide. She crashes into them and I embrace her. She nuzzles her nose against my neck. I feel her breath and sweet, tender kisses on my skin. I could do this, want to do this, every morning until the end of days.

"Do you know the first thing I noticed about you when my parents brought you home?"

"My cute ass?"

She chuckles. "That was the second thing. The first was your eyes, golden brown, like honey. I thought they were beautiful. And sad." She lifts her head, cups my cheek and makes me look at her. "They're better now. I don't ever want to see them like that again, because I..." She hesitates, but only for an instant. "I love you."

My eyes well up without warning. The tears are rolling down my face before I have the chance to blink them away. No one has ever said those words to me. I didn't realize how much I longed to hear them until I heard them; I was incomplete before and now I'm whole. "Say it again."

"I love you."

"One more time."

She wipes at my sodden eyes. "I. Love. You."

I kiss her so deeply. I can't not.

Then there's the sound of the door swooshing open, Cate cooing, "Knock, knock! How was the—"

CHAPTER FORTY-FOUR

Holy-fucking-shit! *That's right, the bedroom doors don't lock.* I move away from Avery faster than I have ever moved in my life. My breath leaves my body with such swiftness I am sure I am going to die right here on her bed, naked as the day I was born.

"Mom!" She yanks the sheet over herself, grips it so firmly that her fists are red.

Cate's expression… Shock and confusion. There's no disgust, but that's cold comfort. "Both of you, living room. Five minutes." She disappears.

Avery leaps to her feet, claws for a T-shirt from the pile of folded laundry on her desk chair. Her face is a death mask. "That did not just happen. I did not get caught again."

I'm standing next to her now. "I'm so sorry. I should've gone back to my room when I first woke up."

"I asked you to stay." She touches my face, then gives me a neon green shirt and a pair of white short-shorts. "Let's get this over with."

"It'll be okay." Please, God or Zeus or Jupiter or Whoever, it has to be okay!

Cate and Tom are next to each other on the couch. Avery and I are on the love seat. Tom is uneasy, studying me as I sport his daughter's clothes. Cate is trying her hardest to keep her features unreadable.

It's working. She leans forward, clasps her hands together, points at us with her index fingers. "What did I walk in on?"

Like she doesn't know. Of course she does; she wants confirmation. *She wants honesty.*

Avery's jaw is clenched tight. I can hardly look at Cate or Tom; forget about speaking. Anyway, I should leave it up to Avery to decide what she wants to tell them, a lie or the truth. We're not in school surrounded by kids whose judgments can aggravate but not actually damage her. Her parents are the most important people in her life; she needs and loves them.

They need and love her—she is their only surviving child, and they'll make decisions based on what they feel is best for her. I'm uniquely qualified to say all of this with certainty.

Silence has clamped its ugly maw down on the room and is consuming us—a slow, painful death. What kind of lie could explain away being naked in bed together, and me kissing her?

"Alright," Cate continues, "I'll tell you what I think, and you tell me if I'm wrong." *Objection, leading the witness!* "I think the two of you had sex last night, and I walked in on the morning after. Is that correct?"

Tom fidgets.

Avery inhales noisily. I can see her gathering every scrap of courage she can find. She closes her eyes, opens them, exhales. "Yes."

"How long has this been going on?"

"We've been together more than a month, but last night was the first time we were *together*."

Tom makes that *puffpuffpuff* sound, air being blown out through loosely closed lips.

Avery rubs her forehead, and her truth comes spilling out of her like it's impossible to suppress: "I'm in love with her. She sees me, the real me, and I see her. I know this isn't what either of you were expecting or hoping for. I couldn't help it. It wasn't going to be any other way."

Cate nods and nods and nods. "Britton, do you have anything to say?"

Avery and I look at each other. There are tears in her eyes. I will not lose her. I don't want to lose Tom and Cate, either. If I have to choose who I get to keep, it's going to be Avery—no question. I've lived this long without parents, without a home, and I've been fine. I won't be fine without her. I scoop her hand into mine and squeeze it. "I love you." Those words seem insufficient, pale compared to the intensity of the color she's brought to my life; I don't know any better ones. To Cate and Tom, I say, "I need you to know I'm not going to give her up. I understand if that means I can't live here anymore. Where I sleep at night doesn't matter to me. She does. That's... That's it."

Tom's brow wrinkles as he digests my mini speech. Then, he smiles at me. It's the most jarring smile I have ever received. "I'm glad that you feel the same way about each other, and I want you both to be happy." He stops, glances at his wife. "We have to set some new rules."

These are Tom and Cate's rules, for which Cate, in true lawyer fashion, draws up an actual document: 1) If either of us is in the other's bedroom when they are home, the door to said bedroom is to remain open. 2) Sleepovers in each other's bedrooms are not permitted, as they wouldn't be if either or both of us were boys. Addendum, per Avery's dispute: Sleepovers on the couch are permissible, provided complete abstinence from 'funny business.' Cuddling while fully clothed does not meet the definition of 'funny business,' and is acceptable. 3) They do not want to know what we get up to when they are not home. 4) When our bedroom doors are closed, they will knock and wait for a response before entering. 5) If we break the first rule under full knowledge of their whereabouts, or the second rule under any circumstance, there will be hell to pay.

I find all of these fair and agreeable. Being told to pack my bags and get the fuck out would've been fair and agreeable, too, so this is nothing short of a miracle.

Avery has no complaints. "Anything else?"

"Yes. No more lying to us," Cate says. "You should understand now how unnecessary it is. There's nothing you could tell us that would make us love you any less. Either of you."

They... Love me. Gulp. *Cry if you must.*

Avery gives her a headshake. "No more lying."

Tom slaps his knees. "Well, I need a glass of wine."

"It's eight in the morning, dear."

"Irish coffee it is." He hops up. "Anyone else?"

Cate, Avery and I raise our hands.

"Drinks all around." He points at Avery. "Your car keys are staying on the hook today."

"I'm good with that."

I love this family. I really do. Someday, I'm going to find the guts to tell them.

CHAPTER FORTY-FIVE

Everyone is talking about us at school on Monday. I know because every time I walk into a room the conversations get hushed. It was wicked fun this morning when we strolled into English class holding hands; I thought some of the boys were gonna bust in their jeans. *Hornt up tools.* It's like no one has ever seen two girls together in real life—untrue, because there are other gay couples at this school—and they're letting their Pornhub-hive mind run wild. No one's shocked by the homosexuality, they're shocked because it's Avery, and probably because she's with me. I can understand that. We're very different, aesthetically. People can't see how much we have in common on the inside.

I haven't had a chance to talk to my friends about it yet. I opt to ignore all the kids gawping at me in the cafeteria and bring it up to them at lunch. "I'm just gonna put it on the table. Is everyone cool with my girlfriend?" I love saying that word out loud. And to an audience! It's magical, an immediate mood-brightener.

"Frankly, my dear, I don't give a damn," Mack responds, then pops a celery stick into her mouth.

I snort. "How long have you been waiting to use that line?"

"Girl, for-fucking-ever."

Olivia goes, "I did not see that shit coming. But you look happy, sis, so I'm happy for you."

Hannah says, "I had a feeling there was something going on. You're cute together."

"She didn't tell me she was into chicks, too." Noah shrugs. "Not tryna be gross or anything, but you guys are mad sexy."

"You're a caveman." Mack glowers at him.

Hannah sniggers. "She's gotcha there."

Spence smiles at me. She is never going to tell them that she and Avery were a thing. She's gotten over too much pain to dredge it up again with all the questions she'd have to field. Also, she's the type of person who likes to look forward, not back. I hope someday she meets someone who makes her deliriously happy. She deserves that.

My friends are dope. Even Noah the Neanderthal.

After the last bell rings, Avery saunters up to my locker with the most amused grin on her face. I shoulder my bag, turn to her. "What's up?"

"Someone named our ship. I overheard this junior say it in study."

Ugh. I hate that, it's so stupid. I mean, I guess it's okay for famous people, but we're not famous. *Your girlfriend sort of is, at least here, so you are by association.* I sigh. "Lay it on me."

"BrAvery."

Okay, that's actually awesome. "You know what? I like it."

"I do, too." She pulls me in for a kiss—there's nothing hindering her anymore, not even the group of underclass girls down the hall who are blatantly staring. "Whatever," she says as we pass them, "we're hot and you're jelly about it."

She's the best. Yes, she is.

She's quiet on the way out of the parking lot. I see her wheels spinning. They shouldn't be; everything's good, and she's just driving. "Tell me what you're thinking."

"When something big happens in my life, I usually visit my sister. I feel like I owe it to her because I didn't always tell her things when she was here. This weekend was... really big." She lets out a lone *ha*.

"You wanna go now?"

"Can we?"

"Yeah. Let's stop to get her some flowers on the way."

She takes a hand off the steering wheel and picks up mine. "Thanks for being so sweet."

The cemetery is sprawling; the lawn is well maintained, green and trimmed. We walk through a section of weathered headstones, until we come to her sister's—unblemished and glossy. It's obsidian granite with a white marble cherub eternally perched on its flat top.

Reese Cahill. Beloved daughter and sister. July 15, 2003—August 8, 2020.

Avery gets down on her haunches, places the bouquet of white carnations into the flower vase protruding from the ground, then pats the gravestone. "Hey, Sissy."

Sissy. I'm going to bawl.

She stands up, peers at me. "I, uh, I talk to her. It might seem weird."

"That isn't weird at all. Do what you'd normally do."

She turns back to Reese. Inhales, exhales. "It's been a while. A lot's changed since the last time I was here. I came out to literally everyone—my friends, everybody at school, Mom and Dad—they caught me with my girlfriend, it was mortifying! Her name is Britton, and I am totally gaga for her. You would not believe how we met..."

*

As we're walking back to the car she says, "I'm going to tell my parents what happened the night Reese died. I've spent too much time hating myself for all of it. It's exhausting. I want to feel better, and I know I can't unless I'm honest, even if they blame me."

"There's no way they'll blame you. You'll see."

"Will you be there with me when I talk to them? I'm gonna need to borrow some of your strength."

"You have enough strength of your own, but yes, I'll be there." I'll never *not* be there when she wants me to be.

We give Tom and Cate a minute after they get home from work, and then we sit them down in the living room. Avery cries from the beginning of the story straight through to the end. Cate starts to cry once she realizes how much misplaced blame Avery's been carrying in her heart for the last two years. "Sweetheart, sometimes things just happen," she says.

"Maybe it wouldn't have if—"

"You let go of that thought right this minute." Tom reaches for his daughter's hands; they seem so small clasped in his giant Papa Bear paws. "Do you know how many times Uncle Jimmy and I nearly came to blows when we were teenagers? I'd have to get in the car and go for a drive to make sure I wouldn't beat the hell out of him. It's a wonder I never got in a wreck. What happened to your sister was an accident, Avery. No one caused it. Repeat after me: It was an accident."

Avery huffs. "It was an accident."

Everyone's silent for a bit, letting the heavy topic lose some of its weightiness. Then Cate breaks it. "I wondered why Spence stopped coming around. It must have been hard on her, to lose you both."

"I know it was." Avery nods, then scopes me. "We're working on becoming friends again."

"That's good. You'll help each other hang onto all the good memories of Reese, the experiences that only the two of you shared with her."

Avery's face lights up. That hadn't dawned on her before. "You're right. There were a ton." She recounts a time the three of them came across a tall, branchy oak tree behind the mall. Reese looked at it, at Spence, and said, "Race you to the top!" She had the head start, but Spence caught up to her. Reese was farther up the tree than Spence when she lost her grip and slipped down a few branches. Spence ultimately beat her—climbing being a talent of hers. "You cheated!" Reese yelled across the treetop. Spence barked back, "I cheated? You were running before you even challenged me!"

"Yep, that sounds like them," Cate responds. She laughs. So does Tom, and then Avery and I join in.

I think Avery's going to be okay.

CHAPTER FORTY-SEVEN

Dinner at Fantasy Island is a Cahill Thanksgiving Eve tradition. Chinese food is one of my favorites, therefore, in my opinion, it is the best tradition ever. Cate pulls the Mercedes into the restaurant's parking lot and flips on the interior lights. She digs inside her purse, then twists around in her seat. "Happy Thanksgiving." She hands me a sealed yellow legal envelope. It's from the Massachusetts Registry of Vital Records and Statistics.

"That was fast." My Biologicals must not have had any protests.

"Now that we know which hospital you were born in and have your parents' names, it should be easy to find them."

I don't even care about finding them, anymore. They gave me their DNA, but Tom and Cate are the closest things to parents I've ever had, and they're more than enough—all I've ever wished for. They've shown me so much affection and acceptance. The void has been forever filled.

Every member of the Cahill family has their attention on me. Avery takes my free hand. "Are you gonna open it?"

I shrug, place the envelope on the seat beside me. "I'll get around to it. I'm way too stoked about food."

They all chortle. Tom says, "Me, too!" He and Cate move to exit the car.

I thrust my arm out to stop them. "Hold up, guys…"

They turn around to face me again.

"I love you."

Cate gets teary. Tom reaches back and ruffles my hair. "We love you too, kiddo."

After we get back from dinner, I resolve to finish my Bay State Rainbow Coalition Scholarship application. As its name implies, it awards grants to prospective college students who are LGBTQI identified. It might be a long shot—I don't have much in the way of a résumé—but I'm going to need some financial aid regardless of what school I go to, so I'm gonna try for it. It can't hurt.

I am dying over the essay, not getting anywhere with writing. It's open-topic, yet my mind is as blank as the damn Word document. The blinking cursor taunts me. "Screw you, too, stupid little line."

I can't concentrate. My focus keeps shifting to the Registry of Stats mailer I tossed onto my bed. *Let's get 'er done!* I yank the thing off the comforter and rip it open. The paper inside is slightly thicker than standard copy paper; the file clerk went through the trouble of recreating the original document. I pull it out. Scrawled across the top, *Certificate of Live Birth, Brigham and Women's Hospital—Boston, MA.* At the bottom left corner is the official Seal of the Commonwealth. Above that, two lines. *Father's Name: Christopher Walsh. Mother's Name: Melissa Britton.* Britton Walsh… They didn't even bother to think up a proper first name for me.

Hahaha! Hohoho! Oh, fuck 'em, I've got more important shit to do than dwell, like live the life they gave me. That's all I needed from them—the rest is mine to make of it what I please, and to love the people who want to love me.

I am Britton Walsh, and I am pretty damn exceptional.

"Hey, Scrawny." Avery peeks her head through my cracked door. It's gotten easier for her to be in here since we had the room repainted last weekend—a subtle blue called Aqua Mist, as close to the color of her irises as I could find. Tom and Cate wanted to have new carpet installed, too, but I insisted on keeping the original, preserving some of Reese's flair.

"Yeah, babe?" I toss my birth certificate in a drawer. I'll need it when I get my driver's license, and my passport, and every other form of ID.

She bounces in, throws her arms around my neck and kisses my cheek. "Do you have a second?"

"For you? Always."

"Can you come downstairs with me?"

"You bet."

Tom and Cate are in the living room enjoying the bottle of mijiu they bought at the restaurant. *Alright, turnt family meeting!*

"Hi, you two." Tom's voice has a seriousness to it. His eyes—Avery's eyes—are deep and earnest. "Britton, the three of us have been talking."

"We have!" *Cate's tipsy.*

"…And we've decided that whatever happens in the future with you and Avery, ah—we want you to know you'll always have a place with us. You're part of our family, and if it's okay with you, we'd like this to be your permanent home."

Once again, they're all looking at me with expectant eyes. These three wonderful people are my family. I've finally found it—Home. "I'd like that, too."

EPILOGUE

I've finished up my work-study for the day—my idea, I wouldn't let Tom and Cate shoulder the expenses of my education that weren't covered by my scholarships—and am waiting for Avery at Forsyth Park. It's the perfect location, halfway between MassArt and Northeastern, and just four blocks from the small apartment we share in the Fenway–Kenmore neighborhood. I was ready and willing to live in the dorms, but Cate suggested off-campus housing would be best for both of us. "That way you'll have your privacy," she said. It was code for 'you don't want any potential roommates to walk in on you screwing like bunnies.' Tom agreed it was a good idea, adding, "Cuts out that freaky meningitis stuff, too." So, off-campus it was. And why not live together? We'd been doing that from the very beginning, anyway.

Avery comes ambling down the sidewalk looking beyond wrecked. Her arms are stuffed with books she couldn't fit in her bag, despite its ridiculous size. "Hi." She leans in, greets me with a peck on the cheek.

All I have to carry is my Nikon, and its case is dangling from my shoulder. "Give me some of those." I take three books from her: *European History: Antiquity to the Renaissance*, *Research Writing*, *Intro to Queer Studies*.

"Thanks," she says with a tired smile. "God, I am so glad it's a long weekend. I need four days off."

"Same."

"Shit, when is Spence's game, again?"

"Babygirl, for real? She's playing your school." She puffs, rolls her eyes. "Saturday," I remind her.

Spence is on a full ride soccer scholarship at UConn—no surprise she was scouted by a Division 1, multiple championship-winning school—and the Connecticut Huskies will be in town this weekend for a match against the Northeastern Huskies. We're supposed to meet the new girl she's dating, too—Kaylen, a teammate she seems to really like. I don't care if it's anti-school spirit for Avery, I'll be rooting for UConn to win.

"Okay."

There's something else for us this weekend. Something important, on Monday. I steal a glimpse of her, wondering if she remembers. She's been swamped with schoolwork lately; she didn't even want to do anything for her birthday. I wouldn't blame her if she's forgotten.

"What?" She can always feel my gaze like it's a corporeal thing. I love, and sometimes, like right now, hate it. She hits me with an expression that says, *Out with it.*

"About Monday."

Her face drops, lips pouting. "You think I forgot our anniversary? Seriously? Our first anniversary."

I can feel that my skin is bright pink. "Well…"

"I was going to try to surprise you, but I can ruin it for you, if you want."

"You know how I feel about surprises."

She does a you're-no-fun-at-all groan. "This is the plan. After working up an appetite via an athletic-sex filled day, we will end the evening at Sorellina. We have a reservation at seven o'clock."

Hell yes to the sex. Sorellina, though? It's the hottest, most expensive fine dining restaurant in Boston. The food is supposed to be legendary, and I have been wanting to try it, but still… "You're crazy."

"Yeah. About you, Scrawny."

I can't believe it's already been a year. Or that it's *only* been a year. That's something about being in love I didn't see coming—time with Avery goes by so quickly yet feels infinite. I know so much about her: If she doesn't put her keys on the hook as soon as she walks through the door, she'll misplace them; she changes her socks twice a day because she hates how they feel when they get even a little bit sweaty; she's one of those unfortunate people for whom cilantro tastes like soap. Still, she surprises me every day—the things that make her laugh that no one else finds funny, the way she randomly interrupts me with a kiss when she thinks I'm saying something cute… "Can we get a cat?" I have no idea why this is the moment I've chosen to bring it up; it feels right. I know we're solid. We can provide a safe, loving home for a furbaby.

"A cat?"

"Mmhmm. I really want a pet. I've been thinking about it since we moved into the apartment. The lease says it's cool."

"I've always wanted a cat. I couldn't have one growing up because Reese was super allergic. She felt bad about it, the dumbass."

"Is that a yes?"

She nods. "Let's go to the shelter tomorrow and see if we fall in love with a sweet little fluffball. Preferably an older one, or one that's, like, missing an eye or something—there're always so many special needs cats up for adoption."

Her heart is so big and beautiful.

That's it, I am going to marry this girl someday. *Yeah, you probably will.* I take her by the elbow, stop us both in our tracks and kiss her a bit too zealously. "I love you."

She smiles, touches her finger to the tip of my nose. "I love you, too."

LETTER FROM KRISTEN

Thank you so much for reading *When Sparks Fly*. I hope that you loved Britton's story as much as I loved writing it. If you'd like to be notified by e-mail when my next book is released, please sign up for e-mail notifications at the link below.

www.bookouture.com/kristen-zimmer

For regular updates on my writing process, or if you just feel like saying hello, feel free to follow me on Facebook or Twitter.

If you did enjoy the journey, I'd be grateful if you would write a review. Getting feedback from readers is incredibly gratifying and also helps to persuade other readers to pick up one of my books for the first time!

Thanks again!
Kristen

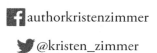

authorkristenzimmer

@kristen_zimmer

ACKNOWLEDGMENTS

Thank you to Mark Falkin for his continued hard work and for once again finding my book the perfect home. Thank you to my editors, Jessie Botterill and Natasha Hodgson, for their incredible insights and for making the publishing process truly delightful. And thank you to the entire Bookouture family; your dedication to bringing beautiful literature into the world is inspiring.

Printed in Great Britain
by Amazon